A Study in Terror:
Sir Arthur Conan Doyle's Revolutionary Stories of Fear and the Supernatural
Vol. 2

Paperback ISBN 9781780926650
ePub ISBN 9781780926667
PDF ISBN 9781780926674

Published in the UK by MX Publishing
335 Princess Park Manor, Royal Drive, London, N11 3GX
www.mxpublishing.co.uk

Cover Illustration by Brian Belanger
Cover Compilation by www.staunch.com

TABLE OF CONTENTS

VOLUME TWO INTRODUCTION: *HOLMES, HORROR, AND H.P. LOVECRAFT*

BY DERRICK BELANGER

> *"...Poe's non-detective writings are very highly regarded; Conan Doyle's are not."*
>
> *-James O'Brien*

As I was compiling the second volume of this anthology, I came across the above quote as well as another in a similar vein from Michael Dirda. In his short masterpiece, On Conan Doyle, Dirda notes:

"Today much of Conan Doyle's substantial oeuvre-his bibliography runs to over 700 pages- suffers readerly neglect because of the widespread misconception that he only rose above the conventions of his time when he wrote about the dynamic duo of Baker Street. His other works are consequently dismissed as period pieces, of interest mainly to professional Doyleans."[1]

It is this dismissal that is most concerning. One must wonder why it is that one of the most popular authors of the

---

[1] The James O'Brien quote is from The Scientific Sherlock Holmes pg.11; the Michael Dirda quote is from On Conan Doyle pg. 51

Victorian-Edwardian period only has a small portion of his writings read today. Why is it that the stories such as *Lot No. 249* and *The Ring of Thoth* are largely unknown when they were the inspiration for the Universal film, *The Mummy*? Why is it that the story *J. Habakuk Jephson's Statement* is largely unknown as the origin to the Mary Celeste mystery? Why are Doyle's pieces of weird fiction left out of most genre studies and collections when he was known as an influence on H.P. Lovecraft? Mostly I wondered, why do those who love Sherlock Holmes so much ignore Doyle's other works?

I posed these and other questions to a mix of Holmesian and Sherlockian experts and scholars to see if they might have an answer. When asked why the Sherlock Holmes stories are so much more read than Doyle's other works, many scratched their heads that I would even ask the question. "The mystique of the Canon? It's such a great game, and Conan Doyle's other work doesn't lend itself to anything like it,"[2] responded crime novelist Wick Downing when I posed my question in a Facebook forum.

Most responded with the fact that the friendship of Holmes and Watson, the wonderful characterizations in the stories, and the viewpoint of Watson telling the stories all weaved together to make stories of literary giants. "I think people connected with the character of Holmes. He's an enigma…people are drawn to because they want to figure him out, or want to be the one to melt his heart (for us females,) and I think that outshined his other works," responded Sherlockian author Kate Workman.

---

[2] Most of the quotes from authors were obtained through informal interview sources such as Facebook postings and e-mails. Because of this format, many typos and punctuation errors were corrected in composing this introduction; however, all quotes are direct.

While there are no continuous main characters throughout the horror and supernatural fiction of Doyle, there is a strong sense of style that did carry over into Doyle's writings on Holmes. All of the writers who read an advanced copy of the first volume of this anthology commented on how the stories are well written and entertaining; some even consented that Doyle's best horror and supernatural stories were at least as good as the weaker Holmes stories. In fact, it was noted that some of Holmes best cases interweaved the genres of horror and mystery together. It helps to be a master writer in multiple genres, such was Doyle. When asked which Holmes stories stand out for blending horror and mystery most respondents had a favorite that came directly to mind. "Horror and mystery . . . surely "The Devil's Foot," responded Chris Redmond of Sherlockian.net. "Its strong point is the motif (which ACD uses in a number of places, both Sherlockian and otherwise) of the experimenter putting himself at mortal risk."

Several respondents expressed how well The Hound of the Baskervilles stands as a mystery-horror blend. Author Jennifer Petkus notes, "*The Hound* is the best story because it epitomizes the triumph of reason over horror while still managing to raise goose bumps. Without actually stating his famous dictum, the great detective nevertheless eliminates the impossible—that a spectral hound is responsible for the death of Sir Charles Baskerville—and proceeds from there to the realm of the possible." And Merrily Taylor, retired university librarian, states, "I am torn between The Hound of the Baskervilles and "The Creeping Man." They both have a nice blend of something scary enough to make us think that indeed, either the supernatural or the horrific might be involved, yet at the end we find out that "real world" evil is involved. I suppose I would say that Professor Presbury has the edge, as he actually uses the tools of science to transform himself into something Other and terrifying. Shades of Dr. Jekyll and Mr. Hyde!"

It is this blend of horror and mystery that makes the above mentioned stories stand out in the canon. My hope with this two volume anthology is that more Sherlockians and Holmesians will read Doyle's works of horror and supernatural fiction and see some shadows from Baker Street creeping into the mix. The short novella The Mystery of Cloomber included in this volume of the anthology can even be seen as a precursor to Doyle's Sherlock Holmes novels.

The Lovecraft Connection

Besides Arthur Conan Doyle, H.P. Lovecraft is arguably the most mimicked writer for pastiches composed in his style. Lovecraft is the number one most influential horror writer of the twentieth century, and his cosmic tales still send chills down the spines of modern day readers. When reading Doyle's stories *The Horror of the Heights* and *The Terror of Blue John Gap,* I noted a similarity in his style and that of Lovecraft and wondered if there was an influence. I asked author and noted Doyle-Lovecraft expert Stephen Seitz, "I'd say ACD was a very strong influence on Lovecraft. As a kid, HPL was an avid fan, and the similarity in prose styles is sometimes uncanny."

When I looked further, I found some very interesting statements. Lovecraft wrote in a letter, "I used to write detective stories very often, the works of A. Conan Doyle being my model so far as plot was concerned." In the book

More Annotated Lovecraft authors S.T. Joshi and Peter Cannon state of Lovecraft's story, *The Hound* that the writing has an "echo of Conan Doyle's Hound of the Baskervilles."[3] They add that Lovecraft wrote, "As to 'Sherlock Holmes' – I used to be infatuated with him! I read every Sherlock Holmes story published…"[4]

While Lovecraft's major influences were authors such as Poe, Machen, Bierce, Chambers, and Blackwood, Doyle should be added to the mix. Fans of Lovecraft will find comparable chills in the stories contained within these anthology volumes even if they do not rise to the cosmic level of Lovecraft.

I hope Lovecraft fans, Sherlock Holmes fans, and lovers of great literature enjoy the works contained within these volumes. Enjoy!

---

[3] This letter is quoted in the Lovecraft collection, The Doom That Came to Sarnath and Other Stories pg.21.
[4] This information can be found in the footnote of More Annotated H.P. Lovecraft pg. 71.

Works Cited

Brien, James F.. *The scientific Sherlock Holmes: cracking the Case with Science and Forensics*. Oxford: Oxford University Press, 2013. Print.

Dirda, Michael. *On Conan Doyle, or, The whole Art of Storytelling*. Princeton, N.J.: Princeton University Press, 2012. Print.

Lovecraft, H. P., and Lin Carter. *The Doom that Came to Sarnath*. New York: Ballantine Books, 1971. Print.

Lovecraft, H. P., P. H. Cannon, and S. T. Joshi. *More Annotated H.P. Lovecraft*. New York: A Dell Trade Paperback, 1999. Print.

Section 1: Doyle's Undead

INTRODUCTION

Perhaps Doyle's greatest literary creation beyond Sherlock Holmes was that of the monster mummy. Before Doyle's writing, Mummies were seen as romantic, a throwback to an enlightened Egyptian era. While stories of Egyptian curses were known, most stories of mummies were on the positive, even humorous side. Then enters Doyle, and once again the author changes everything.

The story *The Ring of Thoth* bears an uncanny resemblance to the story contained in the 1932 Universal horror film, *The Mummy*. Both stories contain immortal men pining for the lovers they lost to the sands of time, and both try to bridge the gap in time and bring their romantic partners back to life. While the film is not "officially" based on Doyle's work, one can see the influence. The second story *Lot No. 249* is perhaps even more influential depicting for the first time the mummy as the mindless brute swathed in bandages, killing anyone who dares challenge its master. My essay *The Making of the Modern Mummy* explains the evolution of the mummy character from romantic icon to shambling monstrosity. Anyone who pictures the traditional mummy, whether it is the image of Boris Karloff emerging from his tomb to the modern take of Imhotep fighting off Brendan

Fraser and company, they are picturing an image first conceived by Sir Arthur Conan Doyle.

--Derrick Belanger

THE RING OF THOTH

Mr. John Vansittart Smith, F.R.S., of 147A Gower Street, was a man whose energy of purpose and clearness of thought might have placed him in the very first rank of scientific observers. He was the victim, however, of a universal ambition which prompted him to aim at distinction in many subjects rather than pre-eminence in one. In his early days he had shown an aptitude for zoology and for botany which caused his friends to look upon him as a second Darwin, but when a professorship was almost within his reach he had suddenly discontinued his studies and turned his whole attention to chemistry. Here his researches upon the spectra of the metals had won him his fellowship in the Royal Society; but again he played the coquette with his subject, and after a year's absence from the laboratory he joined the Oriental Society, and delivered a paper on the Hieroglyphic and Demotic inscriptions of El Kab, thus giving a crowning example both of the versatility and of the inconstancy of his talents.

The most fickle of wooers, however, is apt to be caught at last, and so it was with John Vansittart Smith. The more he burrowed his way into Egyptology the more impressed he became by the vast field which it opened to the inquirer, and by the extreme importance of a subject which promised to throw a light upon the first germs of human civilisation and the origin of the greater part of our arts and sciences. So struck was Mr. Smith that he straightway married an Egyptological young lady who had written upon the sixth dynasty, and having thus secured a sound base of operations he set himself to collect materials for a work which should unite the research of Lepsius and the ingenuity of

Champollion. The preparation of this *magnum opus* entailed many hurried visits to the magnificent Egyptian collections of the Louvre, upon the last of which, no longer ago than the middle of last October, he became involved in a most strange and noteworthy adventure.

The trains had been slow and the Channel had been rough, so that the student arrived in Paris in a somewhat befogged and feverish condition. On reaching the Hotel de France, in the Rue Laffitte, he had thrown himself upon a sofa for a couple of hours, but finding that he was unable to sleep, he determined, in spite of his fatigue, to make his way to the Louvre, settle the point which he had come to decide, and take the evening train back to Dieppe. Having come to his conclusion, he donned his greatcoat, for it was a raw rainy day, and made his way across the Boulevard des Italiens and down the Avenue de l'Opera. Once in the Louvre he was on familiar ground, and he speedily made his way to the collection of papyri which it was his intention to consult.

The warmest admirers of John Vansittart Smith could hardly claim for him that he was a handsome man. His high-beaked nose and prominent chin had something of the same acute and incisive character which distinguished his intellect. He held his head in a birdlike fashion, and birdlike, too, was the pecking motion with which, in conversation, he threw out his objections and retorts. As he stood, with the high collar of his greatcoat raised to his ears, he might have seen from the reflection in the glass-case before him that his appearance was a singular one. Yet it came upon him as a sudden jar when an English voice behind him exclaimed in very audible tones, "What a queer-looking mortal!"

The student had a large amount of petty vanity in his composition which manifested itself by an ostentatious and overdone disregard of all personal considerations. He straightened his lips and looked rigidly at the roll of papyrus, while his heart filled with bitterness against the whole race of travelling Britons.

"Yes," said another voice, "he really is an extraordinary fellow."

"Do you know," said the first speaker, "one could almost believe that by the continual contemplation of mummies the chap has become half a mummy himself?"

"He has certainly an Egyptian cast of countenance," said the other.

John Vansittart Smith spun round upon his heel with the intention of shaming his countrymen by a corrosive remark or two. To his surprise and relief, the two young fellows who had been conversing had their shoulders turned towards him, and were gazing at one of the Louvre attendants who was polishing some brass-work at the other side of the room.

"Carter will be waiting for us at the Palais Royal," said one tourist to the other, glancing at his watch, and they clattered away, leaving the student to his labours.

"I wonder what these chatterers call an Egyptian cast of countenance," thought John Vansittart Smith, and he moved his position slightly in order to catch a glimpse of the man's face. He started as his eyes fell upon it. It was indeed the very face with which his studies had made him familiar. The regular statuesque features, broad brow, well-rounded chin, and dusky complexion were the exact counterpart of the innumerable statues, mummy-cases, and pictures which adorned the walls of the apartment. The thing was beyond all coincidence. The man must be an Egyptian. The national angularity of the shoulders and narrowness of the hips were alone sufficient to identify him.

John Vansittart Smith shuffled towards the attendant with some intention of addressing him. He was not light of touch in conversation, and found it difficult to strike the happy mean between the brusqueness of the superior and the geniality of the equal. As he came nearer, the man presented his side face to him, but kept his gaze still bent upon his work. Vansittart Smith, fixing his eyes upon the fellow's skin, was conscious of a sudden impression that there was something inhuman and preternatural about its appearance. Over the temple and cheek-bone it was as glazed and as shiny as varnished parchment. There was no suggestion of pores. One could not fancy a drop of moisture upon that arid surface. From brow to chin, however, it was cross-hatched by a million delicate wrinkles, which shot and interlaced as though Nature in some Maori mood had tried how wild and intricate a pattern she could devise.

"Ou est la collection de Memphis?" asked the student, with the awkward air of a man who is devising a question merely for the purpose of opening a conversation.

"C'est la," replied the man brusquely, nodding his head at the other side of the room.

"Vous etes un Egyptien, n'est-ce pas?" asked the Englishman.

The attendant looked up and turned his strange dark eyes upon his questioner. They were vitreous, with a misty dry shininess, such as Smith had never seen in a human head before. As he gazed into them he saw some strong emotion gather in their depths, which rose and deepened until it broke into a look of something akin both to horror and to hatred.

"Non, monsieur; je suis francais." The man turned abruptly and bent low over his polishing. The student gazed at him for a moment in astonishment, and then turning to a chair in a retired corner behind one of the doors he proceeded to make notes of his researches among the papyri. His thoughts, however, refused to return into their natural groove. They would run upon the enigmatical attendant with the sphinx-like face and the parchment skin.

"Where have I seen such eyes?" said Vansittart Smith to himself. "There is something saurian about them, something reptilian. There's the membrana nictitans of the snakes," he mused, bethinking himself of his zoological studies. "It gives a shiny effect. But there was something more here. There was a sense of power, of wisdom--so I read them--and of weariness, utter weariness, and ineffable despair. It may be all imagination, but I never had so strong an impression. By Jove, I must have another look at them!" He rose and paced round the Egyptian rooms, but the man who had excited his curiosity had disappeared.

The student sat down again in his quiet corner, and continued to work at his notes. He had gained the information which he required from the papyri, and it only remained to write it down while it was still fresh in his memory. For a time his pencil travelled rapidly over the paper, but soon the lines became less level, the words more blurred, and finally the pencil tinkled down upon the floor, and the head of the student dropped heavily forward upon his chest. Tired out by his journey, he slept so soundly in his lonely post behind the door that neither the clanking civil guard, nor the footsteps of sightseers, nor even the loud hoarse bell which gives the signal for closing, were sufficient to arouse him.

Twilight deepened into darkness, the bustle from the Rue de Rivoli waxed and then waned, distant Notre Dame clanged out the hour of midnight, and still the dark and lonely figure sat silently in the shadow. It was not until close upon one in the morning that, with a sudden gasp and an intaking of the breath, Vansittart Smith returned to consciousness. For a moment it flashed upon him that he had dropped asleep in his study-chair at home. The moon was shining fitfully through the unshuttered window, however, and as his eye ran along the lines of mummies and the endless array of polished cases, he remembered clearly where he was and how he came there. The student was not a nervous man. He possessed that love of a novel situation which is peculiar to his race. Stretching out his cramped limbs, he looked at his watch, and burst into a chuckle as he observed the hour. The episode would make an admirable anecdote to be introduced into his next paper as a relief to the graver and heavier speculations. He was a little cold, but wide awake and much refreshed. It was no wonder that the guardians had overlooked him, for the door threw its heavy black shadow right across him.

The complete silence was impressive. Neither outside nor inside was there a creak or a murmur. He was alone with the dead men of a dead civilisation. What though the outer city reeked of the garish nineteenth century! In all this chamber there was scarce an article, from the shrivelled ear of wheat to the pigment-box of the painter, which had not held its own against four thousand years. Here was the flotsam and jetsam washed up by the great ocean of time from that far-off empire. From stately Thebes, from lordly Luxor, from the great temples of Heliopolis, from a hundred rifled tombs, these relics had been brought. The student glanced round at the long-silent figures who flickered vaguely up through the gloom, at the busy toilers who were now so restful, and he fell into a reverent and thoughtful mood. An unwonted sense of his own youth and insignificance came over him. Leaning back in his chair, he gazed dreamily down the long vista of rooms, all silvery with the moonshine, which extend through the whole wing of the widespread building. His eyes fell upon the yellow glare of a distant lamp.

John Vansittart Smith sat up on his chair with his nerves all on edge. The light was advancing slowly towards him, pausing from time to time, and then coming jerkily onwards. The bearer moved noiselessly. In the utter silence there was no suspicion of a footfall. An idea of robbers entered the Englishman's head. He snuggled up farther into the corner. The light was two rooms off. Now it was in the next chamber, and still there was no sound. With something approaching to a thrill of fear the student observed a face, floating in the air as it were, behind the flare of the lamp. The figure was wrapped in shadow, but the light fell full upon the strange, eager face. There was no mistaking the metallic, glistening eyes and the cadaverous skin. It was the attendant with whom he had conversed.

Vansittart Smith's first impulse was to come forward and address him. A few words of explanation would set the matter clear, and lead doubtless to his being conducted to some side-door from which he might make his way to his hotel. As the man entered the chamber, however, there was something so stealthy in his movements, and so furtive in his expression, that the Englishman altered his intention. This was clearly no ordinary official walking the rounds. The fellow wore felt-soled slippers, stepped with a rising chest, and glanced quickly from left to right, while his hurried, gasping breathing thrilled the flame of his lamp. Vansittart

Smith crouched silently back into the corner and watched him keenly, convinced that his errand was one of secret and probably sinister import.

There was no hesitation in the other's movements. He stepped lightly and swiftly across to one of the great cases, and, drawing a key from his pocket, he unlocked it. From the upper shelf he pulled down a mummy, which he bore away with him, and laid it with much care and solicitude upon the ground. By it he placed his lamp, and then squatting down beside it in Eastern fashion he began with long, quivering fingers to undo the cerecloths and bandages which girt it round. As the crackling rolls of linen peeled off one after the other, a strong aromatic odour filled the chamber, and fragments of scented wood and of spices pattered down upon the marble floor.

It was clear to John Vansittart Smith that this mummy had never been unswathed before. The operation interested him keenly. He thrilled all over with curiosity, and his bird-like head protruded farther and farther from behind the door. When, however, the last roll had been removed from the four-thousand-year-old head, it was all that he could do to stifle an outcry of amazement. First, a cascade of long, black, glossy tresses poured over the workman's hands and arms. A second turn of the bandage revealed a low, white forehead, with a pair of delicately arched eyebrows. A third uncovered a pair of bright, deeply fringed eyes, and a straight, well-cut nose, while a fourth and last showed a sweet, full, sensitive mouth, and a beautifully curved chin. The whole face was one of extraordinary loveliness, save for the one blemish that in the centre of the forehead there was a single irregular, coffee-coloured splotch. It was a triumph of the embalmer's art. Vansittart Smith's eyes grew larger and larger as he gazed upon it, and he chirruped in his throat with satisfaction.

Its effect upon the Egyptologist was as nothing, however, compared with that which it produced upon the strange attendant. He threw his hands up into the air, burst into a harsh clatter of words, and then, hurling himself down upon the ground beside the mummy, he threw his arms round her, and kissed her repeatedly upon the lips and brow. "Ma petite!" he groaned in French. "Ma pauvre petite!" His voice broke with emotion, and his innumerable wrinkles quivered and writhed, but the student observed in the lamp-light that his shining eyes were still dry and tearless as two beads of steel. For some minutes he lay, with a twitching face, crooning and moaning over the beautiful head. Then he broke into a sudden smile, said some words in an unknown tongue, and sprang to his feet with the vigorous air of one who has braced himself for an effort.

In the centre of the room there was a large, circular case which contained, as the student had frequently remarked, a magnificent collection of early Egyptian rings and precious stones. To this the attendant strode, and, unlocking it, threw it open. On the ledge at the side he placed his lamp, and beside it a small, earthenware jar which he had drawn from his pocket. He then took a handful of rings from the case, and with a most serious and anxious face he proceeded to smear each in turn with some liquid substance from the earthen pot, holding them to the light as he did so. He was clearly disappointed with the first lot, for he threw them petulantly back into the case and drew out some more. One of these, a massive ring with a large crystal set in it, he seized and eagerly tested with the contents of the jar. Instantly he uttered a cry of joy, and threw out his arms in a wild gesture which upset the pot and set the liquid streaming across the floor to the very feet of the Englishman. The attendant drew a red handkerchief from his bosom, and, mopping up the mess, he followed it into the corner, where in a moment he found himself face to face with his observer.

"Excuse me," said John Vansittart Smith, with all imaginable politeness; "I have been unfortunate enough to fall asleep behind this door."

"And you have been watching me?" the other asked in English, with a most venomous look on his corpse-like face.

The student was a man of veracity. "I confess," said he, "that I have noticed your movements, and that they have aroused my curiosity and interest in the highest degree."

The man drew a long, flamboyant-bladed knife from his bosom. "You have had a very narrow escape," he said; "had I seen you ten minutes ago, I should have driven this through your heart. As it is, if you touch me or interfere with me in any way you are a dead man."

"I have no wish to interfere with you," the student answered. "My presence here is entirely accidental. All I ask is that you will have the extreme kindness to show me out through some side-door." He spoke with great suavity, for the man was still pressing the tip of his dagger against the palm of his left hand, as though to assure himself of its sharpness, while his face preserved its malignant expression.

"If I thought----" said he. "But no, perhaps it is as well. What is your name?"

The Englishman gave it.

"Vansittart Smith," the other repeated. "Are you the same Vansittart Smith who gave a paper in London upon El Kab? I saw a report of it. Your knowledge of the subject is contemptible."

"Sir!" cried the Egyptologist.

"Yet it is superior to that of many who make even greater pretensions. The whole keystone of our old life in Egypt was not the inscriptions or monuments of which you make so much, but was our hermetic philosophy and mystic knowledge of which you say little or nothing."

"Our old life!" repeated the scholar, wide-eyed; and then suddenly, "Good God, look at the mummy's face!"

The strange man turned and flashed his light upon the dead woman, uttering a long, doleful cry as he did so. The action of the air had already undone all the art of the embalmer. The skin had fallen away, the eyes had sunk inwards, the discoloured lips had writhed away from the yellow teeth, and the brown mark upon the forehead alone showed that it was indeed the same face which had shown such youth and beauty a few short minutes before.

The man flapped his hands together in grief and horror. Then mastering himself by a strong effort he turned his hard eyes once more upon the Englishman.

"It does not matter," he said, in a shaking voice. "It does not really matter. I came here to-night with the fixed determination to do something. It is now done. All else is as nothing. I have found my quest. The old curse is broken. I can rejoin her. What matter about her inanimate shell so long as her spirit is awaiting me at the other side of the veil!"

"These are wild words," said Vansittart Smith. He was becoming more and more convinced that he had to do with a madman.

"Time presses, and I must go," continued the other. "The moment is at hand for which I have waited this weary time. But I must show you out first. Come with me."

Taking up the lamp, he turned from the disordered chamber, and led the student swiftly through the long series of the Egyptian, Assyrian, and Persian apartments. At the end of the latter he pushed open a small door let into the wall and descended a winding, stone stair. The Englishman felt the cold, fresh air of the night upon his brow. There was a door opposite him which appeared to communicate with the street. To the right of this another door stood ajar, throwing a spurt of yellow light across the passage. "Come in here!" said the attendant shortly.

Vansittart Smith hesitated. He had hoped that he had come to the end of his adventure. Yet his curiosity was strong within him. He could not leave the matter unsolved, so he followed his strange companion into the lighted chamber.

It was a small room, such as is devoted to a *concierge*. A wood fire sparkled in the grate. At one side stood a truckle bed, and at the other a coarse, wooden chair, with a round table in the centre, which bore the remains of a meal. As the visitor's eye glanced round he could not but remark with an ever-recurring thrill that all the small details of the room were of the most quaint design and antique workmanship. The candlesticks, the vases upon the chimney-piece, the fire-irons, the ornaments upon the walls, were all such as he had been wont to associate with the remote past. The gnarled, heavy-eyed man sat himself down upon the edge of the bed, and motioned his guest into the chair.

"There may be design in this," he said, still speaking excellent English. "It may be decreed that I should leave some account behind as a warning to all rash mortals who would set their wits up against workings of Nature. I leave it with you. Make such use as you will of it. I speak to you now with my feet upon the threshold of the other world.

"I am, as you surmised, an Egyptian--not one of the drown-trodden race of slaves who now inhabit the Delta of the Nile, but a survivor of that fiercer and harder people who tamed the Hebrew, drove the Ethiopian back into the southern deserts, and built those mighty works which have been the envy and the wonder of all after generations. It was in the reign of Tuthmosis, sixteen hundred years before the birth of Christ, that I first saw the light. You shrink away from me. Wait, and you will see that I am more to be pitied than to be feared.

"My name was Sosra. My father had been the chief priest of Osiris in the great temple of Abaris, which stood in those days upon the Bubastic branch of the Nile. I was brought up in the temple and was trained in all those mystic arts which are spoken of in your own Bible. I was an apt pupil. Before I was sixteen I had learned all which the wisest priest could teach me. From that time on I studied Nature's secrets for myself, and shared my knowledge with no man.

"Of all the questions which attracted me there were none over which I laboured so long as over those which concern themselves with the nature of life. I probed deeply into the vital principle. The aim of medicine had been to drive away disease when it appeared. It seemed to me that a method might be devised which should so fortify the body as to prevent weakness or death from ever taking hold of it. It is useless that I should recount my researches. You would scarce comprehend them if I did. They were carried out partly upon animals, partly upon slaves, and partly on myself. Suffice it that their result was to furnish me with a substance which, when injected into the blood, would endow the body with strength to resist the effects of time, of violence, or of disease. It would not indeed confer immortality, but its potency would endure for many thousands of years. I used it upon a cat, and afterwards drugged the creature with the most deadly poisons. That cat is alive in Lower Egypt at the present moment. There was nothing of mystery or magic in the matter. It was simply a chemical discovery, which may well be made again.

"Love of life runs high in the young. It seemed to me that I had broken away from all human care now that I had abolished pain and driven death to such a distance. With a light heart I poured the accursed stuff into my veins. Then I looked round for someone whom I could benefit. There was a young priest of Thoth, Parmes by name, who had won my goodwill by his earnest nature and his devotion to his studies. To him I whispered my secret, and at his request I injected him with my elixir. I should now, I reflected, never be without a companion of the same age as myself.

"After this grand discovery I relaxed my studies to some extent, but Parmes continued his with redoubled energy. Every day I could see him working with his flasks and his distiller in the Temple of Thoth, but he said little to me as to the result of his labours. For my own part, I used to walk through the city and look around me with exultation as I reflected that all this was destined to pass away, and that only I should remain. The people would bow to me as they passed me, for the fame of my knowledge had gone abroad.

"There was war at this time, and the Great King had sent down his soldiers to the eastern boundary to drive away the Hyksos. A Governor, too, was sent to Abaris, that he might hold it for the King. I had heard much of the beauty of the daughter of this Governor, but one day as I walked out with

Parmes we met her, borne upon the shoulders of her slaves. I was struck with love as with lightning. My heart went out from me. I could have thrown myself beneath the feet of her bearers. This was my woman. Life without her was impossible. I swore by the head of Horus that she should be mine. I swore it to the Priest of Thoth. He turned away from me with a brow which was as black as midnight.

"There is no need to tell you of our wooing. She came to love me even as I loved her. I learned that Parmes had seen her before I did, and had shown her that he, too, loved her, but I could smile at his passion, for I knew that her heart was mine. The white plague had come upon the city and many were stricken, but I laid my hands upon the sick and nursed them without fear or scathe. She marvelled at my daring. Then I told her my secret, and begged her that she would let me use my art upon her.

"'Your flower shall then be unwithered, Atma,' I said. 'Other things may pass away, but you and I, and our great love for each other, shall outlive the tomb of King Chefru.'

"But she was full of timid, maidenly objections. 'Was it right?' she asked, 'was it not a thwarting of the will of the gods? If the great Osiris had wished that our years should be so long, would he not himself have brought it about?'

"With fond and loving words I overcame her doubts, and yet she hesitated. It was a great question, she said. She would think it over for this one night. In the morning I should know of her resolution. Surely one night was not too much to ask. She wished to pray to Isis for help in her decision.

"With a sinking heart and a sad foreboding of evil I left her with her tirewomen. In the morning, when the early sacrifice was over, I hurried to her house. A frightened slave met me upon the steps. Her mistress was ill, she said, very ill. In a frenzy I broke my way through the attendants, and rushed through hall and corridor to my Atma's chamber. She lay upon her couch, her head high upon the pillow, with a pallid face and a glazed eye. I knew that hell-mark of old. It was the scar of the white plague, the sign-manual of death.

"Why should I speak of that terrible time? For months I was mad, fevered, delirious, and yet I could not die. Never did an Arab thirst after the sweet wells as I longed after death. Could poison or steel have shortened the thread of my existence, I should soon have rejoined my love in the land with the narrow portal. I tried, but it was of no avail. The accursed influence was too strong upon me. One night as I lay upon my couch, weak and weary, Parmes, the priest of Thoth, came to my chamber. He stood in the circle of the lamp-light, and he looked down upon me with eyes which were bright with a mad joy.

"'Why did you let the maiden die?' he asked; 'why did you not strengthen her as you strengthened me?'

"'I was too late,' I answered. 'But I had forgot. You also loved her. You are my fellow in misfortune. Is it not terrible to think of the centuries which must pass ere we look upon her again? Fools, fools, that we were to take death to be our enemy!'

"'You may say that,' he cried with a wild laugh; 'the words come well from your lips. For me they have no meaning.'

"'What mean you?' I cried, raising myself upon my elbow. 'Surely, friend, this grief has turned your brain.' His face was aflame with joy, and he writhed and shook like one who hath a devil.

"'Do you know whither I go?' he asked.

"'Nay,' I answered, 'I cannot tell.'

"'I go to her,' said he. 'She lies embalmed in the farther tomb by the double palm-tree beyond the city wall.'

"'Why do you go there?' I asked.

"'To die!' he shrieked, 'to die! I am not bound by earthen fetters.'

"'But the elixir is in your blood,' I cried.

"'I can defy it,' said he; 'I have found a stronger principle which will destroy it. It is working in my veins at this moment, and in an hour I shall be a dead man. I shall join her, and you shall remain behind.'

"As I looked upon him I could see that he spoke words of truth. The light in his eye told me that he was indeed beyond the power of the elixir.

"'You will teach me!' I cried.

"'Never!' he answered.

"'I implore you, by the wisdom of Thoth, by the majesty of Anubis!'

"'It is useless,' he said coldly.

"'Then I will find it out,' I cried.

"'You cannot,' he answered; 'it came to me by chance. There is one ingredient which you can never get. Save that which is in the ring of Thoth, none will ever more be made.'

"'In the ring of Thoth!' I repeated, 'where then is the ring of Thoth?'

"'That also you shall never know,' he answered. 'You won her love. Who has won in the end? I leave you to your sordid earth life. My chains are broken. I must go!' He turned upon his heel and fled from the chamber. In the morning came the news that the Priest of Thoth was dead.

"My days after that were spent in study. I must find this subtle poison which was strong enough to undo the elixir. From early dawn to midnight I bent over the test-tube and the furnace. Above all, I collected the papyri and the chemical flasks of the Priest of Thoth. Alas! They taught me little. Here and there some hint or stray expression would raise hope in my bosom, but no good ever came of it. Still, month after month, I struggled on. When my heart grew faint I would make my way to the tomb by the palm-trees. There, standing by the dead casket from which the jewel had been rifled, I would feel her sweet presence, and would whisper to her that I would rejoin her if mortal wit could solve the riddle.

"Parmes had said that his discovery was connected with the ring of Thoth. I had some remembrance of the trinket. It was a large and weighty circlet, made, not of gold, but of a rarer and heavier metal brought from the mines of Mount Harbal. Platinum, you call it. The ring had, I remembered, a hollow crystal set in it, in which some few drops of liquid might be stored. Now, the secret of Parmes could not have to do with the metal alone, for there were many rings of that metal in the Temple. Was it not more likely that he had stored his precious poison within the cavity of the crystal? I had scarce come to this conclusion before, in hunting through his papers, I came upon one which told me that it was indeed so, and that there was still some of the liquid unused.

"But how to find the ring? It was not upon him when he was stripped for the embalmer. Of that I made sure. Neither was it among his private effects. In vain I searched every room that he had entered, every box and vase and chattel that he had owned. I sifted the very sand of the desert in the places where he had been wont to walk; but, do what I would, I could come upon no traces of the ring of Thoth. Yet it may be that my labours would have overcome all obstacles had it not been for a new and unlooked-for misfortune.

"A great war had been waged against the Hyksos, and the Captains of the Great King had been cut off in the desert, with all their bowmen and horsemen. The shepherd tribes were upon us like the locusts in a dry year. From the wilderness of Shur to the great, bitter lake there was blood by day and fire by night. Abaris was the bulwark of Egypt, but we could not keep the savages back. The city fell. The Governor and the soldiers were put to the sword, and I, with many more, was led away into captivity.

"For years and years I tended cattle in the great plains by the Euphrates. My master died, and his son grew old, but I was still as far from death as ever. At last I escaped upon a swift camel, and made my way back to Egypt. The Hyksos had settled in the land which they had conquered, and their own King ruled over the country. Abaris had been torn down, the city had been burned, and of the great Temple there was nothing left save an unsightly mound. Everywhere the tombs had been rifled and the monuments destroyed. Of my Atma's grave no sign was left. It was buried in the sands of the desert, and the palm-trees which marked the spot had long disappeared. The papers of Parmes and the remains of the Temple of Thoth were either destroyed or scattered far and wide over the deserts of Syria. All search after them was vain.

"From that time I gave up all hope of ever finding the ring or discovering the subtle drug. I set myself to live as patiently as might be until the effect of the elixir should wear away. How can you understand how terrible a thing time is, you who have experience only of the narrow course which lies between the cradle and the grave! I know it to my cost, I who have floated down the whole stream of history. I was old when Ilium fell. I was very old when Herodotus came to Memphis. I was bowed down with years when the new gospel came upon the earth. Yet you see me much as other men are, with the cursed elixir still sweetening my blood, and guarding me against that which I would court. Now, at last, at last I have come to the end of it!

"I have travelled in all lands and I have dwelt with all nations. Every tongue is the same to me. I learned them all to help pass the weary time. I need not tell you how slowly they drifted by, the long dawn of modern civilization, the dreary middle years, the dark times of barbarism. They are all behind me now. I have never looked with the eyes of love upon another woman. Atma knows that I have been constant to her.

"It was my custom to read all that the scholars had to say upon Ancient Egypt. I have been in many positions, sometimes affluent, sometimes poor, but I have always found enough to enable me to buy the journals which deal with such matters. Some nine months ago I was in San Francisco, when I read an account of some discoveries made in the neighbourhood of Abaris. My heart leapt into my mouth as I read it. It said that the excavator had busied himself in exploring some tombs recently unearthed. In one there had been found an unopened mummy with an inscription upon the outer case setting forth that it contained the body of the daughter of the Governor of the city in the days of Tuthmosis. It added that on removing the outer case there had been exposed a large platinum ring set with a crystal, which had been laid upon the breast of the embalmed woman. This, then, was where Parmes had hid the ring of Thoth. He might well say that it was safe, for no Egyptian would ever stain his soul by moving even the outer case of a buried friend.

"That very night I set off from San Francisco, and in a few weeks I found myself once more at Abaris, if a few sand-heaps and crumbling walls may retain the name of the great city. I hurried to the Frenchmen who were digging there and asked them for the ring. They replied that both the ring and the mummy had been sent to the Boulak Museum at Cairo. To Boulak I went, but only to be told that Mariette Bey had claimed them and had shipped them to the Louvre. I followed them, and there, at last, in the Egyptian chamber, I came, after close upon four thousand years, upon the remains of my Atma, and upon the ring for which I had sought so long.

"But how was I to lay hands upon them? How was I to have them for my very own? It chanced that the office of attendant was vacant. I went to the Director. I convinced him that I knew much about Egypt. In my eagerness I said too much. He remarked that a Professor's chair would suit me better than a seat in the conciergerie. I knew more, he said, than he did. It was only by blundering, and letting him think that he had over-estimated my knowledge, that I prevailed upon him to let me move the few effects which I have retained into this chamber. It is my first and my last night here.

"Such is my story, Mr. Vansittart Smith. I need not say more to a man of your perception. By a strange chance you have this night looked upon the face of the woman whom I loved in those far-off days. There were many rings with crystals in the case, and I had to test for the platinum to be sure of the one which I wanted. A glance at the crystal has shown me that the liquid is indeed within it, and that I shall at last be able to shake off that accursed health which has been worse to me than the foulest disease. I have nothing more to say to you. I have unburdened myself. You may tell my story or you may withhold it at your pleasure. The choice rests with you. I owe you some amends, for you have had a narrow escape of your life this night. I was a desperate man, and not to be baulked in my purpose. Had I seen you before the thing was done, I might have put it beyond your power to oppose me or to raise an alarm. This is the door. It leads into the Rue de Rivoli. Good night."

The Englishman glanced back. For a moment the lean figure of Sosra the Egyptian stood framed in the narrow doorway. The next the door slammed, and the heavy rasping of a bolt broke on the silent night.

It was on the second day after his return to London that Mr. John Vansittart Smith saw the following concise narrative in the Paris correspondence of *The Times* :--

"*Curious Occurrence in the Louvre.* --Yesterday morning a strange discovery was made in the principal Eastern chamber. The *ouvriers* who are employed to clean out the rooms in the morning found one of the attendants lying dead upon the floor with his arms round one of the mummies. So close was his embrace that it was only with the utmost difficulty that they were separated. One of the cases containing valuable rings had been opened and rifled. The authorities are of opinion that the man was bearing away the mummy with some idea of selling it to a private collector, but that he was struck down in the very act by long-standing disease of the heart. It is said that he was a man of uncertain age and eccentric habits, without any living relations to mourn over his dramatic and untimely end."

LOT NO. 249

Of the dealings of Edward Bellingham with William Monkhouse Lee, and of the cause of the great terror of Abercrombie Smith, it may be that no absolute and final judgment will ever be delivered. It is true that we have the full and clear narrative of Smith himself, and such corroboration as he could look for from Thomas Styles the servant, from the Reverend Plumptree Peterson, Fellow of Old's, and from such other people as chanced to gain some passing glance at this or that incident in a singular chain of events. Yet, in the main, the story must rest upon Smith alone, and the most will think that it is more likely that one brain, however outwardly sane, has some subtle warp in its texture, some strange flaw in its workings, than that the path of Nature has been overstepped in open day in so famed a centre of learning and light as the University of Oxford. Yet when we think how narrow and how devious this path of Nature is, how dimly we can trace it, for all our lamps of science, and how from the darkness which girds it round great and terrible possibilities loom ever shadowly upwards, it is a bold and confident man who will put a limit to the strange by-paths into which the human spirit may wander.

In a certain wing of what we will call Old College in Oxford there is a corner turret of an exceeding great age. The heavy arch which spans the open door has bent downwards in the centre under the weight of its years, and the grey, lichen-blotched blocks of stone are, bound and knitted together with withes and strands of ivy, as though the old mother had set herself to brace them up against wind and weather. From the door a stone stair curves upward spirally, passing two landings, and terminating in a third one, its steps all shapeless and hollowed by the tread of so many generations of the seekers after knowledge. Life has flowed like water down this winding stair, and, waterlike, has left these smooth-worn grooves behind it. From the long-gowned, pedantic scholars of Plantagenet days down to the young bloods of a later age, how full and strong had been that tide of young English life. And what was left now of all those hopes, those strivings, those fiery energies, save here and there in some old-world churchyard a few scratches upon a stone, and perchance a handful of dust in a mouldering coffin? Yet here were the silent stair and the grey old wall, with bend and saltire and many another heraldic device still to be read upon its surface, like grotesque shadows thrown back from the days that had passed.

In the month of May, in the year 1884, three young men occupied the sets of rooms which opened on to the separate landings of the old stair. Each set consisted simply of a sitting-room and of a bedroom, while the two corresponding rooms upon the ground-floor were used, the one as a coal-cellar, and the other as the living-room of the servant, or gyp, Thomas Styles, whose duty it was to wait upon the three men above him. To right and to left was a line of lecture-rooms and of offices, so that the dwellers in the old turret enjoyed a certain seclusion, which made the chambers popular among the more studious undergraduates. Such were the three who occupied them now—Abercrombie Smith above, Edward Bellingham beneath him, and William Monkhouse Lee upon the lowest storey.

It was ten o'clock on a bright spring night, and Abercrombie Smith lay back in his arm-chair, his feet upon the fender, and his briar-root pipe between his lips. In a similar chair, and equally at his ease, there lounged on the other side of the fireplace his old school friend Jephro Hastie. Both men were in flannels, for they had spent their evening upon the river, but apart from their dress no one could look at their hard-cut, alert faces without seeing that they were open-air men—men whose minds and tastes turned naturally to all that was manly and robust. Hastie, indeed, was stroke of his college boat, and Smith was an even better oar, but a coming examination had already cast its shadow over him and held him to his work, save for the few hours a week which health demanded. A litter of medical books upon the table, with scattered bones, models and anatomical plates, pointed to the extent as well as the nature of his studies, while a couple of single-sticks and a set of boxing-gloves above the mantelpiece hinted at the means by which, with Hastie's help, he might take his exercise in its most compressed and least distant form. They knew each other very well—so well that they could sit now in that soothing silence which is the very highest development of companionship.

"Have some whisky," said Abercrombie Smith at last between two cloudbursts. "Scotch in the jug and Irish in the bottle."

"No, thanks. I'm in for the sculls. I don't liquor when I'm training. How about you?"

"I'm reading hard. I think it best to leave it alone."

Hastie nodded, and they relapsed into a contented silence.

"By-the-way, Smith," asked Hastie, presently, "have you made the acquaintance of either of the fellows on your stair yet?"

"Just a nod when we pass. Nothing more."

"Hum! I should be inclined to let it stand at that. I know something of them both. Not much, but as much as I want. I don't think I should take them to my bosom if I were you. Not that there's much amiss with Monkhouse Lee."

"Meaning the thin one?"

"Precisely. He is a gentlemanly little fellow. I don't think there is any vice in him. But then you can't know him without knowing Bellingham."

"Meaning the fat one?"

"Yes, the fat one. And he's a man whom I, for one, would rather not know."

Abercrombie Smith raised his eyebrows and glanced across at his companion.

"What's up, then?" he asked. "Drink? Cards? Cad? You used not to be censorious."

"Ah! You evidently don't know the man, or you wouldn't ask. There's something damnable about him—something reptilian. My gorge always rises at him. I should put him down as a man with secret vices—an evil liver. He's no fool, though. They say that he is one of the best men in his line that they have ever had in the college."

"Medicine or classics?"

"Eastern languages. He's a demon at them. Chillingworth met him somewhere above the second cataract last long, and he told me that he just prattled to the Arabs as if he had been born and nursed and weaned among them. He talked Coptic to the Copts, and Hebrew to the Jews, and Arabic to the Bedouins, and they were all ready to kiss the hem of his frock-coat. There are some old hermit Johnnies up in those parts who sit on rocks and scowl and spit at the casual stranger. Well, when they saw this chap Bellingham, before he had said five words they just lay down on their bellies and wriggled. Chillingworth said that he never saw anything like it. Bellingham seemed to take it as his right, too, and strutted about among them and talked down to them like a Dutch uncle. Pretty good for an undergrad. Of Old's, wasn't it?"

"Why do you say you can't know Lee without knowing Bellingham?"

"Because Bellingham is engaged to his sister Eveline. Such a bright little girl, Smith! I know the whole family well. It's disgusting to see that brute with her. A toad and a dove, that's what they always remind me of."

Abercrombie Smith grinned and knocked his ashes out against the side of the grate.

"You show every card in your hand, old chap," said he. "What a prejudiced, green-eyed, evil-thinking old man it is! You have really nothing against the fellow except that."

"Well, I've known her ever since she was as long as that cherry-wood pipe, and I don't like to see her taking risks. And it is a risk. He looks beastly. And he has a beastly temper, a venomous temper. You remember his row with Long Norton?"

"No; you always forget that I am a freshman."

"Ah, it was last winter. Of course. Well, you know the towpath along by the river. There were several fellows going along it, Bellingham in front, when they came on an old market-woman coming the other way. It had been raining—you know what those fields are like when it has rained—and the path ran between the river and a great puddle that was nearly as broad. Well, what does this swine do but keep the path, and push the old girl into the mud, where she and her marketings came to terrible grief. It was a blackguard thing to do, and Long Norton, who is as gentle a fellow as ever stepped, told him what he thought of it. One word led to another, and it ended in Norton laying his stick across the fellow's shoulders. There was the deuce of a fuss about it, and it's a treat to see the way in which Bellingham looks at Norton when they meet now. By Jove, Smith, it's nearly eleven o'clock!"

"No hurry. Light your pipe again."

"Not I. I'm supposed to be in training. Here I've been sitting gossiping when I ought to have been safely tucked up. I'll borrow your skull, if you can share it. Williams has had mine for a month. I'll take the little bones of your ear, too, if you are sure you won't need them. Thanks very much. Never mind a bag, I can carry them very well under my arm. Good-night, my son, and take my tip as to your neighbour."

When Hastie, bearing his anatomical plunder, had clattered off down the winding stair, Abercrombie Smith hurled his pipe into the wastepaper basket, and drawing his chair nearer to the lamp, plunged into a formidable green-covered volume, adorned with great colored maps of that strange internal kingdom of which we are the hapless and helpless monarchs. Though a freshman at Oxford, the student was not so in medicine, for he had worked for four years at Glasgow and at Berlin, and this coming examination would place him finally as a member of his profession. With his firm mouth, broad forehead, and clear-cut, somewhat hard-featured face, he was a man who, if he had no brilliant talent, was yet so dogged, so patient, and so strong that he might in the end overtop a more showy genius. A man who can hold his own among Scotchmen and North Germans is not a man to be easily set back. Smith had left a name at Glasgow and at

Berlin, and he was bent now upon doing as much at Oxford, if hard work and devotion could accomplish it.

He had sat reading for about an hour, and the hands of the noisy carriage clock upon the side table were rapidly closing together upon the twelve, when a sudden sound fell upon the student's ear—a sharp, rather shrill sound, like the hissing intake of a man's breath who gasps under some strong emotion. Smith laid down his book and slanted his ear to listen. There was no one on either side or above him, so that the interruption came certainly from the neighbour beneath—the same neighbour of whom Hastie had given so unsavoury an account. Smith knew him only as a flabby, pale-faced man of silent and studious habits, a man, whose lamp threw a golden bar from the old turret even after he had extinguished his own. This community in lateness had formed a certain silent bond between them. It was soothing to Smith when the hours stole on towards dawning to feel that there was another so close who set as small a value upon his sleep as he did. Even now, as his thoughts turned towards him, Smith's feelings were kindly. Hastie was a good fellow, but he was rough, strong-fibred, with no imagination or sympathy. He could not tolerate departures from what he looked upon as the model type of manliness. If a man could not be measured by a public-school standard, then he was beyond the pale with Hastie. Like so many who are themselves robust, he was apt to confuse the constitution with the character, to ascribe to want of principle what was really a want of circulation. Smith, with his stronger mind, knew his friend's habit, and made allowance for it now as his thoughts turned towards the man beneath him.

There was no return of the singular sound, and Smith was about to turn to his work once more, when suddenly there broke out in the silence of the night a hoarse cry, a positive scream—the call of a man who is moved and shaken beyond all control. Smith sprang out of his chair and dropped his book. He was a man of fairly firm fibre, but there was something in this sudden, uncontrollable shriek of horror which chilled his blood and pringled in his skin. Coming in such a place and at such an hour, it brought a thousand fantastic possibilities into his head. Should he rush down, or was it better to wait? He had all the national hatred of making a scene, and he knew so little of his neighbour that he would not lightly intrude upon his affairs. For a moment he stood in doubt and even as he balanced the matter there was a quick rattle of footsteps upon the stairs, and young Monkhouse Lee, half dressed and as white as ashes, burst into his room.

"Come down!" he gasped. "Bellingham's ill."

Abercrombie Smith followed him closely down stairs into the sitting-room which was beneath his own, and intent as he was upon the matter in hand, he could not but take an amazed glance around him as he crossed the threshold. It was such a chamber as he had never seen before—a museum rather than a study. Walls and ceiling were thickly covered with a thousand strange relics from Egypt and the East. Tall, angular figures bearing burdens or weapons stalked in an uncouth frieze round the apartments. Above were bull-headed, stork-headed, cat-headed, owl-headed statues, with viper-crowned, almond-eyed monarchs, and strange, beetle-like deities cut out of the blue Egyptian lapis lazuli. Horus and Isis and Osiris peeped down from every niche and shelf, while across the ceiling a true son of Old Nile, a great, hanging-jawed crocodile, was slung in a double noose.

In the centre of this singular chamber was a large, square table, littered with papers, bottles, and the dried leaves of some graceful, palm-like plant. These varied objects had all been heaped together in order to make room for a mummy case, which had been conveyed from the wall, as was evident from the gap there, and laid across the front of the table. The mummy itself, a horrid, black, withered thing, like a charred head on a gnarled bush, was lying half out of the case, with its clawlike hand and bony forearm resting upon the table. Propped up against the sarcophagus was an old yellow scroll of papyrus, and in front of it, in a wooden armchair, sat the owner of the room, his head thrown back, his widely-opened eyes directed in a horrified stare to the crocodile above him, and his blue, thick lips puffing loudly with every expiration.

"My God! He's dying!" cried Monkhouse Lee distractedly.

He was a slim, handsome young fellow, olive-skinned and dark-eyed, of a Spanish rather than of an English type, with a Celtic intensity of manner which contrasted with the Saxon phlegm of Abercombie Smith.

"Only a faint, I think," said the medical student. "Just give me a hand with him. You take his feet. Now on to the sofa. Can you kick all those little wooden devils off? What a litter it is! Now he will be all right if we undo his collar and give him some water. What has he been up to at all?"

"I don't know. I heard him cry out. I ran up. I know him pretty well, you know. It is very good of you to come down."

"His heart is going like a pair of castanets," said Smith, laying his hand on the breast of the unconscious man. "He seems to me to be frightened all to pieces. Chuck the water over him! What a face he has got on him!"

It was indeed a strange and most repellent face, for colour and outline were equally unnatural. It was white, not with the ordinary pallor of fear but with an absolutely bloodless white, like the underside of a sole. He was very fat, but gave the impression of having at some time been considerably fatter, for his skin hung loosely increases and folds, and was shot with a meshwork of wrinkles. Short, stubbly brown hair bristled up from his scalp, with a pair of thick, wrinkled ears protruding on either side. His light grey eyes were still open, the pupils dilated and the balls projecting in a fixed and horrid stare. It seemed to Smith as he looked down upon him that he had never seen nature's danger signals flying so plainly upon a man's countenance, and his thoughts turned more seriously to the warning which Hastie had given him an hour before.

"What the deuce can have frightened him so?" he asked.

"It's the mummy."

"The mummy? How, then?"

"I don't know. It's beastly and morbid. I wish he would drop it. It's the second fright he has given me. It was the same last winter. I found him just like this, with that horrid thing in front of him."

"What does he want with the mummy, then?"

"Oh, he's a crank, you know. It's his hobby. He knows more about these things than any man in England. But I wish he wouldn't! Ah, he's beginning to come to."

A faint tinge of colour had begun to steal back into Bellingham's ghastly cheeks, and his eyelids shivered like a sail after a calm. He clasped and unclasped his hands, drew a long, thin breath between his teeth, and suddenly jerking up his head, threw a glance of recognition around him. As his eyes fell upon the mummy, he sprang off the sofa, seized the roll of papyrus, thrust it into a drawer, turned the key, and then staggered back on to the sofa.

"What's up?" he asked. "What do you chaps want?"

"You've been shrieking out and making no end of a fuss," said Monkhouse Lee. "If our neighbour here from above hadn't come down, I'm sure I don't know what I should have done with you."

"Ah, it's Abercrombie Smith," said Bellingham, glancing up at him. "How very good of you to come in! What a fool I am! Oh, my God, what a fool I am!"

He sunk his head on to his hands, and burst into peal after peal of hysterical laughter.

"Look here! Drop it!" cried Smith, shaking him roughly by the shoulder.

"Your nerves are all in a jangle. You must drop these little midnight games with mummies, or you'll be going off your chump. You're all on wires now."

"I wonder," said Bellingham, "whether you would be as cool as I am if you had seen——"

"What then?"

"Oh, nothing. I meant that I wonder if you could sit up at night with a mummy without trying your nerves. I have no doubt that you are quite right. I dare say that I have been taking it out of myself too much lately. But I am all right now. Please don't go, though. Just wait for a few minutes until I am quite myself."

"The room is very close," remarked Lee, throwing open the window and letting in the cool night air.

"It's balsamic resin," said Bellingham. He lifted up one of the dried palmate leaves from the table and frizzled it over the chimney of the lamp. It broke away into heavy smoke wreaths, and a pungent, biting odour filled the chamber. "It's the sacred plant—the plant of the priests," he remarked. "Do you know anything of Eastern languages, Smith?"

"Nothing at all. Not a word."

The answer seemed to lift a weight from the Egyptologist's mind.

"By-the-way," he continued, "how long was it from the time that you ran down, until I came to my senses?"

"Not long. Some four or five minutes."

"I thought it could not be very long," said he, drawing a long breath. "But what a strange thing unconsciousness is! There is no measurement to it. I could not tell from my own sensations if it were seconds or weeks. Now that gentleman on the table was packed up in the days of the eleventh dynasty, some forty centuries ago, and yet if he could find his tongue he would tell us that this lapse of time has been but a closing of the eyes and a reopening of them. He is a singularly fine mummy, Smith."

Smith stepped over to the table and looked down with a professional eye at the black and twisted form in front of him. The features, though horribly discoloured, were perfect, and two little nut-like eyes still lurked in the depths of the black, hollow sockets. The blotched skin was drawn tightly from bone to bone, and a tangled wrap of black coarse hair fell over the ears. Two thin teeth, like those of a rat, overlay the shrivelled lower lip. In its crouching position, with bent joints and craned head, there was a suggestion of energy about the horrid thing which made Smith's gorge rise. The gaunt ribs, with their parchment-like covering, were exposed, and the sunken, leaden-hued abdomen, with the long slit where the embalmer had left his mark; but the lower limbs were wrapt round with coarse yellow bandages. A number of little clove-like pieces of myrrh and of cassia were sprinkled over the body, and lay scattered on the inside of the case.

"I don't know his name," said Bellingham, passing his hand over the shrivelled head. "You see the outer sarcophagus with the inscriptions is missing. Lot 249 is all the title he has now. You see it printed on his case. That was his number in the auction at which I picked him up."

"He has been a very pretty sort of fellow in his day," remarked Abercrombie Smith.

"He has been a giant. His mummy is six feet seven in length, and that would be a giant over there, for they were never a very robust race. Feel these great knotted bones, too. He would be a nasty fellow to tackle."

"Perhaps these very hands helped to build the stones into the pyramids," suggested Monkhouse Lee, looking down with disgust in his eyes at the crooked, unclean talons.

"No fear. This fellow has been pickled in natron, and looked after in the most approved style. They did not serve hodsmen in that fashion. Salt or bitumen was enough for them. It has been calculated that this sort of thing cost about seven hundred and thirty pounds in our money. Our friend was a noble at the least. What do you make of that small inscription near his feet, Smith?"

"I told you that I know no Eastern tongue."

"Ah, so you did. It is the name of the embalmer, I take it. A very conscientious worker he must have been. I wonder how many modern works will survive four thousand years?"

He kept on speaking lightly and rapidly, but it was evident to Abercrombie Smith that he was still palpitating with fear. His hands shook, his lower lip trembled, and look where he would, his eye always came sliding round to his gruesome companion. Through all his fear, however, there was a suspicion of triumph in his tone and manner. His eye shone, and his footstep, as he paced the room, was brisk and jaunty. He gave the impression of a man who has gone through an ordeal, the marks of which he still bears upon him, but which has helped him to his end.

"You're not going yet?" he cried, as Smith rose from the sofa.

At the prospect of solitude, his fears seemed to crowd back upon him, and he stretched out a hand to detain him.

"Yes, I must go. I have my work to do. You are all right now. I think that with your nervous system you should take up some less morbid study."

"Oh, I am not nervous as a rule; and I have unwrapped mummies before."

"You fainted last time," observed Monkhouse Lee.

"Ah, yes, so I did. Well, I must have a nerve tonic or a course of electricity. You are not going, Lee?"

"I'll do whatever you wish, Ned."

"Then I'll come down with you and have a shake-down on your sofa. Good-night, Smith. I am so sorry to have disturbed you with my foolishness."

They shook hands, and as the medical student stumbled up the spiral and irregular stair he heard a key turn in a door, and the steps of his two new acquaintances as they descended to the lower floor.

In this strange way began the acquaintance between Edward Bellingham and Abercrombie Smith, an acquaintance which the latter, at least, had no desire to push further. Bellingham, however, appeared to have taken a fancy to his rough-spoken neighbour, and made his advances in such a way that he could hardly be repulsed without absolute brutality. Twice he called to thank Smith for his assistance, and many times afterwards he looked in with books, papers, and such other civilities as two bachelor neighbours can offer each other. He was, as Smith soon found, a man of wide reading, with catholic tastes and an extraordinary memory. His manner, too, was so pleasing and suave that one came, after a time, to overlook his repellent appearance. For a jaded and wearied man he was no unpleasant companion, and Smith found himself, after a time, looking forward to his visits, and even returning them.

Clever as he undoubtedly was, however, the medical student seemed to detect a dash of insanity in the man. He broke out at times into a high, inflated style of talk which was in contrast with the simplicity of his life.

"It is a wonderful thing," he cried, "to feel that one can command powers of good and of evil—a ministering angel or a demon of vengeance." And again, of Monkhouse Lee, he said,—"Lee is a good fellow, an honest fellow, but he is without strength or ambition. He would not make a fit partner for a man with a great enterprise. He would not make a fit partner for me."

At such hints and innuendoes stolid Smith, puffing solemnly at his pipe, would simply raise his eyebrows and shake his head, with little interjections of medical wisdom as to earlier hours and fresher air.

One habit Bellingham had developed of late which Smith knew to be a frequent herald of a weakening mind. He appeared to be forever talking to himself. At late hours of the night, when there could be no visitor with him, Smith could still hear his voice beneath him in a low, muffled monologue, sunk almost to a whisper, and yet very audible in the silence. This solitary babbling annoyed and distracted the student, so that he spoke more than once to his neighbour about it. Bellingham, however, flushed up at the charge, and denied curtly that he had uttered a sound; indeed, he showed more annoyance over the matter than the occasion seemed to demand.

Had Abercrombie Smith had any doubt as to his own ears he had not to go far to find corroboration. Tom Styles, the little wrinkled man-servant who had attended to the wants of the lodgers in the turret for a longer time than any man's memory could carry him, was sorely put to it over the same matter.

"If you please, sir," said he, as he tidied down the top chamber one morning, "do you think Mr. Bellingham is all right, sir?"

"All right, Styles?"

"Yes sir. Right in his head, sir."

"Why should he not be, then?"

"Well, I don't know, sir. His habits has changed of late. He's not the same man he used to be, though I make free to say that he was never quite one of my gentlemen, like Mr. Hastie or yourself, sir. He's took to talkin' to himself something awful. I wonder it don't disturb you. I don't know what to make of him, sir."

"I don't know what business it is of yours, Styles."

"Well, I takes an interest, Mr. Smith. It may be forward of me, but I can't help it. I feel sometimes as if I was mother and father to my young gentlemen. It all falls on me when things go wrong and the relations come. But Mr. Bellingham, sir. I want to know what it is that walks about his room sometimes when he's out and when the door's locked on the outside."

"Eh! you're talking nonsense, Styles."

"Maybe so, sir; but I heard it more'n once with my own ears."

"Rubbish, Styles."

"Very good, sir. You'll ring the bell if you want me."

Abercrombie Smith gave little heed to the gossip of the old man-servant, but a small incident occurred a few days later which left an unpleasant effect upon his mind, and brought the words of Styles forcibly to his memory.

Bellingham had come up to see him late one night, and was entertaining him with an interesting account of the rock tombs of Beni Hassan in Upper Egypt, when Smith, whose hearing was remarkably acute, distinctly heard the sound of a door opening on the landing below.

"There's some fellow gone in or out of your room," he remarked.

Bellingham sprang up and stood helpless for a moment, with the expression of a man who is half incredulous and half afraid.

"I surely locked it. I am almost positive that I locked it," he stammered. "No one could have opened it."

"Why, I hear someone coming up the steps now," said Smith.

Bellingham rushed out through the door, slammed it loudly behind him, and hurried down the stairs. About half-way down Smith heard him stop, and thought he caught the sound of whispering. A moment later the door beneath him shut, a key creaked in a lock, and Bellingham, with beads of moisture upon his pale face, ascended the stairs once more, and re-entered the room.

"It's all right," he said, throwing himself down in a chair. "It was that fool of a dog. He had pushed the door open. I don't know how I came to forget to lock it."

"I didn't know you kept a dog," said Smith, looking very thoughtfully at the disturbed face of his companion.

"Yes, I haven't had him long. I must get rid of him. He's a great nuisance."

"He must be, if you find it so hard to shut him up. I should have thought that shutting the door would have been enough, without locking it."

"I want to prevent old Styles from letting him out. He's of some value, you know, and it would be awkward to lose him."

"I am a bit of a dog-fancier myself," said Smith, still gazing hard at his companion from the corner of his eyes. "Perhaps you'll let me have a look at it."

"Certainly. But I am afraid it cannot be to-night; I have an appointment. Is that clock right? Then I am a quarter of an hour late already. You'll excuse me, I am sure."

He picked up his cap and hurried from the room. In spite of his appointment, Smith heard him re-enter his own chamber and lock his door upon the inside.

This interview left a disagreeable impression upon the medical student's mind. Bellingham had lied to him, and lied so clumsily that it looked as if he had desperate reasons for concealing the truth. Smith knew that his neighbour had no dog. He knew, also, that the step which he had heard upon the stairs was not the step of an animal. But if it were not, then what could it be? There was old Styles's statement about the something which used to pace the room at times when the owner was absent. Could it be a woman? Smith rather inclined to the view. If so, it would mean disgrace and expulsion to Bellingham if it were discovered by the authorities, so that his anxiety and falsehoods might be accounted for. And yet it was inconceivable that an undergraduate could keep a woman in his rooms without being instantly detected. Be the explanation what it might, there was something ugly about it, and Smith determined, as he turned to his books, to discourage all further attempts at intimacy on the part of his soft-spoken and ill-favoured neighbour.

But his work was destined to interruption that night. He had hardly caught tip the broken threads when a firm, heavy footfall came three steps at a time from below, and Hastie, in blazer and flannels, burst into the room.

"Still at it!" said he, plumping down into his wonted arm-chair. "What a chap you are to stew! I believe an earthquake might come and knock Oxford into a cocked hat, and you would sit perfectly placid with your books among the rains. However, I won't bore you long. Three whiffs of baccy, and I am off."

"What's the news, then?" asked Smith, cramming a plug of bird's-eye into his briar with his forefinger.

"Nothing very much. Wilson made 70 for the freshmen against the eleven. They say that they will play him instead of Buddicomb, for Buddicomb is clean off colour. He used to be able to bowl a little, but it's nothing but half-vollies and long hops now."

"Medium right," suggested Smith, with the intense gravity which comes upon a 'varsity man when he speaks of athletics.

"Inclining to fast, with a work from leg. Comes with the arm about three inches or so. He used to be nasty on a wet wicket. Oh, by-the-way, have you heard about Long Norton?"

"What's that?"

"He's been attacked."

"Attacked?"

"Yes, just as he was turning out of the High Street, and within a hundred yards of the gate of Old's."

"But who——"

"Ah, that's the rub! If you said 'what,' you would be more grammatical. Norton swears that it was not human, and, indeed, from the scratches on his throat, I should be inclined to agree with him."

"What, then? Have we come down to spooks?"

Abercrombie Smith puffed his scientific contempt.

"Well, no; I don't think that is quite the idea, either. I am inclined to think that if any showman has lost a great ape lately, and the brute is in these parts, a jury would find a true bill against it. Norton passes that way every night, you know, about the same hour. There's a tree that hangs low over the path—the big elm from Rainy's garden. Norton thinks the thing dropped on him out of the tree. Anyhow, he was nearly strangled by two arms, which, he says, were as strong and as thin as steel bands. He saw nothing; only those beastly arms that tightened and tightened on him. He yelled his head nearly off, and a couple of chaps came running, and the thing went over the wall like a cat. He never got a fair sight of it the whole time. It gave Norton a shake up, I can tell you. I tell him it has been as good as a change at the sea-side for him."

"A garrotter, most likely," said Smith.

"Very possibly. Norton says not; but we don't mind what he says. The garrotter had long nails, and was pretty smart at swinging himself over walls. By-the-way, your beautiful neighbour would be pleased if he heard about it. He had a grudge against Norton, and he's not a man, from what I know of him, to forget his little debts. But hallo, old chap, what have you got in your noddle?"

"Nothing," Smith answered curtly.

He had started in his chair, and the look had flashed over his face which comes upon a man who is struck suddenly by some unpleasant idea.

"You looked as if something I had said had taken you on the raw. By-the-way, you have made the acquaintance of Master B. since I looked in last, have you not? Young Monkhouse Lee told me something to that effect."

"Yes; I know him slightly. He has been up here once or twice."

"Well, you're big enough and ugly enough to take care of yourself. He's not what I should call exactly a healthy sort of Johnny, though, no doubt, he's very clever, and all that. But you'll soon find out for yourself. Lee is all right; he's a very decent little fellow. Well, so long, old chap! I row Mullins for the Vice-Chancellor's pot on Wednesday week, so mind you come down, in case I don't see you before."

Bovine Smith laid down his pipe and turned stolidly to his books once more. But with all the will in the world, he found it very hard to keep his mind upon his work. It would slip away to brood upon the man beneath him, and upon the little mystery which hung round his chambers. Then his thoughts turned to this singular attack of which Hastie had spoken, and to the grudge which Bellingham was said to owe the object of it. The two ideas would persist in rising together in his mind, as though there were some close and intimate connection between them. And yet the suspicion was so dim and vague that it could not be put down in words.

"Confound the chap!" cried Smith, as he shied his book on pathology across the room. "He has spoiled my night's reading, and that's reason enough, if there were no other, why I should steer clear of him in the future."

For ten days the medical student confined himself so closely to his studies that he neither saw nor heard anything of either of the men beneath him. At the hours when

Bellingham had been accustomed to visit him, he took care to sport his oak, and though he more than once heard a knocking at his outer door, he resolutely refused to answer it. One afternoon, however, he was descending the stairs when, just as he was passing it, Bellingham's door flew open, and young Monkhouse Lee came out with his eyes sparkling and a dark flush of anger upon his olive cheeks. Close at his heels followed Bellingham, his fat, unhealthy face all quivering with malignant passion.

"You fool!" he hissed. "You'll be sorry."

"Very likely," cried the other. "Mind what I say. It's off! I won't hear of it!"

"You've promised, anyhow."

"Oh, I'll keep that! I won't speak. But I'd rather little Eva was in her grave. Once for all, it's off. She'll do what I say. We don't want to see you again."

So much Smith could not avoid hearing, but he hurried on, for he had no wish to be involved in their dispute. There had been a serious breach between them, that was clear enough, and Lee was going to cause the engagement with his sister to be broken off. Smith thought of Hastie's comparison of the toad and the dove, and was glad to think that the matter was at an end. Bellingham's face when he was in a passion was not pleasant to look upon. He was not a man to whom an innocent girl could be trusted for life. As he walked, Smith wondered languidly what could have caused the quarrel, and what the promise might be which Bellingham had been so anxious that Monkhouse Lee should keep.

It was the day of the sculling match between Hastie and Mullins, and a stream of men were making their way down to the banks of the Isis. A May sun was shining brightly, and the yellow path was barred with the black shadows of the tall elm-trees. On either side the grey colleges lay back from the road, the hoary old mothers of minds looking out from their high, mullioned windows at the tide of young life which swept so merrily past them. Black-clad tutors, prim officials, pale reading men, brown-faced, straw-hatted young athletes in white sweaters or many-coloured blazers, all were hurrying towards the blue winding river which curves through the Oxford meadows.

Abercrombie Smith, with the intuition of an old oarsman, chose his position at the point where he knew that the struggle, if there were a struggle, would come. Far off he heard the hum which announced the start, the gathering roar of the approach, the thunder of running feet, and the shouts of the men in the boats beneath him. A spray of half-clad, deep-breathing runners shot past him, and craning over their shoulders, he saw Hastie pulling a steady thirty-six, while his opponent, with a jerky forty, was a good boat's length behind him. Smith gave a cheer for his friend, and pulling out his watch, was starting off again for his chambers, when he felt a touch upon his shoulder, and found that young Monkhouse Lee was beside him.

"I saw you there," he said, in a timid, deprecating way. "I wanted to speak to you, if you could spare me a half-hour. This cottage is mine. I share it with Harrington of King's. Come in and have a cup of tea."

"I must be back presently," said Smith. "I am hard on the grind at present. But I'll come in for a few minutes with pleasure. I wouldn't have come out only Hastie is a friend of mine."

"So he is of mine. Hasn't he a beautiful style? Mullins wasn't in it. But come into the cottage. It's a little den of a place, but it is pleasant to work in during the summer months."

It was a small, square, white building, with green doors and shutters, and a rustic trellis-work porch, standing back some fifty yards from the river's bank. Inside, the main room was roughly fitted up as a study—deal table, unpainted shelves with books, and a few cheap oleographs upon the wall. A kettle sang upon a spirit-stove, and there were tea things upon a tray on the table.

"Try that chair and have a cigarette," said Lee. "Let me pour you out a cup of tea. It's so good of you to come in, for I know that your time is a good deal taken up. I wanted to say to you that, if I were you, I should change my rooms at once."

"Eh?"

Smith sat staring with a lighted match in one hand and his unlit cigarette in the other.

"Yes; it must seem very extraordinary, and the worst of it is that I cannot give my reasons, for I am under a solemn promise—a very solemn promise. But I may go so far as to say that I don't think Bellingham is a very safe man to live near. I intend to camp out here as much as I can for a time."

"Not safe! What do you mean?"

"Ah, that's what I mustn't say. But do take my advice, and move your rooms. We had a grand row to-day. You must have heard us, for you came down the stairs."

"I saw that you had fallen out."

"He's a horrible chap, Smith. That is the only word for him. I have had doubts about him ever since that night when he fainted—you remember, when you came down. I taxed him to-day, and he told me things that made my hair rise, and wanted me to stand in with him. I'm not strait-laced, but I am a clergyman's son, you know, and I think there are some things which are quite beyond the pale. I only thank God that I found him out before it was too late, for he was to have married into my family."

"This is all very fine, Lee," said Abercrombie Smith curtly. "But either you are saying a great deal too much or a great deal too little."

"I give you a warning."

"If there is real reason for warning, no promise can bind you. If I see a rascal about to blow a place up with dynamite no pledge will stand in my way of preventing him."

"Ah, but I cannot prevent him, and I can do nothing but warn you."

"Without saying what you warn me against."

"Against Bellingham."

"But that is childish. Why should I fear him, or any man?"

"I can't tell you. I can only entreat you to change your rooms. You are in danger where you are. I don't even say that Bellingham would wish to injure you. But it might happen, for he is a dangerous neighbour just now."

"Perhaps I know more than you think," said Smith, looking keenly at the young man's boyish, earnest face.

"Suppose I tell you that someone else shares Bellingham's rooms."

Monkhouse Lee sprang from his chair in uncontrollable excitement.

"You know, then?" he gasped.

"A woman."

Lee dropped back again with a groan.

"My lips are sealed," he said. "I must not speak."

"Well, anyhow," said Smith, rising, "it is not likely that I should allow myself to be frightened out of rooms which suit me very nicely. It would be a little too feeble for me to move out all my goods and chattels because you say that Bellingham might in some unexplained way do me an injury. I think that I'll just take my chance, and stay where I am, and as I see that it's nearly five o'clock, I must ask you to excuse me."

He bade the young student adieu in a few curt words, and made his way homeward through the sweet spring evening feeling half-ruffled, half-amused, as any other strong, unimaginative man might who has been menaced by a vague and shadowy danger.

There was one little indulgence which Abercrombie Smith always allowed himself, however closely his work might press upon him. Twice a week, on the Tuesday and the Friday, it was his invariable custom to walk over to Farlingford, the residence of Dr. Plumptree Peterson, situated about a mile and a half out of Oxford. Peterson had been a close friend of Smith's elder brother Francis, and as he was a bachelor, fairly well-to-do, with a good cellar and a better library, his house was a pleasant goal for a man who was in need of a brisk walk. Twice a week, then, the medical student would swing out there along the dark country roads, and spend a pleasant hour in Peterson's comfortable study, discussing, over a glass of old port, the gossip of the 'varsity or the latest developments of medicine or of surgery.

On the day which followed his interview with Monkhouse Lee, Smith shut up his books at a quarter past eight, the hour when he usually started for his friend's house. As he was leaving his room, however, his eyes chanced to fall upon one of the books which Bellingham had lent him, and his conscience pricked him for not having returned it. However repellent the man might be, he should not be treated with discourtesy. Taking the book, he walked downstairs and knocked at his neighbour's door. There was no answer; but on turning the handle he found that it was unlocked. Pleased at the thought of avoiding an interview, he stepped inside, and placed the book with his card upon the table.

The lamp was turned half down, but Smith could see the details of the room plainly enough. It was all much as he had seen it before—the frieze, the animal-headed gods, the banging crocodile, and the table littered over with papers and dried leaves. The mummy case stood upright against the wall, but the mummy itself was missing. There was no sign of any second occupant of the room, and he felt as he withdrew that he had probably done Bellingham an injustice. Had he a guilty secret to preserve, he would hardly leave his door open so that all the world might enter.

The spiral stair was as black as pitch, and Smith was slowly making his way down its irregular steps, when he was suddenly conscious that something had passed him in the darkness. There was a faint sound, a whiff of air, a light brushing past his elbow, but so slight that he could scarcely be certain of it. He stopped and listened, but the wind was rustling among the ivy outside, and he could hear nothing else.

"Is that you, Styles?" he shouted.

There was no answer, and all was still behind him. It must have been a sudden gust of air, for there were crannies and cracks in the old turret. And yet he could almost have sworn that he heard a footfall by his very side. He had emerged into the quadrangle, still turning the matter over in his head, when a man came running swiftly across the smooth-cropped lawn.

"Is that you, Smith?"

"Hullo, Hastie!"

"For God's sake come at once! Young Lee is drowned! Here's Harrington of King's with the news. The doctor is out. You'll do, but come along at once. There may be life in him."

"Have you brandy?"

"No."

"I'll bring some. There's a flask on my table."

Smith bounded up the stairs, taking three at a time, seized the flask, and was rushing down with it, when, as he passed Bellingham's room, his eyes fell upon something which left him gasping and staring upon the landing.

The door, which he had closed behind him, was now open, and right in front of him, with the lamp-light shining upon it, was the mummy case. Three minutes ago it had been empty. He could swear to that. Now it framed the lank body of its horrible occupant, who stood, grim and stark, with his black shrivelled face towards the door. The form was lifeless and inert, but it seemed to Smith as he gazed that there still lingered a lurid spark of vitality, some faint sign of consciousness in the little eyes which lurked in the depths of the hollow sockets. So astounded and shaken was he that he had forgotten his errand, and was still staring at the lean, sunken figure when the voice of his friend below recalled him to himself.

"Come on, Smith!" he shouted. "It's life and death, you know. Hurry up! Now, then," he added, as the medical student reappeared, "let us do a sprint. It is well under a mile, and we should do it in five minutes. A human life is better worth running for than a pot."

Neck and neck they dashed through the darkness, and did not pull up until, panting and spent, they had reached the little cottage by the river. Young Lee, limp and dripping like a broken water-plant, was stretched upon the sofa, the green scum of the river upon his black hair, and a fringe of white foam upon his leaden-hued lips. Beside him knelt his fellow-student Harrington, endeavouring to chafe some warmth back into his rigid limbs.

"I think there's life in him," said Smith, with his hand to the lad's side. "Put your watch glass to his lips. Yes, there's dimming on it. You take one arm, Hastie. Now work it as I do, and we'll soon pull him round."

For ten minutes they worked in silence, inflating and depressing the chest of the unconscious man. At the end of that time a shiver ran through his body, his lips trembled, and he opened his eyes. The three students burst out into an irrepressible cheer.

"Wake up, old chap. You've frightened us quite enough."

"Have some brandy. Take a sip from the flask."

"He's all right now," said his companion Harrington. "Heavens, what a fright I got! I was reading here, and he had gone for a stroll as far as the river, when I heard a scream and a splash. Out I ran, and by the time that I could find him and fish him out, all life seemed to have gone. Then Simpson couldn't get a doctor, for he has a game-leg, and I had to run, and I don't know what I'd have done without you fellows. That's right, old chap. Sit up."

Monkhouse Lee had raised himself on his hands, and looked wildly about him.

"What's up?" he asked. "I've been in the water. Ah, yes; I remember."

A look of fear came into his eyes, and he sank his face into his hands.

"How did you fall in?"

"I didn't fall in."

"How, then?"

"I was thrown in. I was standing by the bank, and something from behind picked me up like a feather and hurled me in. I heard nothing, and I saw nothing. But I know what it was, for all that."

"And so do I," whispered Smith.

Lee looked up with a quick glance of surprise. "You've learned, then!" he said. "You remember the advice I gave you?"

"Yes, and I begin to think that I shall take it."

"I don't know what the deuce you fellows are talking about," said Hastie, "but I think, if I were you, Harrington, I should get Lee to bed at once. It will be time enough to discuss the why and the wherefore when he is a little stronger. I think, Smith, you and I can leave him alone now. I am walking back to college; if you are coming in that direction, we can have a chat."

But it was little chat that they had upon their homeward path. Smith's mind was too full of the incidents of the evening, the absence of the mummy from his neighbour's rooms, the step that passed him on the stair, the reappearance—the extraordinary, inexplicable reappearance of the grisly thing—and then this attack upon Lee, corresponding so closely to the previous outrage upon another man against whom Bellingham bore a grudge. All this settled in his thoughts, together with the many little incidents which had previously turned him against his neighbour, and the singular circumstances under which he was first called in to him. What had been a dim suspicion, a vague, fantastic conjecture, had suddenly taken form, and stood out in his mind as a grim fact, a thing not to be denied. And yet, how monstrous it was! How unheard of! How entirely beyond all bounds of human experience. An impartial judge, or even the friend who walked by his side, would simply tell him that his eyes had deceived him, that the mummy had been there all the time, that young Lee had tumbled into the river as any other man tumbles into a river, and that a blue pill was the best thing for a disordered liver. He felt that he would have said as much if the positions had been reversed. And yet he could swear that Bellingham was a murderer at heart, and that he wielded a weapon such as no man had ever used in all the grim history of crime.

Hastie had branched off to his rooms with a few crisp and emphatic comments upon his friend's unsociability, and Abercrombie Smith crossed the quadrangle to his corner turret with a strong feeling of repulsion for his chambers and their associations. He would take Lee's advice, and move his quarters as soon as possible, for how could a man study when his ear was ever straining for every murmur or footstep in the room below? He observed, as he crossed over the lawn that the light was still shining in Bellingham's window, and as he passed up the staircase the door opened, and the man himself looked out at him. With his fat, evil face he was like some bloated spider fresh from the weaving of his poisonous web.

"Good-evening," said he. "Won't you come in?"

"No," cried Smith, fiercely.

"No? You are busy as ever? I wanted to ask you about Lee. I was sorry to hear that there was a rumour that something was amiss with him."

His features were grave, but there was the gleam of a hidden laugh in his eyes as he spoke. Smith saw it, and he could have knocked him down for it.

"You'll be sorrier still to hear that Monkhouse Lee is doing very well, and is out of all danger," he answered. "Your hellish tricks have not come off this time. Oh, you needn't try to brazen it out. I know all about it."

Bellingham took a step back from the angry student, and half-closed the door as if to protect himself.

"You are mad," he said. "What do you mean? Do you assert that I had anything to do with Lee's accident?"

"Yes," thundered Smith. "You and that bag of bones behind you; you worked it between you. I tell you what it is, Master B., they have given up burning folk like you, but we still keep a hangman, and, by George! If any man in this college meets his death while you are here, I'll have you up, and if you don't swing for it, it won't be my fault. You'll find that your filthy Egyptian tricks won't answer in England."

"You're a raving lunatic," said Bellingham.

"All right. You just remember what I say, for you'll find that I'll be better than my word."

The door slammed, and Smith went fuming up to his chamber, where he locked the door upon the inside, and spent half the night in smoking his old briar and brooding over the strange events of the evening.

Next morning Abercrombie Smith heard nothing of his neighbour, but Harrington called upon him in the afternoon to say that Lee was almost himself again. All day Smith stuck fast to his work, but in the evening he determined to pay the visit to his friend Dr. Peterson upon which he had started upon the night before. A good walk and a friendly chat would be welcome to his jangled nerves.

Bellingham's door was shut as he passed, but glancing back when he was some distance from the turret, he saw his neighbour's head at the window outlined against the lamp-light, his face pressed apparently against the glass as he gazed out into the darkness. It was a blessing to be away from all contact with him, but if for a few hours, and Smith stepped out briskly, and breathed the soft spring air into his lungs. The half-moon lay in the west between two Gothic pinnacles, and threw upon the silvered street a dark tracery from the stone-work above. There was a brisk breeze, and light, fleecy clouds drifted swiftly across the sky. Old's was on the very border of the town, and in five minutes Smith found himself beyond the houses and between the hedges of a May-scented Oxfordshire lane.

It was a lonely and little frequented road which led to his friend's house. Early as it was, Smith did not meet a single soul upon his way. He walked briskly along until he came to the avenue gate, which opened into the long gravel drive leading up to Farlingford. In front of him he could see the cosy red light of the windows glimmering through the foliage. He stood with his hand upon the iron latch of the swinging gate, and he glanced back at the road along which he had come. Something was coming swiftly down it.

It moved in the shadow of the hedge, silently and furtively, a dark, crouching figure, dimly visible against the black background. Even as he gazed back at it, it had lessened its distance by twenty paces, and was fast closing upon him. Out of the darkness he had a glimpse of a scraggy neck, and of two eyes that will ever haunt him in his dreams. He turned, and with a cry of terror he ran for his life up the avenue. There were the red lights, the signals of safety, almost within a stone's throw of him. He was a famous runner, but never had he run as he ran that night.

The heavy gate had swung into place behind him, but he heard it dash open again before his pursuer. As he rushed madly and wildly through the night, he could hear a swift, dry patter behind him, and could see, as he threw back a glance, that this horror was bounding like a tiger at his heels, with blazing eyes and one stringy arm outthrown. Thank God, the door was ajar. He could see the thin bar of light which shot from the lamp in the hall. Nearer yet sounded the clatter from behind. He heard a hoarse gurgling at his very shoulder. With a shriek he flung himself against the door, slammed and bolted it behind him, and sank half-fainting on to the hall chair.

"My goodness, Smith, what's the matter?" asked Peterson, appearing at the door of his study.

"Give me some brandy!"

Peterson disappeared, and came rushing out again with a glass and a decanter.

"You need it," he said, as his visitor drank off what he poured out for him. "Why, man, you are as white as a cheese."

Smith laid down his glass, rose up, and took a deep breath.

"I am my own man again now," said he. "I was never so unmanned before. But, with your leave, Peterson, I will sleep here to-night, for I don't think I could face that road again except by daylight. It's weak, I know, but I can't help it."

Peterson looked at his visitor with a very questioning eye.

"Of course you shall sleep here if you wish. I'll tell Mrs. Burney to make up the spare bed. Where are you off to now?"

"Come up with me to the window that overlooks the door. I want you to see what I have seen."

They went up to the window of the upper hall whence they could look down upon the approach to the house. The drive and the fields on either side lay quiet and still, bathed in the peaceful moonlight.

"Well, really, Smith," remarked Peterson, "it is well that I know you to be an abstemious man. What in the world can have frightened you?"

"I'll tell you presently. But where can it have gone? Ah, now look, look! See the curve of the road just beyond your gate."

"Yes, I see; you needn't pinch my arm off. I saw someone pass. I should say a man, rather thin, apparently, and tall, very tall. But what of him? And what of yourself? You are still shaking like an aspen leaf."

"I have been within hand-grip of the devil, that's all. But come down to your study, and I shall tell you the whole story."

He did so. Under the cheery lamplight, with a glass of wine on the table beside him, and the portly form and florid face of his friend in front, he narrated, in their order, all the events, great and small, which had formed so singular a chain, from the night on which he had found Bellingham fainting in front of the mummy case until his horrid experience of an hour ago.

"There now," he said as he concluded, "that's the whole black business. It is monstrous and incredible, but it is true."

Dr. Plumptree Peterson sat for some time in silence with a very puzzled expression upon his face.

"I never heard of such a thing in my life, never!" he said at last. "You have told me the facts. Now tell me your inferences."

"You can draw your own."

"But I should like to hear yours. You have thought over the matter, and I have not."

"Well, it must be a little vague in detail, but the main points seem to me to be clear enough. This fellow Bellingham, in his Eastern studies, has got hold of some infernal secret by which a mummy—or possibly only this particular mummy—can be temporarily brought to life. He was trying this disgusting business on the night when he fainted. No doubt the sight of the creature moving had shaken his nerve, even though he had expected it. You remember that almost the first words he said were to call out upon himself as a fool. Well, he got more hardened afterwards, and carried the matter through without fainting. The vitality which he could put into it was evidently only a passing thing, for I have seen it continually in its case as dead as this table. He has some elaborate process, I fancy, by which he brings the thing to pass. Having done it, he naturally bethought him that he might use the creature as an agent. It has intelligence and it has strength. For some purpose he took Lee into his confidence; but Lee, like a decent Christian, would have nothing to do with such a business. Then they had a row, and Lee vowed that he would tell his sister of Bellingham's true character. Bellingham's game was to prevent him, and he nearly managed it, by setting this creature of his on his track. He had already tried its powers upon another man—Norton—towards whom he had a grudge. It is the merest chance that he has not two murders upon his soul. Then, when I taxed him with the matter, he had the strongest reasons for wishing to get me out of the way before I could convey my knowledge to anyone else. He got his chance when I went out, for he knew my habits, and where I was bound for. I have had a narrow shave, Peterson, and it is mere luck you didn't find me on your doorstep in the morning. I'm not a nervous man as a rule, and I never thought to have the fear of death put upon me as it was to-night."

"My dear boy, you take the matter too seriously," said his companion. "Your nerves are out of order with your work, and you make too much of it. How could such a thing as this stride about the streets of Oxford, even at night, without being seen?"

"It has been seen. There is quite a scare in the town about an escaped ape, as they imagine the creature to be. It is the talk of the place."

"Well, it's a striking chain of events. And yet, my dear fellow, you must allow that each incident in itself is capable of a more natural explanation."

"What! even my adventure of to-night?"

"Certainly. You come out with your nerves all unstrung, and your head full of this theory of yours. Some gaunt, half-famished tramp steals after you, and seeing you run, is emboldened to pursue you. Your fears and imagination do the rest."

"It won't do, Peterson; it won't do."

"And again, in the instance of your finding the mummy case empty, and then a few moments later with an occupant, you know that it was lamplight, that the lamp was half turned down, and that you had no special reason to look hard at the case. It is quite possible that you may have overlooked the creature in the first instance."

"No, no; it is out of the question."

"And then Lee may have fallen into the river, and Norton been garrotted. It is certainly a formidable indictment that you have against Bellingham; but if you were to place it before a police magistrate, he would simply laugh in your face."

"I know he would. That is why I mean to take the matter into my own hands."

"Eh?"

"Yes; I feel that a public duty rests upon me, and, besides, I must do it for my own safety, unless I choose to allow myself to be hunted by this beast out of the college, and that would be a little too feeble. I have quite made up my mind what I shall do. And first of all, may I use your paper and pens for an hour?"

"Most certainly. You will find all that you want upon that side table."

Abercrombie Smith sat down before a sheet of foolscap, and for an hour, and then for a second hour his pen travelled swiftly over it. Page after page was finished and tossed aside while his friend leaned back in his arm-chair, looking across at him with patient curiosity. At last, with an exclamation of satisfaction, Smith sprang to his feet, gathered his papers up into order, and laid the last one upon Peterson's desk.

"Kindly sign this as a witness," he said.

"A witness? Of what?"

"Of my signature, and of the date. The date is the most important. Why, Peterson, my life might hang upon it."

"My dear Smith, you are talking wildly. Let me beg you to go to bed."

"On the contrary, I never spoke so deliberately in my life. And I will promise to go to bed the moment you have signed it."

"But what is it?"

"It is a statement of all that I have been telling you tonight. I wish you to witness it."

"Certainly," said Peterson, signing his name under that of his companion. "There you are! But what is the idea?"

"You will kindly retain it, and produce it in case I am arrested."

"Arrested? For what?"

"For murder. It is quite on the cards. I wish to be ready for every event. There is only one course open to me, and I am determined to take it."

"For Heaven's sake, don't do anything rash!"

"Believe me, it would be far more rash to adopt any other course. I hope that we won't need to bother you, but it will ease my mind to know that you have this statement of my motives. And now I am ready to take your advice and to go to roost, for I want to be at my best in the morning."

Abercrombie Smith was not an entirely pleasant man to have as an enemy. Slow and easytempered, he was formidable when driven to action. He brought to every purpose in life the same deliberate resoluteness which had distinguished him as a scientific student. He had laid his studies aside for a day, but he intended that the day should not be wasted. Not a word did he say to his host as to his plans, but by nine o'clock he was well on his way to Oxford.

In the High Street he stopped at Clifford's, the gun-maker's, and bought a heavy revolver, with a box of central-fire cartridges. Six of them he slipped into the chambers, and half-cocking the weapon, placed it in the pocket of his coat. He then made his way to Hastie's rooms, where the big oarsman was lounging over his breakfast, with the Sporting Times propped up against the coffeepot.

"Hullo! What's up?" he asked. "Have some coffee?"

"No, thank you. I want you to come with me, Hastie, and do what I ask you."

"Certainly, my boy."

"And bring a heavy stick with you."

"Hullo!" Hastie stared. "Here's a hunting-crop that would fell an ox."

"One other thing. You have a box of amputating knives. Give me the longest of them."

"There you are. You seem to be fairly on the war trail. Anything else?"

"No; that will do." Smith placed the knife inside his coat, and led the way to the quadrangle. "We are neither of us chickens, Hastie," said he. "I think I can do this job alone, but I take you as a precaution. I am going to have a little talk with Bellingham. If I have only him to deal with, I won't, of course, need you. If I shout, however, up you come, and lam out with your whip as hard as you can lick. Do you understand?"

"All right. I'll come if I hear you bellow."

"Stay here, then. It may be a little time, but don't budge until I come down."

"I'm a fixture."

Smith ascended the stairs, opened Bellingham's door and stepped in. Bellingham was seated behind his table, writing. Beside him, among his litter of strange possessions, towered the mummy case, with its sale number 249 still stuck upon its front, and its hideous occupant stiff and stark within it. Smith looked very deliberately round him, closed the door, locked it, took the key from the inside, and then stepping across to the fireplace, struck a match and set the fire alight. Bellingham sat staring, with amazement and rage upon his bloated face.

"Well, really now, you make yourself at home," he gasped.

Smith sat himself deliberately down, placing his watch upon the table, drew out his pistol, cocked it, and laid it in his lap. Then he took the long amputating knife from his bosom, and threw it down in front of Bellingham.

"Now, then," said he, "just get to work and cut up that mummy."

"Oh, is that it?" said Bellingham with a sneer.

"Yes, that is it. They tell me that the law can't touch you. But I have a law that will set matters straight. If in five minutes you have not set to work, I swear by the God who made me that I will put a bullet through your brain!"

"You would murder me?"

Bellingham had half risen, and his face was the colour of putty.

"Yes."

"And for what?"

"To stop your mischief. One minute has gone."

"But what have I done?"

"I know and you know."

"This is mere bullying."

"Two minutes are gone."

"But you must give reasons. You are a madman—a dangerous madman. Why should I destroy my own property? It is a valuable mummy."

"You must cut it up, and you must burn it."

"I will do no such thing."

"Four minutes are gone."

Smith took up the pistol and he looked towards Bellingham with an inexorable face. As the second-hand stole round, he raised his hand, and the finger twitched upon the trigger.

"There! There! I'll do it!" screamed Bellingham.

In frantic haste he caught up the knife and hacked at the figure of the mummy, ever glancing round to see the eye and the weapon of his terrible visitor bent upon him. The creature crackled and snapped under every stab of the keen blade. A thick yellow dust rose up from it. Spices and dried essences rained down upon the floor. Suddenly, with a rending crack, its backbone snapped asunder, and it fell, a brown heap of sprawling limbs, upon the floor.

"Now into the fire!" said Smith.

The flames leaped and roared as the dried and tinderlike debris was piled upon it. The little room was like the stoke-hole of a steamer and the sweat ran down the faces of the two men; but still the one stooped and worked, while the other sat watching him with a set face. A thick, fat smoke oozed out from the fire, and a heavy smell of burned rosin and singed hair filled the air. In a quarter of an hour a few charred and brittle sticks were all that was left of Lot No. 249.

"Perhaps that will satisfy you," snarled Bellingham, with hate and fear in his little grey eyes as he glanced back at his tormenter.

"No; I must make a clean sweep of all your materials. We must have no more devil's tricks. In with all these leaves! They may have something to do with it."

"And what now?" asked Bellingham, when the leaves also had been added to the blaze.

"Now the roll of papyrus which you had on the table that night. It is in that drawer, I think."

"No, no," shouted Bellingham. "Don't burn that! Why, man, you don't know what you do. It is unique; it contains wisdom which is nowhere else to be found."

"Out with it!"

"But look here, Smith, you can't really mean it. I'll share the knowledge with you. I'll teach you all that is in it. Or, stay, let me only copy it before you burn it!"

Smith stepped forward and turned the key in the drawer. Taking out the yellow, curled roll of paper, he threw it into the fire, and pressed it down with his heel. Bellingham screamed, and grabbed at it; but Smith pushed him back, and stood over it until it was reduced to a formless grey ash.

"Now, Master B.," said he, "I think I have pretty well drawn your teeth. You'll hear from me again, if you return to your old tricks. And now good-morning, for I must go back to my studies."

And such is the narrative of Abercrombie Smith as to the singular events which occurred in Old College, Oxford, in the spring of '84. As Bellingham left the university immediately afterwards, and was last heard of in the Soudan, there is no one who can contradict his statement. But the wisdom of men is small, and the ways of nature are strange, and who shall put a bound to the dark things which may be found by those who seek for them?

THE MAKING OF THE MODERN MUMMY

BY DERRICK BELANGER

The Mummy! That vile, mindless creature that rises from the dead to attack the living! A being made up of nothing but bone and dust held together by loosening bandages! A seemingly frail monster that shambles along, arms extended, impenetrable to bullets or axes flung into its body, using superhuman strength to strangle or smother its prey!

This is the most common image of the mummy seen in everything from chilling movies to cereal commercials. Used as a foil for adventurers, a partner to Dracula and Frankenstein, a precursor to the zombies so prevalent in today's pop culture, the mummy is one of the most famous monsters to rise from the rich horror period of the 19th century. Yet the mummy was not always depicted this way; in fact, it tended to be used as a source of romance, a gateway to the unknown, and the butt end of jokes. How did the mummy change from this harmless image to one of nightmares? The answer lies in two stories by Sir Arthur Conan Doyle. Without these works, the mummy as a horror icon may never have emerged in the films of the 20th century, and therefore, never become the monstrous creature we know today.

Egyptomania and Mummy Stories Before Doyle

At the turn of the 19th century, the Western world was enamored with a mania for all things Egyptian, "inspired by the Napoleonic invasion of Egypt in 1798 and the subsequent

British intervention in the region."[5] Egyptian motifs began appearing on pottery, jewelry and clothing. Mummy unrollings became popular social events. In fact, Thomas Pettigrew, a famous mummy unroller was "unwrapping to standing room only crowds in such places as the lecture hall of the Royal Institute."[6] It is no surprise with Egyptomania capturing the minds of the European and American public that their fascination with mummies would seep into the literature of the day.

There tended to be three types of stories centering on ancient Egypt and Egyptian mummies throughout the 19th century. The first involved comedy and parody. The first known publication of a 19th century story involving mummies was entitled *The Mummy!: Or, a Tale of the Twenty-Second Century* by Jane Loudon (at the time Jane Webb). This novel involved a mummy named Cheops brought to life by means of electricity in the 22nd century. The book shows a wacky world of London with a lower class too educated to do work, where robotic lawyers and doctors run on steam power, and where suborbital balloon flight is possible. The mummy in this book is the protagonist acting as tourist and being shown an England of which the author clearly disapproves.

Another story in this vein is Poe's "Some Words With a Mummy." In this story the mummy Allamistakeo is resurrected by a group of men at a mummy unwrapping who decide to hook up a Voltaic pile (i.e. a battery) to the Count. Once revived the mummy and the men go about trying to prove which time period is better that of modern England or that of ancient Egypt. The story then becomes a series of one

---

[5] Curran "Egyptomania: Egypt in Western Art 1730-1930."
[6] Kristek "The UnMuseum - Mummys in Entertainment."

liners. For example, when Count Allamistakeo is told he should be dead, he replies, "I am little more than seven hundred years old! My father lived a thousand and was by no means in his dotage when he died."[7] Many of the lines also make fun of Victorian London. When the Mummy is told modern clothing is better than that of ancient England, Count Allamistakeo "glanced downward to the straps of his pantaloons...his mouth extended itself from ear to ear."[8] While these tales do have resurrected corpses from ancient Egypt, they are a far cry from the horror tales of the 20th century.

A second type of Victorian mummy story involved romance usually as some form of love across the barriers of time. An excellent example of this type of story is *The Romance of a Mummy* by Theophile Gautier. In this novel, an Egyptian mummy is unearthed by Dr. Rumphias and Lord Evandale, two explorers attempting to find an unplundered Egyptian tomb. Unlike most mummy tales, this creature is not shriveled skin and bones but one of the most beautiful women the men had ever laid eyes upon. Once her wrappings were removed, "the young woman showed in the chaste nudity of her lovely form, preserving, in spite of so many centuries that had passed away the fullness of her contours."[9] Dr. Rumphias finds a scroll in the tomb that contains the story of the woman and how she ended up as a mummy. Thus begins the tale within a tale that involves a love triangle between the woman whom we discover is named Tahoser, her lover Poeri, and the Pharaoh who wants to win her heart. The story is melodramatic and includes lots of twists and turns of the soap opera kind as well as the story of Moses added to the mix. In

---

[7] Poe, Edgar Allan. *Some Words With a Mummy*

[8] ibid

[9] Gautier, Theophile. *The Romance of the Mummy. Complete Works Vol. 5.*

the end, Lord Evandale declares his love for Tahoser and cannot look at another woman again. The book ends by stating, "Lord Evandale is retrospectively in love with Tahoser...who dies three thousand five hundred years ago."[10] This story makes the mummy into an item of beauty and fits more in line with the 21st century tales of vampires and Frankensteins who are gorgeous and romantic. Horror remains absent, or is at least greatly reduced, from these stories.

The third type of 19th century mummy story does involve horror. These stories, known as Pharaoh's Curse stories, are tales of supernatural revenge as explorers and Egyptologists are killed or harmed by seemingly unnatural means for ignoring a warning on the outside of a tomb. An excellent example of this story is "Lost in a Pyramid or The Mummy's Curse," by none other than Louisa May Alcott. Alcott, known more for *Little Women,* crafts an eerie tale which begins with Egyptian explorer Paul Forsyth telling his fiancée how he came in possession of seeds from an unknown Egyptian plant. He explains that when he was in Egypt with his partner, Professor Niles, they became lost while exploring one of the larger passages below the Cheops pyramid. Completely befuddled and not sure what to do, the Professor comes up with a plan. He remembered a story of a group that was lost in a tunnel that saved themselves by building a fire. When they built the fire, "the smoke penetrated further than sound or light."[11] Without any firewood, the duo decides to burn a mummy they had discovered in the passage. The plan works and the two are saved by their guide. Before leaving, Professor Niles takes with him several seeds of an unknown

---

[10] ibid

[11] Alcott, Louisa May. "Lost in a Pyramid, or the Mummy's Curse." Project Gutenberg Australia.

plant and a scroll that said the mummy they burned "was that of a sorceress who bequeathed her curse to whoever should disturb her rest."[12] Section one ends with Evelyn, Forsyth's fiancée, convincing him to plant the unknown seeds.

The second part of the story begins three months later on Evelyn and Forsyth's wedding day. Evelyn surprises Forsyth by showing him that she has grown flowers from his seeds, the flowers being ghostly white with no scent. The two are married and that afternoon, Forsyth receives a chilling letter about Niles. The professor has died and his final words are, "beware the mummy's curse, for this fatal flower has killed me."[13] The plant, it ends up, is extremely poisonous to those who hold it for two or three hours. The tale ends with Forsyth discovering Evelyn in a coma, wearing one of the flowers. Forsyth spends the rest of his life tending to his bride who remains in a state between life and death. This terrifying story is much closer to the modern mummy tale. Many modern stories involve curses which cause the mummy to come to life. Even the 1932 Universal film, *The Mummy*, was written to be a mummy's curse story.[14] However, we still do not have the shambling mummy monster. That would come from the mind of Sir Arthur Conan Doyle.

"The Book of Thoth" and "Lot No. 249"

In the autumn of 1888, Doyle took a family vacation to Paris where he toured the Louvre. The Egyptian artifacts in the art museum inspired Doyle to pen his first supernatural mummy story, "The Ring of Thoth." Doyle wrote that it was,

---

[12] ibid

[13] ibid

[14] Even though the film uses a curse, it is a minor part of the story.

"A queer story- powerful I think."[15] The tale, more on the supernatural side than horror side, would nonetheless be a major influence on Mummy fiction. The plot involves a Mr. Jon Vansittart Smith, a bit of a Renaissance man in the fields of Zoology, Chemistry, and Egyptology, who is working on a book that would, "unite the research of Lepsius with the ingenuity of Champollion."[16] Smith ends up visiting the Egyptian collections at the Louvre where he overhears two Britons talking about one of the museum guards. One notes "that by continual contemplation of mummies the chap has become one himself."[17] Smith believes the attendant does look Egyptian and tries to strike up a conversation with the man. The conversation goes nowhere and Smith sits down in a dark corner of the room, looks over his notes, and accidentally falls asleep. It is here where the supernatural element enters.

Smith awakens in the Louvre at night, overlooked, he assumes, because the chair he fell asleep in was in a very dark corner. As Smith rises from his chair he spies the Egyptian attendant sneaking across the exhibit floor. The man takes a mummy out of its case and unwraps its bandages. Like in the novel *The Romance of a Mummy*, the woman below the wrappings is not decrepit but is extremely beautiful. Smith notes, the "face was one of extraordinary loveliness, save for that one blemish in the centre of its forehead."[18] The Egyptian attendant upon seeing the unwrapped woman, "kissed her repeatedly upon the lips and brow."[19] Smith reveals himself to the attendant, and he tells Smith the story behind what he is doing. Another similarity to *The Romance of a Mummy* is that

---

[15] Qtd. in Lellenberg Pg 255
[16] Doyle, pg. 5401
[17] ibid. pg. 5402
[18] ibid. 5406
[19] See note 13

we get a tale within a tale as the attendant explains his real name is Sosra and he is 3,600 years old. By a twist of fate, he and the Priest of Thoth in ancient Egypt, discovered the secret of immortality. They also both fell in love with the same woman, Atma. As Sosra wins Atma's hand, he asks to share the secret elixir of immortality with her. Before Atma can answer, she succumbs to "the white plague, the sign manual of death."[20]The Priest of Thoth finds a way to thwart immortality and dies, but he refuses to let Sosra know his secret. Finally, after thousands of years, Sosra has found his lost love and The Ring of Thoth which contains the antidote to his immortality. The story ends with the body of Sosra discovered in the Louvre the next day with his arms wrapped around Atma.

Doyle's tale seems to follow the typical "Love beyond the boundaries of time," mummy story except for several changes. The first is the concept of the immortal lover from Egypt living for centuries and looking like a living mummy. The second is the underlying implication of necrophilia. Both of these ideas would be borrowed and used for the Universal Mummy film in 1932, the basis for all future mummy stories.

Doyle's second mummy story is also one of his most memorable works beyond that of the great detective. Published in 1892 the story casts away the ideas of funny mummies, romantic mummies, or even Egyptian curses. Here, for the first time, we have the mummy as a blood thirsty rotting corpse out for revenge.[21]The tale begins with Abercrombie Smith, an athletic first year Oxford medical student, being warned by his friend Jephro Hastie about the strange student living in the dorm room directly below Smith.

---

[20] ibid 5412

[21] Wikimedia Foundation. *Lot No. 249.*

The student, Edward Bellingham, is studying to become an Egyptologist and already has a masterful command of Eastern languages as well as mesmerizing powers. Hastie explains, he "talked Coptic to the Copts, and Hebrew to the Jews, and Arabic to the Bedouins, and they were all ready to kiss the hem of his frock-coat."[22] Hastie also says the shocking news that Bellingham is engaged to the beautiful sister of one of their good friends. Hastie says, "It's disgusting to see that brute with her. A toad and a dove..."[23] Later that night after Hastie leaves, Smith is disturbed by a scream from the room below him. Smith goes down to the lower room to help and bursts into a room covered in Egyptian decor. It is here where the reader is first introduced to the mummy, "a horrid, black, withered thing, like a charred head on a gnarled bush...with its clawlike hand and bony forearm."[24] This mummy is no ancient beauty.

Smith helps revive Bellingham who we later learn fainted because he was able to bring the mummy to life using an ancient spell. The story then goes on to have the mummy terrorize the town of Oxford under the guidance of Bellingham. The student uses the mummy to seek revenge on people who have wronged him. Eventually, Smith figures out that Bellingham is using the mummy to attack others. He tries to persuade Bellingham to stop, and one night, he finds himself being pursued by the beast. Smith, trying to outrun the creature, says "this horror was bounding like a tiger at his heels, with blazing eyes and one stringy arm out-thrown."[25] Smith is able to evade the predator. He returns to Bellingham's room later that night and at gun point forces Bellingham to

[22] Doyle pg. 5430
[23] ibid 5406
[24] Doyle 5433
[25] Doyle 5449

destroy and burn the mummy as well as the roll of papyrus that contains the spell to raise the dead. The story ends with Bellingham fleeing to the Sudan perhaps to return someday with more ancient and cursed knowledge.

While both of Doyle's stories were successful in their time, it would be several decades before their influence was felt in the increasingly popular medium of film. Throughout the early 20th century, silent films still followed the formulas for Mummy stories from the Victorian era. These movies were either comedies (*Elixer of Life*), romances (*Through the Centuries*), or curse stories (*Made for Love*). It is quite possible that Doyle's tales would have been remembered just as great pieces of literature but those bearing little influence on the future of fiction; however, Doyle's influence would ripple throughout the remainder of the 20th century due to the advent of the Universal horror films and one in particular simply titled, *The Mummy*.

Doyle's Impact - Universal's Mummy

Without a doubt, the number one most influential mummy story of the 20th Century was the 1932 Universal film, *The Mummy*. The feature focuses on Boris Karloff rising from the dead as Imhotep, a mummy resurrected by a reading from the Scroll of Thoth. The film then jumps ten years into the future with Imhotep, now going under the guise of Ardath Bey, showing a team of archaeologists where to find the tomb of Princess Ankh-es-en-amon. Imhotep's goal is to resurrect the princess, a task he tried once before in ancient Egypt and was entombed for what was considered a sacrilegious act. Eventually, Imhotep discovers Helen Grosvenor, a woman who is revealed to be the reincarnation of Ankh-es-en-amon. Imhotep schemes to kill Helen, then bring her back to life with the Scroll of Thoth, so that she will once again be the princess and live an immortal life with Imhotep. In the end, Imhotep is thwarted (interestingly enough by a statue of Isis that comes to life) and the scroll is burned, never to be used again.[26]

The film, while a unique story, borrows heavily from Doyle.[27] As Richard Freeman notes in his essay, "The Mummy in Context," "there is little doubt that there are many plot points in common, and the popularity of Conan Doyle would indicate that his stories are likely to have been known, at least by John L. Balderston, the final scenarist on the 1932 film."[28] Both the film and "The Ring of Thoth" deal with an ancient man (one an immortal, the other a revived mummy), trying to reconnect with their lost lover. Doyle's story has the two reconnect through death; *The Mummy* has Imhotep attempt to reconnect with his lover through immortality. Even with these differences, ""Doyle's story is obviously a source for the 1932 movie."[29]

In "The Ring of Thoth" and "Lot No. 249," there is also a hint of forbidden love further than the theme of love beyond the ages. This is a more sinister love, that of necrophilia. When Sosra unwraps the mummified remains of Atma, "he kissed her repeatedly upon the lips and brow."[30] As well preserved as Atma is, this scene still has Sosra kissing a corpse. When Sosra's body is discovered at the end of the story, it is written that he is holding Atma so tightly that, "it

---

[26] Freund, *The Mummy*

[27] Interestingly though, according to the book *Hollywood Horror,* when story editor Richard Schayer was assigned to find a work of literature as a basis for *The Mummy*, he claimed that he could not find one. This leads to speculation that perhaps Universal did not want to pay royalties to the Doyle estate.

[28] Freeman, *The Mummy in Context.*

[29] Delahoyde, *Mummies: An Introduction*

[30] See note 18

was only with the utmost difficulty that they were separated."[31] While the story never specifically states if Sosra was fully dressed, the fact that we know Atma was naked does leave the mind to speculate on a darker conclusion. In "Lot No. 249," the reader learns that Bellingham is engaged to a woman yet she never makes an appearance in the story. Instead, Bellingham is shown fawning over his mummy. At one point when Smith is asked if he knows what is making noise in Bellingham's room when the student is away from his room, Smith responds, "A woman."[32] The implication is that the male mummy has taken the place of Bellingham's fiancé. The story ends with "the academic colleagues of the necrophiliac professor"[33] forcing him to destroy his mummy "with hate and fear in his little grey eyes."[34] The hate and fear go beyond the humiliation to the fact that Bellingham was forced to destroy the object of his obsession, perhaps even of his romantic love.

The Universal film also hints at this taboo. In the film, *The Mummy*, when the story of Imhotep's entombment is retold, we discover that his captors found him trying to revive the body of Ankh-es-en-amon. Imhotep briefly explains, "They broke in upon me and found me doing questionable things." Was the questionable thing violating nature by bringing his loved one back to life or was there something even more sinister going on? The fact that Imhotep uses the plural in saying questionable things makes one wonder what more besides raising the dead was he caught doing. Professor Michael Delahoyde thinks this might be one of the reasons that mummies have stood the test of time as memorable

---

[31] pg. 5416
[32] ibid. pg. 5444
[33] Higham pg. 139
[34] Doyle 5455

monsters. He writes, "This perhaps is the potential psychosexual creepiness, since other monsters seem to involve other taboos."[35] This does fit in with the sexualized idea of the vampire so prevalent in today's culture.

Beyond the plot of *The Mummy* film is the one visual that is more famous than the movie itself, that of the mummified corpse of Imhotep rising out of his sarcophas and so startling his guard that the man's mind snaps. All the guard can say is, "It went for a little walk."[36]This little walk, mere seconds of film time, would inscribe itself on the minds of all viewers now and forever, redefining the mummy s a monster. Once again, this concept did not first arise in the minds of the screenwriters but in the mind of Arthur Conan Doyle in his second Mummy story, "Lot No. 249." The image of the monster mummy is etched in the reader's mind after reading the narrative and it is clear to see its reflection in Karloff's screen appearance. As Charles Higham writes in *The Adventures of Conan Doyle*, "*The Ring of Thoth* and *Lot No. 249* are echoed loudly in the film *The Mummy*."[37] The idea of a mindless monster mummy seeking revenge is used in most mummy films and stories that come after *The Mummy*. In fact, *Lot No. 249* is seen as having "a profound influence on the horror movie genre throughout the 20th century."[38] This profound influence is seen in the later Universal mummy films as well as the Hammer films of the 1960s. These movies, such as Universal's *The Mummy's* Hand and Hammer's *The Mummy,* combine the monster mummy from "Lot No. 249," with the resurrection of an ancient lover seen in "The Ring of Thoth." Even other mummy genres closer to the 19th century

---

[35] See note 18
[36] See note 16
[37] Higham 309 (italics from text).
[38] See note 23

stories such as *Abbott and Costello Meet the Mummy,* still use the monster mummy introduced in "Lot No. 249." After Universal's 1932 film, the monster mummy was expected in any story or film in the genre.[39] One can only speculate how different the mummy horror genre would have been, if it even came to exist at all, without Doyle's contributions.

Conclusion

When Arthur Conan Doyle drafted the stories *The Ring of Thoth* and *Lot No. 249*, he did not set out to have a profound impact in the world of horror writings; he simply wanted to tell great tales. The fact these stories are still known today and were extremely impactful shows just how successful Doyle was at his aim. Both stories continue to be collected in horror anthologies and *Lot No. 249* has twice been captured on film. With Universal's popular reboot of the Mummy films at the end of the 20th century, one can see that the monster mummy will be around for years to come. One can even say, due to Doyle's influence, the mummy has now reached its own form of immortality.

---

[39] It is important to note that there were exceptions to this rule. The 1980 film *The Awakening* is an excellent example of the 19th century curse tale (it was adapted from *Jewel of the Seven Stars* by Brahm Stoker) sans monster mummy.

Works Cited

Alcott, Louisa May. "Lost in a Pyramid, or the Mummy's
    Curse." *Project Gutenberg Australia*. N.p., n.d.
    Web. 18 July 2013.
    <http://gutenberg.net.au/ebooks06/0603041h.html>.
The Awakening. Dir. Mike Newell. Perf. Charlton Heston.
    Warner Home Video, 1980. Film.
Curran, Brian. "Egyptomania:Egypt in Western Art 1730-
    1930." *Access My Library*. Gale, 1 Dec. 1996. Web.
    18 July 2013.
    <http://www.accessmylibrary.com/article-1G1-
    19178143/egyptomania-egypt-western-art.html>.
Delahoyde, Michael. "Mummies: Introduction." *Washington
    State University - Pullman, Washington*   .
    Washington state University, 4 Dec. 2009. Web. 19
    July 2013.
    <http://public.wsu.edu/~delahoyd/mummy.intro.ht
    ml>.
Doyle, Sir Arthur Conan. *Delphi Complete Works of Sir
    Arthur Conan Doyle*. Ebook: Delphi Classics, 2011.
    Print.
Freeman, Richard . "THE MUMMY in context." *European
    journal of American studies*. Version 1. Europena
    Association for American Studies, n.d. Web. 19
    July 2013. <http://ejas.revues.org/7566>.
Gautier, Theophile. *Complete Works of Theophile Gautier
    Volume 5*. S.l.: Hardpress Ltd, 2013. Print.
Higham, Charles. *The Adventures of Conan Doyle: the Life
    of the Creator of Sherlock Holmes*. New York:
    Norton, 1976. Print.
Kristek, Lee. "The UnMuseum - Mummys in

Entertainment." *The Museum of UnNatural Mystery*. N.p., n.d. Web. 18 July 2013. <http://www.unmuseum.org/mumwrap.htm>.

"Lot No. 249 - Wikipedia, the free encyclopedia." *Wikipedia, the free encyclopedia*. Wikimedia Foundation, n.d. Web. 19 July 2013. <http://en.wikipedia.org/wiki/Lot_No._249>.

The Mummy. Dir. Karl Freund. Perf. Boris Karloff. 1932. Universal, 2004. DVD.

Poe, Edgar Allan. "Some Words With a Mummy - Edgar Allan Poe." *Books & Literature Classics*. About.com, n.d. Web. 18 July 2013. <http://classiclit.about.com/library/bl-etexts/eapoe/bl-eapoe-some.htm>.

Vieira, Mark A.. *Hollywood Horror: From Gothic to Cosmic*. New York: Harry N. Abrams, 2003. Print.

Section 2: The Dawn of the Doyle Detective

INTRODUCTION

It would be remiss to release this anthology sans any stories in the genre for which Sir Arthur Conan Doyle is most famously known, that of the detective story. This anthology includes Doyle's least known work of detective fiction, *The Mystery of Cloomber.* By most accounts, Doyle hated it; or at the very least, found his own novel to be a huge disappointment. Thus, *The Mystery of Cloomber* was the only novel of Doyle's excluded from the 24 volume Crowborough edition of his fiction published in 1930. It is not entirely clear whether Doyle was upset by the novel's sales, by the story itself, or a combination of the two; however, despite Doyle's personal criticism, the novel has developed a small but growing fan base over a century after its initial publication.

Like some of Doyle's later detective fiction including that of Sherlock Holmes and Professor Challenger, *The Mystery of Cloomber* is a mystery, a horror story, a supernatural piece, and a revenge tale rolled into one. The story focuses on the new owner of a Scottish estate -- secretive, paranoid; and ultimately resolved to a sinister fate. The detective, John Fothergill West, is an amateur who uses modes of deduction similar to the logic used by Holmes and Challenger in Doyle's later works. While most readers would be hard pressed not to solve the case long before West, one can see in *Cloomber* Doyle's first foray into the multi-genre mystery that would make him the most famous detective fiction writer of all time.

--Derrick Belanger

THE MYSTERY OF CLOOMBER

CHAPTER 1 - *THE HEGIRA OF THE WESTS FROM EDINBURGH*

I, John Fothergill West, student of law in the University of St. Andrews, have endeavoured in the ensuing pages to lay my statement before the public in a concise and business-like fashion.

It is not my wish to achieve literary success, nor have I any desire by the graces of my style, or by the artistic ordering of my incidents, to throw a deeper shadow over the strange passages of which I shall have to speak. My highest ambition is that those who know something of the matter should, after reading my account, be able to conscientiously indorse it without finding a single paragraph in which I have either added to or detracted from the truth.

Should I attain this result, I shall rest amply satisfied with the outcome of my first, and probably my last, venture in literature.

It was my intention to write out the sequence of events in due order, depending on trustworthy hearsay when I was describing that which was beyond my own personal knowledge. I have now, however, through the kind cooperation of friends, hit upon a plan which promises to be less onerous to me and more satisfactory to the reader. This is nothing less than to make use of the various manuscripts which I have by me bearing upon the subject, and to add to them the first-hand evidence contributed by those who had the best opportunities of knowing Major-General J. B. Heatherstone.

In pursuance of this design I shall lay before the public the testimony of Israel Stakes, formerly coachman at Cloomber Hall, and of John Easterling, F.R.C.P. Edin., now practising at Stranraer, in Wigtownshire. To these I shall add a verbatim account extracted from the journal of the late John Berthier Heatherstone, of the events which occurred in the Thul Valley in the autumn of '41 towards the end of the first Afghan War, with a description of the skirmish in the Terada defile, and of the death of the man Ghoolab Shah.

To myself I reserve the duty of filling up all the gaps and chinks which may be left in the narrative. By this arrangement I have sunk from the position of an author to that of a compiler, but on the other hand my work has ceased to be a story and has expanded into a series of affidavits.

My Father, John Hunter West, was a well-known Oriental and Sanskrit scholar, and his name is still of weight with those who are interested in such matters. He it was who first after Sir William Jones called attention to the great value of early Persian literature, and his translations from the Hafiz and from Ferideddin Atar have earned the warmest commendations from the Baron von Hammer-Purgstall, of Vienna, and other distinguished Continental critics.

In the issue of the *Orientalisches Scienzblatt* for January, 1861, he is described as *"Der beruhmte und sehr gelhernte Hunter West von Edinburgh"*—a passage which I well remember that he cut out and stowed away, with a pardonable vanity, among the most revered family archives.

He had been brought up to be a solicitor, or Writer to the Signet, as it is termed in Scotland, but his learned hobby absorbed so much of his time that he had little to devote to the pursuit of his profession.

When his clients were seeking him at his chambers in George Street, he was buried in the recesses of the Advocates' Library, or poring over some mouldy manuscript at the Philosophical Institution, with his brain more exercised over the code which Menu propounded six hundred years before the birth of Christ than over the knotty problems of Scottish law in the nineteenth century. Hence it can hardly be wondered at that as his learning accumulated his practice dissolved, until at the very moment when he had attained the zenith of his celebrity he had also reached the nadir of his fortunes.

There being no chair of Sanscrit in any of his native universities, and no demand anywhere for the only mental wares which he had to dispose of, we should have been forced to retire into genteel poverty, consoling ourselves with the aphorisms and precepts of Firdousi, Omar Khayyam, and others of his Eastern favourites, had it not been for the kindness and liberality of his half-brother William Farintosh, the Laird of Branksome, in Wigtownshire.

This William Farintosh was the proprietor of a landed estate, the acreage which bore, unfortunately, a most disproportional relation to its value, for it formed the bleakest and most barren tract of land in the whole of a bleak and barren shire. As a bachelor, however, his expenses had been small, and he had contrived from the rents of his scattered cottages, and the sale of the Galloway nags, which he bred upon the moors, not only to live as a laird should, but to put by a considerable sum in the bank.

We had heard little from our kinsman during the days of our comparative prosperity, but just as we were at our wit's end, there came a letter like a ministering angel, giving us assurance of sympathy and succour. In it the Laird of Branksome told us that one of his lungs had been growing weaker for some time, and that Dr. Easterling, of Stranraer, had strongly advised him to spend the few years which were left to him in some more genial climate. He had determined, therefore to set out for the South of Italy, and he begged that we should take up our residence at Branksome in his absence, and that my father should act as his land steward and agent at a salary which placed us above all fear of want.

Our mother had been dead for some years, so that there were only myself, my father, and my sister Esther to consult, and it may be readily imagined that it did not take us long to decide upon the acceptance of the laird's generous offer. My father started for Wigtown that very night, while Esther and I followed a few days afterwards, bearing with us two potato-sacksful of learned books, and such other of our household effects that were worth the trouble and expense of transport.

CHAPTER 2 - *OF THE STRANGE MANNER IN WHICH A TENANT CAME TO CLOOMBER*

Branksome might have appeared a poor dwelling-place when compared with the house of an English squire, but to us, after our long residence in stuffy apartments, it was of regal magnificence.

The building was broad-spread and low, with red-tiled roof, diamond-paned windows, and a profusion of dwelling rooms with smoke-blackened ceilings and oaken wainscots. In front was a small lawn, girt round with a thin fringe of haggard and ill grown beeches, all gnarled and withered from the effects of the sea-spray. Behind lay the scattered hamlet of Branksome-Bere—a dozen cottages at most—inhabited by rude fisher-folk who looked upon the laird as their natural protector.

To the west was the broad, yellow beach and the Irish Sea, while in all other directions the desolate moors, greyish-green in the foreground and purple in the distance, stretched away in long, low curves to the horizon.

Very bleak and lonely it was upon this Wigtown coast. A man might walk many a weary mile and never see a living thing except the white, heavy-flapping kittiwakes, which screamed and cried to each other with their shrill, sad voices.

Very lonely and very bleak! Once out of sight of Branksome and there was no sign of the works of man save only where the high, white tower of Cloomber Hall shot up, like a headstone of some giant grave, from amid the firs and larches which girt it round.

This great house, a mile or more from our dwelling, had been built by a wealthy Glasgow merchant of strange tastes and lonely habits, but at the time of our arrival it had been untenanted for many years, and stood with weather-blotched walls and vacant, staring windows looking blankly out over the hill side.

Empty and mildewed, it served only as a landmark to the fishermen, for they had found by experience that by keeping the laird's chimney and the white tower of Cloomber in a line they could steer their way through the ugly reef which raises its jagged back, like that of some sleeping monster, above the troubled waters of the wind-swept bay.

To this wild spot it was that Fate had brought my father, my sister, and myself. For us its loneliness had no terrors. After the hubbub and bustle of a great city, and the weary task of upholding appearances upon a slender income, there was a grand, soul-soothing serenity in the long sky-line and the eager air. Here at least there was no neighbour to pry and chatter.

The laird had left his phaeton and two ponies behind him, with the aid of which my father and I would go the round of the estate doing such light duties as fall to an agent, or "factor" as it was there called, while our gentle Esther looked to our household needs, and brightened the dark old building.

Such was our simple, uneventful existence, until the summer night when an unlooked-for incident occurred which proved to be the herald of those strange doings which I have taken up my pen to describe.

It had been my habit to pull out of an evening in the laird's skiff and to catch a few whiting which might serve for our supper. On this well-remembered occasion my sister came with me, sitting with her book in the stern-sheets of the boat, while I hung my lines over the bows.

The sun had sunk down behind the rugged Irish coast, but a long bank of flushed cloud still marked the spot, and cast a glory upon the waters. The whole broad ocean was seamed and scarred with crimson streaks. I had risen in the boat, and was gazing round in delight at the broad panorama of shore and sea and sky, when my sister plucked at my sleeve with a little, sharp cry of surprise.

"See, John," she cried, "there is a light in Cloomber Tower!"

I turned my head and stared back at the tall, white turret which peeped out above the belt of trees. As I gazed I distinctly saw at one of the windows the glint of a light, which suddenly vanished, and then shone out once more from another higher up. There it flickered for some time, and finally flashed past two successive windows underneath before the trees obscured our view of it. It was clear that someone bearing a lamp or a candle had climbed up the tower stairs and had then returned into the body of the house.

"Who in the world can it be?" I exclaimed, speaking rather to myself than to Esther, for I could see by the surprise upon her face that she had no solution to offer. "Maybe some of the folk from Branksome-Bere have wanted to look over the place."

My sister shook her head.

"There is not one of them would dare to set foot within the avenue gates," she said. "Besides, John, the keys are kept by the house-agent at Wigtown. Were they ever so curious, none of our people could find their way in."

When I reflected upon the massive door and ponderous shutters which guarded the lower storey of Cloomber, I could not but admit the force of my sister's objection. The untimely visitor must either have used considerable violence in order to force his way in, or he must have obtained possession of the keys.

Piqued by the little mystery, I pulled for the beach, with the determination to see for myself who the intruder might be, and what were his intentions. Leaving my sister at Branksome, and summoning Seth Jamieson, an old man-o'-war's-man and one of the stoutest of the fishermen, I set off across the moor with him through the gathering darkness.

"It hasna a guid name after dark, yon hoose," remarked my companion, slackening his pace perceptibly as I explained to him the nature of our errand. "It's no for naething that him wha owns it wunna gang within a Scotch mile o't."

"Well, Seth, there is someone who has no fears about going into it," said I, pointing to the great, white building which flickered up in front of us through the gloom.

The light which I had observed from the sea was moving backwards and forward past the lower floor windows, the shutters of which had been removed. I could now see that a second fainter light followed a few paces behind the other. Evidently two individuals, the one with a lamp and the other with a candle or rushlight, were making a careful examination of the building.

"Let ilka man blaw his ain parritch," said Seth Jamieson doggedly, coming to a dead stop. "What is it tae us if a wraith or a bogle minds tae tak' a fancy tae Cloomber? It's no canny tae meddle wi' such things."

"Why, man," I cried, "you don't suppose a wraith came here in a gig? What are those lights away yonder by the avenue gates?"

"The lamps o' a gig, sure enough!" exclaimed my companion in a less lugubrious voice. "Let's steer for it, Master West, and speer where she hails frae."

By this time night had closed in save for a single long, narrow slit in the westward. Stumbling across the moor together, we made our way into the Wigtown Road, at the point where the high stone pillars mark the entrance to the Cloomber avenue. A tall dog-cart stood in front of the gateway, the horse browsing upon the thin border of grass which skirted the road.

"It's a' richt!" said Jamieson, taking a close look at the deserted vehicle. "I ken it weel. It belongs tae Maister McNeil, the factor body frae Wigtown—him wha keeps the keys."

"Then we may as well have speech with him now that we are here," I answered. "They are coming down, if I am not mistaken."

As I spoke we heard the slam of the heavy door and within a few minutes two figures, the one tall and angular, the other short and thick came towards us through the darkness. They were talking so earnestly that they did not observe us until they had passed through the avenue gate.

"Good evening, Mr. McNeil," said I, stepping forward and addressing the Wigtown factor, with whom I had some slight acquaintance.

The smaller of the two turned his face towards me as I spoke, and showed me that I was not mistaken in his identity, but his taller companion sprang back and showed every sign of violent agitation.

"What is this, McNeil?" I heard him say, in a gasping, choking voice. "Is this your promise? What is the meaning of it?"

"Don't be alarmed, General! Don't be alarmed!" said the little fat factor in a soothing fashion, as one might speak to a frightened child. "This is young Mr. Fothergill West, of Branksome, though what brings him up here tonight is more than I can understand. However, as you are to be neighbours, I can't do better than take the opportunity to introduce you to each other. Mr. West, this is General Heatherstone, who is about to take a lease of Cloomber Hall."

I held out my hand to the tall man, who took it in a hesitating, half-reluctant fashion.

"I came up," I explained, "because I saw your lights in the windows, and I thought that something might be wrong. I am very glad I did so, since it has given me the chance of making the general's acquaintance."

Whilst I was talking, I was conscious that the new tenant of Cloomber Hall was peering at me very closely through the darkness. As I concluded, he stretched out a long, tremulous arm, and turned the gig-lamp in such a way as to throw a flood of light upon my face.

"Good Heavens, McNeil!" he cried, in the same quivering voice as before, "the fellow's as brown as chocolate. He's not an Englishman. You're not an Englishman—you, sir?"

"I'm a Scotchman, born and bred," said I, with an inclination to laugh, which was only checked by my new acquaintance's obvious terror.

"A Scotchman, eh?" said he, with a sigh of relief. "It's all one nowadays. You must excuse me, Mr.—Mr. West. I'm nervous, infernally nervous. Come along, McNeil, we must be back in Wigtown in less than an hour. Good-night, gentlemen, good-night!"

The two clambered into their places; the factor cracked his whip, and the high dog-cart clattered away through the darkness, casting a brilliant tunnel of yellow light on either side of it, until the rumble of its wheels died away in the distance.

"What do you think of our new neighbour, Jamieson?" I asked, after a long silence.

"'Deed, Mr. West, he seems, as he says himsel', to be vera nervous. Maybe his conscience is oot o' order."

"His liver, more likely," said I. "He looks as if he had tried his constitution a bit. But it's blowing chill, Seth, my lad, and it's time both of us were indoors."

I bade my companion good-night, and struck off across the moors for the cheery, ruddy light which marked the parlour windows of Branksome.

CHAPTER 3 - *OF OUR FURTHER ACQUAINTANCE WITH MAJOR-GENERAL J. B. HEATHERSTONE*

There was, as may well be imagined, much stir amongst our small community at the news that the Hall was to be inhabited once more, and considerable speculation as to the new tenants, and their object in choosing this particular part of the country for their residence.

It speedily became apparent that, whatever their motives might be, they had definitely determined upon a lengthy stay, for relays of plumbers and of joiners came down from Wigtown, and there was hammering and repairing going on from morning till night.

It was surprising how quickly the signs of the wind and weather were effaced, until the great, square-set house was all as spick-and-span as though it had been erected yesterday. There were abundant signs that money was no consideration to General Heatherstone, and that it was not on the score of retrenchment that he had taken up his abode among us.

"It may be that he is devoted to study," suggested my father, as we discussed the question round the breakfast table. "Perhaps he has chosen this secluded spot to finish some magnum opus upon which he is engaged. If that is the case I should be happy to let him have the run of my library."

Esther and I laughed at the grandiloquent manner in which he spoke of the two potato-sacksful of books.

"It may be as you say," said I, "but the general did not strike me during our short interview as being a man who was likely to have any very pronounced literary tastes. If I might hazard a guess, I should say that he is here upon medical advice, in the hope that the complete quiet and fresh air may restore his shattered nervous system. If you had seen how he glared at me, and the twitching of his fingers, you would have thought it needed some restoring."

"I do wonder whether he has a wife and a family," said my sister. "Poor souls, how lonely they will be! Why, excepting ourselves, there is not a family that they could speak to for seven miles and more."

"General Heatherstone is a very distinguished soldier," remarked my father.

"Why, papa, however came you to know anything about him?"

"Ah, my dears," said my father, smiling at us over his coffee-cup, "you were laughing at my library just now, but you see it may be very useful at times." As he spoke he took a red-covered volume from a shelf and turned over the pages. "This is an Indian Army List of three years back," he explained, "and here is the very gentleman we want-'Heatherstone, J. B., Commander of the Bath,' my dears, and 'V.C.', think of that, 'V.C.'—'formerly colonel in the Indian Infantry, 41st Bengal Foot, but now retired with the rank of major-general.' In this other column is a record of his services—'capture of Ghuznee and defence of Jellalabad, Sobraon 1848, Indian Mutiny and reduction of Oudh. Five times mentioned in dispatches.' I think, my dears, that we have cause to be proud of our new neighbour."

"It doesn't mention there whether he is married or not, I suppose?" asked Esther.

"No," said my father, wagging his white head with a keen appreciation of his own humour. "It doesn't include that under the heading of 'daring actions'—though it very well might, my dear, it very well might."

All our doubts, however, upon this head were very soon set at rest, for on the very day that the repairing and the furnishing had been completed I had occasion to ride into Wigtown, and I met upon the way a carriage which was bearing General Heatherstone and his family to their new home. An elderly lady, worn and sickly-looking, was by his side, and opposite him sat a young fellow about my own age and a girl who appeared to be a couple of years younger.

I raised my hat, and was about to pass them, when the general shouted to his coachman to pull up, and held out his hand to me. I could see now in the daylight that his face, although harsh and stern, was capable of assuming a not unkindly expression.

"How are you, Mr. Fothergill West?" he cried. "I must apologise to you if I was a little brusque the other night—you will excuse an old soldier who has spent the best part of his life in harness—All the same, you must confess that you are rather dark-skinned for a Scotchman."

"We have a Spanish strain in our blood," said I, wondering at his recurrence to the topic.

"That would, of course, account for it," he remarked. "My dear," to his wife, "allow me to introduce Mr. Fothergill West to you. This is my son and my daughter. We have come here in search of rest, Mr. West—complete rest."

"And you could not possibly have come to a better place," said I.

"Oh, you think so?" he answered. "I suppose it is very quiet indeed, and very lonely. You might walk through these country lanes at night, I dare say, and never meet a soul, eh?"

"Well, there are not many about after dark," I said.

"And you are not much troubled with vagrants or wandering beggars, eh? Not many tinkers or tramps or rascally gipsies—no vermin of that sort about?"

"I find it rather cold," said Mrs. Heatherstone, drawing her thick sealskin mantle tighter round her figure. "We are detaining Mr. West, too."

"So we are, my dear, so we are. Drive on, coachman. Good-day, Mr. West."

The carriage rattled away towards the Hall, and I trotted thoughtfully onwards to the little country metropolis.

As I passed up the High Street, Mr. McNeil ran out from his office and beckoned to me to stop.

"Our new tenants have gone out," he said. "They drove over this morning."

"I met them on the way," I answered.

As I looked down at the little factor, I could see that his face was flushed and that he bore every appearance of having had an extra glass.

"Give me a real gentleman to do business with," he said, with a burst of laughter. "They understand me and I understand them. 'What shall I fill it up for?' says the general, taking a blank cheque out o' his pouch and laying it on the table. 'Two hundred,' says I, leaving a bit o' a margin for my own time and trouble."

"I thought that the landlord had paid you for that," I remarked.

"Aye, aye, but it's well to have a bit margin. He filled it up and threw it over to me as if it had been an auld postage stamp. That's the way business should be done between honest men—though it wouldna do if one was inclined to take an advantage. Will ye not come in, Mr. West, and have a taste of my whisky?"

"No, thank you," said I, "I have business to do."

"Well, well, business is the chief thing. It's well not to drink in the morning, too. For my own part, except a drop before breakfast to give me an appetite, and maybe a glass, or even twa, afterwards to promote digestion, I never touch spirits before noon. What d'ye think o' the general, Mr. West?"

"Why, I have hardly had an opportunity of judging," I answered.

Mr. McNeil tapped his forehead with his forefinger.

"That's what I think of him," he said in a confidential whisper, shaking his head at me. "He's gone, sir, gone, in my estimation. Now what would you take to be a proof of madness, Mr. West?"

"Why, offering a blank cheque to a Wigtown house-agent," said I.

"Ah, you're aye at your jokes. But between oorsel's now, if a man asked ye how many miles it was frae a seaport, and whether ships come there from the East, and whether there were tramps on the road, and whether it was against the lease for him to build a high wall round the grounds, what would ye make of it, eh?"

"I should certainly think him eccentric," said I.

"If every man had his due, our friend would find himsel' in a house with a high wall round the grounds, and that without costing him a farthing," said the agent.

"Where then?" I asked, humouring his joke.

"Why, in the Wigtown County Lunatic Asylum," cried the little man, with a bubble of laughter, in the midst of which I rode on my way, leaving him still chuckling over his own facetiousness.

The arrival of the new family at Cloomber Hall had no perceptible effect in relieving the monotony of our secluded district, for instead of entering into such simple pleasures as the country had to offer, or interesting themselves, as we had hoped, in our attempts to improve the lot of our poor crofters and fisherfolk, they seemed to shun all observation, and hardly ever to venture beyond the avenue gates.

We soon found, too, that the factor's words as to the inclosing of the grounds were founded upon fact, for gangs of workmen were kept hard at work from early in the morning until late at night in erecting a high, wooden fence round the whole estate.

When this was finished and topped with spikes, Cloomber Park became impregnable to anyone but an exceptionally daring climber. It was as if the old soldier had been so imbued with military ideas that, like my Uncle Toby, he could not refrain even in times of peace from standing upon the defensive.

Stranger still, he had victualled the house as if for a siege, for Begbie, the chief grocer of Wigtown, told me himself in a rapture of delight and amazement that the general had sent him an order for hundreds of dozens of every imaginable potted meat and vegetable.

It may be imagined that all these unusual incidents were not allowed to pass without malicious comment. Over the whole countryside and as far away as the English border there was nothing but gossip about the new tenants of Cloomber Hall and the reasons which had led them to come among us.

The only hypothesis, however, which the bucolic mind could evolve, was that which had already occurred to Mr. McNeil, the factor—namely, that the old general and his family were one and all afflicted with madness, or, as an alternative conclusion, that he had committed some heinous offence and was endeavouring to escape the consequences of his misdeeds.

These were both natural suppositions under the circumstances, but neither of them appeared to me to commend itself as a true explanation of the facts.

It is true that General Heatherstone's behaviour on the occasion of our first interview was such as to suggest some suspicion of mental disease, but no man could have been more reasonable or more courteous than he had afterwards shown himself to be.

Then, again, his wife and children led the same secluded life that he did himself, so that the reason could not be one peculiar to his own health.

As to the possibility of his being a fugitive from justice, that theory was even more untenable. Wigtownshire was bleak and lonely, but it was not such an obscure corner of the world that a well-known soldier could hope to conceal himself there, nor would a man who feared publicity set every one's tongue wagging as the general had done.

On the whole, I was inclined to believe that the true solution of the enigma lay in his own allusion to the love of quiet, and that they had taken shelter here with an almost morbid craving for solitude and repose. We very soon had an instance of the great lengths to which this desire for isolation would carry them.

My father had come down one morning with the weight of a great determination upon his brow.

"You must put on your pink frock to-day, Esther," said he, "and you, John, you must make yourself smart, for I have determined that the three of us shall drive round this afternoon and pay our respects to Mrs. Heatherstone and the general."

"A visit to Cloomber," cried Esther, clapping her hands.

"I am here," said my father, with dignity, "not only as the laird's factor, but also as his kinsman. In that capacity I am convinced that he would wish me to call upon these newcomers and offer them any politeness which is in our power. At present they must feel lonely and friendless. What says the great Firdousi? 'The choicest ornaments to a man's house are his friends.'"

My sister and I knew by experience that when the old man began to justify his resolution by quotations from the Persian poets there was no chance of shaking it. Sure enough that afternoon saw the phaeton at the door, with my father perched upon the seat, with his second-best coat on and a pair of new driving-gloves.

"Jump in, my dears," he cried, cracking his whip briskly, "we shall show the general that he has no cause to be ashamed of his neighbours."

Alas! Pride always goes before a fall. Our well-fed ponies and shining harness were not destined that day to impress the tenants of Cloomber with a sense of our importance.

We had reached the avenue gate, and I was about to get out and open it, when our attention was arrested by a very large wooden placard, which was attached to one of the trees in such a manner that no one could possibly pass without seeing it. On the white surface of this board was printed in big, black letters the following hospitable inscription:

GENERAL AND MRS. HEATHERSTONE

HAVE NO WISH

TO INCREASE

THE CIRCLE OF THEIR ACQUAINTANCE.

We all sat gazing at this announcement for some moments in silent astonishment. Then Esther and I, tickled by the absurdity of the thing, burst out laughing, but my father pulled the ponies' heads round, and drove home with compressed lips and the cloud of much wrath upon his brow. I have never seen the good man so thoroughly moved, and I am convinced that his anger did not arise from any petty feeling of injured vanity upon his own part, but from the thought that a slight had been offered to the Laird of Branksome, whose dignity he represented.

CHAPTER 4- *OF A YOUNG MAN WITH A GREY HEAD*

If I had any personal soreness on account of this family snub, it was a very passing emotion, and one which was soon effaced from my mind.

It chanced that on the very next day after the episode I had occasion to pass that way, and stopped to have another look at the obnoxious placard. I was standing staring at it and wondering what could have induced our neighbours to take such an outrageous step, when I became suddenly aware of a sweet, girlish face which peeped out at me from between the bars of the gate, and of a white hand which eagerly beckoned me to approach. As I advanced to her I saw that it was the same young lady whom I had seen in the carriage.

"Mr. West," she said, in a quick whisper, glancing from side to side as she spoke in a nervous, hasty manner, "I wish to apologise to you for the indignity to which you and your family were subjected yesterday. My brother was in the avenue and saw it all, but he is powerless to interfere. I assure you, Mr. West, that if that hateful thing," pointing up at the placard, "has given you any annoyance, it has given my brother and myself far more."

"Why, Miss Heatherstone," said I, putting the matter off with a laugh, "Britain is a free country, and if a man chooses to warn off visitors from his premises there is no reason why he should not."

"It is nothing less than brutal," she broke out, with a petulant stamp of the foot. "To think that your sister, too, should have such an unprovoked insult offered to her! I am ready to sink with shame at the very thought."

"Pray do not give yourself one moment's uneasiness upon the subject," said I earnestly, for I was grieved at her evident distress. "I am sure that your father has some reason unknown to us for taking this step."

"Heaven knows he has!" she answered, with ineffable sadness in her voice, "and yet I think it would be more manly to face a danger than to fly from it. However, he knows best, and it is impossible for us to judge. But who is this?" she exclaimed, anxiously, peering up the dark avenue. "Oh, it is my brother Mordaunt. Mordaunt," she said, as the young man approached us, "I have been apologising to Mr. West for what happened yesterday, in your name as well as my own."

"I am very, very glad to have the opportunity of doing it in person," said he courteously. "I only wish that I could see your sister and your father as well as yourself, to tell them how sorry I am. I think you had better run up to the house, little one, for it's getting near tiffin-time. No—don't you go Mr. West. I want to have a word with you."

Miss Heatherstone waved her hand to me with a bright smile, and tripped up the avenue, while her brother unbolted the gate, and, passing through, closed it again, locking it upon the outside.

"I'll have a stroll down the road with you, if you have no objection. Have a manilla." He drew a couple of cheroots from his pocket and handed one to me. "You'll find they are not bad," he said. "I became a connoisseur in tobacco when I was in India. I hope I am not interfering with your business in coming along with you?"

"Not at all," I answered, "I am very glad to have your company."

"I'll tell you a secret," said my companion. "This is the first time that I have been outside the grounds since we have been down here."

"And your sister?"

"She has never been out, either," he answered. "I have given the governor the slip to-day, but he wouldn't half like it if he knew. It's a whim of his that we should keep ourselves entirely to ourselves. At least, some people would call it a whim, for my own part I have reason to believe that he has solid grounds for all that he does—though perhaps in this matter he may be a little too exacting."

"You must surely find it very lonely," said I. "Couldn't you manage to slip down at times and have a smoke with me? That house over yonder is Branksome."

"Indeed, you are very kind," he answered, with sparkling eyes. "I should dearly like to run over now and again. With the exception of Israel Stakes, our old coachman and gardener, I have not a soul that I can speak to."

"And your sister—she must feel it even more," said I, thinking in my heart that my new acquaintance made rather too much of his own troubles and too little of those of his companion.

"Yes; poor Gabriel feels it, no doubt," he answered carelessly, "but it's a more unnatural thing for a young man of my age to be cooped up in this way than for a woman. Look at me, now. I am three-and-twenty next March, and yet I have never been to a university, nor to a school for that matter. I am as complete an ignoramus as any of these clodhoppers. It seems strange to you, no doubt, and yet it is so. Now, don't you think I deserve a better fate?"

He stopped as he spoke, and faced round to me, throwing his palms forward in appeal.

As I looked at him, with the sun shining upon his face, he certainly did seem a strange bird to be cooped up in such a cage. Tall and muscular, with a keen, dark face, and sharp, finely cut features, he might have stepped out of a canvas of Murillo or Velasquez. There were latent energy and power in his firm-set mouth, his square eyebrows, and the whole pose of his elastic, well-knit figure.

"There is the learning to be got from books and the learning to be got from experience," said I sententiously. "If you have less of your share of the one, perhaps you have more of the other. I cannot believe you have spent all your life in mere idleness and pleasure."

"Pleasure!" he cried. "Pleasure! Look at this!" He pulled off his hat, and I saw that his black hair was all decked and dashed with streaks of grey. "Do you imagine that this came from pleasure?" he asked, with a bitter laugh.

"You must have had some great shock," I said, astonished at the sight, "some terrible illness in your youth. Or perhaps it arises from a more chronic cause—a constant gnawing anxiety. I have known men as young as you whose hair was as grey."

"Poor brutes!" he muttered. "I pity them."

"If you can manage to slip down to Branksome at times," I said, "perhaps you could bring Miss Heatherstone with you. I know that my father and my sister would be delighted to see her, and a change, if only for an hour or two, might do her good."

"It would be rather hard for us both to get away together," he answered. "However, if I see a chance I shall bring her down. It might be managed some afternoon perhaps, for the old man indulges in a siesta occasionally."

We had reached the head of the winding lane which branches off from the high road and leads to the laird's house, so my companion pulled up.

"I must go back," he said abruptly, "or they will miss me. It's very kind of you, West, to take this interest in us. I am very grateful to you, and so will Gabriel be when she hears of your kind invitation. It's a real heaping of coals of fire after that infernal placard of my father's."

He shook my hand and set off down the road, but he came running after me presently, calling me to stop.

"I was just thinking," he said, "that you must consider us a great mystery up there at Cloomber. I dare say you have come to look upon it as a private lunatic asylum, and I can't blame you. If you are interested in the matter, I feel it is unfriendly upon my part not to satisfy your curiosity, but I have promised my father to be silent about it. And indeed if I were to tell you all that I know you might not be very much the wiser after all. I would have you understand this, however—that my father is as sane as you or I, and that he has very good reasons for living the life which he does. I may add that his wish to remain secluded does not arise from any unworthy or dishonourable motives, but merely from the instinct of self-preservation."

"He is in danger, then?" I ejaculated.

"Yes; he is in constant danger."

"But why does he not apply to the magistrates for protection?" I asked. "If he is afraid of any one, he has only to name him and they will bind him over to keep the peace."

"My dear West," said young Heatherstone, "the danger with which my father is threatened is one that cannot be averted by any human intervention. It is none the less very real, and possibly very imminent."

"You don't mean to assert that it is supernatural," I said incredulously.

"Well, hardly that, either," he answered with hesitation. "There," he continued, "I have said rather more than I should, but I know that you will not abuse my confidence. Good-bye!"

He took to his heels and was soon out of sight round a curve in the country road.

A danger which was real and imminent, not to be averted by human means, and yet hardly supernatural—here was a conundrum indeed!

I had come to look upon the inhabitants of the Hall as mere eccentrics, but after what young Mordaunt Heatherstone had just told me, I could no longer doubt that some dark and sinister meaning underlay all their actions. The more I pondered over the problem, the more unanswerable did it appear, and yet I could not get the matter out of my thoughts.

The lonely, isolated Hall, and the strange, impending catastrophe which hung over its inmates, appealed forcibly to my imagination. All that evening, and late into the night, I sat moodily by the fire, pondering over what I had heard, and revolving in my mind the various incidents which might furnish me with some clue to the mystery.

CHAPTER 5 - *HOW FOUR OF US CAME TO BE UNDER THE SHADOW OF CLOOMBER*

I trust that my readers will not set me down as an inquisitive busybody when I say that as the days and weeks went by I found my attention and my thoughts more and more attracted to General Heatherstone and the mystery which surrounded him.

It was in vain that I endeavoured by hard work and a strict attention to the laird's affairs to direct my mind into some more healthy channel. Do what I would, on land or on the water, I would still find myself puzzling over this one question, until it obtained such a hold upon me that I felt it was useless for me to attempt to apply myself to anything until I had come to some satisfactory solution of it.

I could never pass the dark line of five-foot fencing, and the great iron gate, with its massive lock, without pausing and racking my brain as to what the secret might be which was shut in by that inscrutable barrier. Yet, with all my conjectures and all my observations, I could never come to any conclusion which could for a moment be accepted as an explanation of the facts.

My sister had been out for a stroll one night, visiting a sick peasant or performing some other of the numerous acts of charity by which she had made herself beloved by the whole countryside.

"John," she said when she returned, "have you seen Cloomber Hall at night?"

"No," I answered, laying down the book which I was reading. "Not since that memorable evening when the general and Mr. McNeil came over to make an inspection."

"Well, John, will you put your hat on and come a little walk with me?"

I could see by her manner that something had agitated or frightened her.

"Why, bless the girl!" cried I boisterously, "what is the matter? The old Hall is not on fire, surely? You look as grave as if all Wigtown were in a blaze."

"Not quite so bad as that," she said, smiling. "But do come out, Jack. I should very much like you to see it."

I had always refrained from saying anything which might alarm my sister, so that she knew nothing of the interest which our neighbours' doings had for me. At her request I took my hat and followed her out into the darkness. She led the way along a little footpath over the moor, which brought us to some rising ground, from which we could look down upon the

Hall without our view being obstructed by any of the fir-trees which had been planted round it.

"Look at that!" said my sister, pausing at the summit of this little eminence.

Cloomber lay beneath us in a blaze of light. In the lower floors the shutters obscured the illumination, but above, from the broad windows of the second storey to the thin slits at the summit of the tower, there was not a chink or an aperture which did not send forth a stream of radiance. So dazzling was the effect that for a moment I was persuaded that the house was on fire, but the steadiness and clearness of the light soon freed me from that apprehension. It was clearly the result of many lamps placed systematically all over the building.

It added to the strange effect that all these brilliantly illuminated rooms were apparently untenanted, and some of them, so far as we could judge, were not even furnished. Through the whole great house there was no sign of movement or of life—nothing but the clear, unwinking flood of yellow light.

I was still lost in wonder at the sight when I heard a short, quick sob at my side.

"What is it, Esther, dear?" I asked, looking down at my companion.

"I feel so frightened. Oh, John, John, take me home, I feel so frightened!"

She clung to my arm, and pulled at my coat in a perfect frenzy of fear.

"It's all safe, darling," I said soothingly. "There is nothing to fear. What has upset you so?"

"I am afraid of them, John; I am afraid of the Heatherstones. Why is their house lit up like this every night? I have heard from others that it is always so. And why does the old man run like a frightened hare if any one comes upon him. There is something wrong about it, John, and it frightens me."

I pacified her as well as I could, and led her home with me, where I took care that she should have some hot port negus before going to bed. I avoided the subject of the Heatherstones for fear of exciting her, and she did not recur to it of her own accord. I was convinced, however, from what I had heard from her, that she had for some time back been making her own observations upon our neighbours, and that in doing so she had put a considerable strain upon her nerves.

I could see that the mere fact of the Hall being illuminated at night was not enough to account for her extreme agitation, and that it must have derived its importance in her eyes from being one in a chain of incidents, all of which had left a weird or unpleasant impression upon her mind.

That was the conclusion which I came to at the time, and I have reason to know now that I was right, and that my sister had even more cause than I had myself for believing that there was something uncanny about the tenants of Cloomber.

Our interest in the matter may have arisen at first from nothing higher than curiosity, but events soon look a turn which associated us more closely with the fortunes of the Heatherstone family.

Mordaunt had taken advantage of my invitation to come down to the laird's house, and on several occasions he brought with him his beautiful sister. The four of us would wander over the moors together, or perhaps if the day were fine set sail upon our little skiff and stand off into the Irish Sea.

On such excursions the brother and sister would be as merry and as happy as two children. It was a keen pleasure to them to escape from their dull fortress, and to see, if only for a few hours, friendly and sympathetic faces round them.

There could be but one result when four young people were brought together in sweet, forbidden intercourse. Acquaintance-ship warmed into friendship, and friendship flamed suddenly into love.

Gabriel sits beside me now as I write, and she agrees with me that, dear as is the subject to ourselves, the whole story of our mutual affection is of too personal a nature to be more than touched upon in this statement. Suffice it to say that, within a few weeks of our first meeting Mordaunt Heatherstone had won the heart of my dear sister, and Gabriel had given me that pledge which death itself will not be able to break.

I have alluded in this brief way to the double tie which sprang up between the two families, because I have no wish that this narrative should degenerate into anything approaching to romance, or that I should lose the thread of the facts which I have set myself to chronicle. These are connected with General Heatherstone, and only indirectly with my own personal history.

It is enough if I say that after our engagement the visits to Branksome became more frequent, and that our friends were able sometimes to spend a whole day with us when business had called the general to Wigtown, or when his gout confined him to his room.

As to our good father, he was ever ready to greet us with many small jests and tags of Oriental poems appropriate to the occasion, for we had no secrets from him, and he already looked upon us all as his children.

There were times when on account of some peculiarly dark or restless fit of the general's it was impossible for weeks on end for either Gabriel or Mordaunt to get away from the grounds. The old man would even stand on guard, a gloomy and silent sentinel, at the avenue gate, or pace up and down the drive as though he suspected that attempts had been made to penetrate his seclusion.

Passing of an evening I have seen his dark, grim figure flitting about in the shadow of the trees, or caught a glimpse of his hard, angular, swarthy face peering out suspiciously at me from behind the bars.

My heart would often sadden for him as I noticed his uncouth, nervous movements, his furtive glances and twitching features. Who would have believed that this slinking, cowering creature had once been a dashing officer, who had fought the battles of his country and had won the palm of bravery among the host of brave men around him?

In spite of the old soldier's vigilance, we managed to hold communication with our friends.

Immediately behind the Hall there was a spot where the fencing had been so carelessly erected that two of the rails could be removed without difficulty, leaving a broad gap, which gave us the opportunity for many a stolen interview, though they were necessarily short, for the general's movements were erratic, and no part of the grounds was secure from his visitations.

How vividly one of these hurried meetings rises before me! It stands out clear, peaceful, and distinct amid the wild, mysterious incidents which were destined to lead up to the terrible catastrophe which has cast a shade over our lives.

I can remember that as I walked through the fields the grass was damp with the rain of the morning, and the air was heavy with the smell of the fresh-turned earth. Gabriel was waiting for me under the hawthorn tree outside the gap, and we stood hand-in-hand looking down at the long sweep of moorland and at the broad blue channel which encircled it with its fringe of foam.

Far away in the north-west the sun glinted upon the high peak of Mount Throston. From where we stood we could see the smoke of the steamers as they ploughed along the busy water-way which leads to Belfast.

"Is it not magnificent?" Gabriel cried, clasping her hands round my arm. "Ah, John, why are we not free to sail away over these waves together, and leave all our troubles behind us on the shore?"

"And what are the troubles which you would leave behind you, dear one?" I asked. "May I not know them, and help you to bear them?"

"I have no secrets from you, John," she answered. "Our chief trouble is, as you may guess, our poor father's strange behaviour. Is it not a sad thing for all of us that a man who has played such a distinguished part in the world should skulk from one obscure corner of the country to another, and should defend himself with locks and barriers as though he were a common thief flying from justice? This is a trouble, John, which it is out of your power to alleviate."

"But why does he do it, Gabriel?" I asked.

"I cannot tell," she answered frankly. "I only know that he imagines some deadly danger to be hanging over his head, and that this danger was incurred by him during his stay in India. What its nature may be I have no more idea than you have."

"Then your brother has," I remarked. "I am sure from the way in which he spoke to me about it one day that he knows what it is, and that he looks upon it as real."

"Yes, he knows, and so does my mother," she answered, "but they have always kept it secret from me. My poor father is very excited at present. Day and night he is in an agony of apprehension, but it will soon be the fifth of October, and after that he will be at peace."

"How do you know that?" I asked in surprise.

"By experience," she answered gravely. "On the fifth of October these fears of his come to a crisis. For years back he has been in the habit of locking Mordaunt and myself up in our rooms on that date, so that we have no idea what occurs, but we have always found that he has been much relieved afterwards, and has continued to be comparatively in peace until that day begins to draw round again."

"Then you have only ten days or so to wait," I remarked, for September was drawing to a close. "By the way, dearest, why is it that you light up all your rooms at night?"

"You have noticed it, then?" she said. "It comes also from my father's fears. He does not like to have one dark corner in the whole house. He walks about a good deal at night, and inspects everything, from the attics right down to the cellars. He has large lamps in every room and corridor, even the empty ones, and he orders the servants to light them all at dusk."

"I am rather surprised that you manage to keep your servants," I said, laughing. "The maids in these parts are a superstitious class, and their imaginations are easily excited by anything which they don't understand."

"The cook and both housemaids are from London, and are used to our ways. We pay them on a very high scale to make up for any inconvenience to which they may be put. Israel Stakes, the coachman, is the only one who comes from this part of the country, and he seems to be a stolid, honest fellow, who is not easily scared."

"Poor little girl," I exclaimed, looking down at the slim, graceful figure by my side. "This is no atmosphere for you to live in. Why will you not let me rescue you from it? Why won't you allow me to go straight and ask the general for your hand? At the worst he could only refuse."

She turned quite haggard and pale at the very thought.

"For Heaven's sake, John," she cried earnestly, "do nothing of the kind. He would whip us all away in the dead of the night, and within a week we should be settling down again in some wilderness where we might never have a chance of seeing or hearing from you again. Besides, he never would forgive us for venturing out of the grounds."

"I don't think that he is a hard-hearted man," I remarked. "I have seen a kindly look in his eyes, for all his stern face."

"He can be the kindest of fathers," she answered. "But he is terrible when opposed or thwarted. You have never seen him so, and I trust you never will. It was that strength of will and impatience of opposition which made him such a splendid officer. I assure you that in India everyone thought a great deal of him. The soldiers were afraid of him, but they would have followed him anywhere."

"And had he these nervous attacks then?"

"Occasionally, but not nearly so acutely. He seems to think that the danger—whatever it may be—becomes more imminent every year. Oh, John, it is terrible to be waiting like this with a sword over our heads—and all the more terrible to me since I have no idea where the blow is to come from."

"Dear Gabriel," I said, taking her hand and drawing her to my side, "look over all this pleasant countryside and the broad blue sea. Is it not all peaceful and beautiful? In these cottages, with their red-tiled roofs peeping out from the grey moor, there live none but simple, God-fearing men, who toil hard at their crafts and bear enmity to no man. Within seven miles of us is a large town, with every civilised appliance for the preservation of order. Ten miles farther there is a garrison quartered, and a telegram would at any time bring down a company of soldiers. Now, I ask you, dear, in the name of common-sense, what conceivable danger could threaten you in this secluded neighbourhood, with the means of help so near? You assure me that the peril is not connected with your father's health?"

"No, I am sure of that. It is true that Dr. Easterling, of Stranraer, has been over to see him once or twice, but that was merely for some small indisposition. I can assure you that the danger is not to be looked for in that direction."

"Then I can assure you," said I, laughing, "that there is no danger at all. It must be some strange monomania or hallucination. No other hypothesis will cover the facts."

"Would my father's monomania account for the fact of my brother's hair turning grey and my mother wasting away to a mere shadow?"

"Undoubtedly," I answered. "The long continued worry of the general's restlessness and irritability would produce those effects on sensitive natures."

"No, no!" said she, shaking her head sadly, "I have been exposed to his restlessness and irritability, but they have had no such effect upon me. The difference between us lies in the fact that they know this awful secret and I do not."

"My dear girl," said I, "the days of family apparitions and that kind of thing are gone. Nobody is haunted nowadays, so we can put that supposition out of the question. Having done so, what remains? There is absolutely no other theory which could even be suggested. Believe me, the whole mystery is that the heat of India has been too much for your poor father's brain."

What she would have answered I cannot tell, for at that moment she gave a start as if some sound had fallen upon her ear. As she looked round apprehensively, I suddenly saw her features become rigid and her eyes fixed and dilated.

Following the direction of her gaze, I felt a sudden thrill of fear pass through me as I perceived a human face surveying us from behind one of the trees—a man's face, every feature of which was distorted by the most malignant hatred and anger. Finding himself observed, he stepped out and advanced towards us, when I saw that it was none other than the general himself. His beard was all a-bristle with fury, and his deepset eyes glowed from under their heavily veined lids with a most sinister and demoniacal brightness.

CHAPTER 6 - *HOW I CAME TO BE ENLISTED AS ONE OF THE GARRISON OF CLOOMBER*

"To your room, girl!" he cried in a hoarse, harsh voice, stepping in between us and pointing authoritatively towards the house.

He waited until Gabriel, with a last frightened glance at me, had passed through the gap, and then he turned upon me with an expression so murderous that I stepped back a pace or two, and tightened my grasp upon my oak stick.

"You-you—" he spluttered, with his hand twitching at his throat, as though his fury were choking him. "You have dared to intrude upon my privacy! Do you think I built this fence that all the vermin in the country might congregate round it? Oh, you have been very near your death, my fine fellow! You will never be nearer until your time comes. Look at this!" He pulled a squat, thick pistol out of his bosom. "If you had passed through that gap and set foot on my land I'd have let daylight into you. I'll have no vagabonds here. I know how to treat gentry of that sort, whether their faces are black or white."

"Sir," said I, "I meant no harm by coming here, and I do not know how I have deserved this extraordinary outburst. Allow me to observe, however, that you are still covering me with your pistol, and that, as your hand is rather tremulous, it is more than possible that it may go off. If you don't turn the muzzle down I shall be compelled in self-defence to strike you over the wrist with my stick."

"What the deuce brought you here, then?" he asked, in a more composed voice, putting his weapon back into his bosom. "Can't a gentleman live quietly without your coming to peep and pry? Have you no business of your own to look after, eh? And my daughter? How came you to know anything of her? And what have you been trying to squeeze out of her? It wasn't chance that brought you here."

"No," said I boldly, "it was not chance which brought me here. I have had several opportunities of seeing your daughter and of appreciating her many noble qualities. We are engaged to be married to each other, and I came up with the express intention of seeing her."

Instead of blazing into a fury, as I had expected, the general gave a long whistle of astonishment, and then leant up against the railings, laughing softly to himself.

"English terriers are fond of nosing worms," he remarked at last. "When we brought them out to India they used to trot off into the jungle and begin sniffing at what they imagined to be worms there. But the worm turned out to be a venomous snake, and so poor doggy played no more. I think you'll find yourself in a somewhat analogous position if you don't look out."

"You surely don't mean to cast an aspersion upon your own daughter?" I said, flushing with indignation.

"Oh, Gabriel is all right," he answered carelessly. "Our family is not exactly one, however, which I should recommend a young fellow to marry into. And pray how is it that I was not informed of this snug little arrangement of yours?"

"We were afraid, sir, that you might separate us," I replied, feeling that perfect candour was the best policy under the circumstances. "It is possible that we were mistaken. Before coming to any final decision, I implore you to remember that the happiness of both of us is at stake. It is in your power to divide our bodies, but our souls shall be forever united."

"My good fellow," said the general, in a not unkindly tone, "you don't know what you are asking for. There is a gulf between you and any one of the blood of Heatherstone which can never be bridged over."

All trace of anger had vanished now from his manner, and given place to an air of somewhat contemptuous amusement.

My family pride took fire at his words. "The gulf may be less than you imagine," I said coldly. "We are not clodhoppers because we live in this out-of-the-way place. I am of noble descent on one side, and my mother was a Buchan of Buchan. I assure you that there is no such disparity between us as you seem to imagine."

"You misunderstand me," the general answered. "It is on our side that the disparity lies. There are reasons why my daughter Gabriel should live and die single. It would not be to your advantage to marry her."

"But surely, sir," I persisted, "I am the best judge of my own interests and advantages. Since you take this ground all becomes easy, for I do assure you that the one interest which overrides all others is that I should have the woman I love for my wife. If this is your only objection to our match you may surely give us your consent, for any danger or trial which I may incur in marrying Gabriel will not weigh with me one featherweight."

"Here's a young bantam!" exclaimed the old soldier, smiling at my warmth. "It's easy to defy danger when you don't know what the danger is."

"What is it, then?" I asked, hotly. "There is no earthly peril which will drive me from Gabriel's side. Let me know what it is and test me."

"No, no. That would never do," he answered with a sigh, and then, thoughtfully, as if speaking his mind aloud: "He has plenty of pluck and is a well-grown lad, too. We might do worse than make use of him."

He went on mumbling to himself with a vacant stare in his eyes as if he had forgotten my presence.

"Look here, West," he said presently. "You'll excuse me if I spoke hastily a little time ago. It is the second time that I have had occasion to apologise to you for the same offence. It shan't occur again. I am rather over-particular, no doubt, in my desire for complete isolation, but I have good reasons for insisting on the point. Rightly or wrongly, I have got it into my head that someday there might be an organised raid upon my grounds. If anything of the sort should occur I suppose I might reckon upon your assistance?"

"With all my heart."

"So that if ever you got a message such as 'Come up,' or even 'Cloomber,' you would know that it was an appeal for help, and would hurry up immediately, even if it were in the dead of the night?"

"Most certainly I should," I answered. "But might I ask you what the nature of the danger is which you apprehend?"

"There would be nothing gained by your knowing. Indeed, you would hardly understand it if I told you. I must bid you good day now, for I have stayed with you too long. Remember, I count upon you as one of the Cloomber garrison now."

"One other thing, sir," I said hurriedly, for he was turning away, "I hope that you will not be angry with your daughter for anything which I have told you. It was for my sake that she kept it all secret from you."

"All right," he said, with his cold, inscrutable smile. "I am not such an ogre in the bosom of my family as you seem to think. As to this marriage question, I should advise you as a friend to let it drop altogether, but if that is impossible I must insist that it stand over completely for the present. It is impossible to say what unexpected turn events may take. Good-bye."

He plunged into the wood and was quickly out of sight among the dense plantation.

Thus ended this extraordinary interview, in which this strange man had begun by pointing a loaded pistol at my breast and had ended, by partially acknowledging the possibility of my becoming his future son-in-law. I hardly knew whether to be cast down or elated over it.

On the one hand he was likely, by keeping a closer watch over his daughter, to prevent us from communicating as freely as we had done hitherto. Against this there was the advantage of having obtained an implied consent to the renewal of my suit at some future date. On the whole, I came to the conclusion as I walked thoughtfully home that I had improved my position by the incident.

But this danger—this shadowy, unspeakable danger—which appeared to rise up at every turn, and to hang day and night over the towers of Cloomber! Rack my brain as I would, I could not conjure up any solution to the problem which was not puerile and inadequate.

One fact struck me as being significant. Both the father and the son had assured me, independently of each other, that if I were told what the peril was, I would hardly realise its significance. How strange and bizarre must the fear be which can scarcely be expressed in intelligible language!

I held up my hand in the darkness before I turned to sleep that night, and I swore that no power of man or devil should ever weaken my love for the woman whose pure heart I had had the good fortune to win.

CHAPTER 7 - *OF CORPORAL RUFUS SMITH AND HIS COMING TO CLOOMBER*

In making this statement I have purposely couched it in bald and simple language, for fear I should be accused of colouring my narrative for the sake of effect. If, however, I have told my story with any approach to realism, the reader will understand me when I say that by this time the succession of dramatic incidents which had occurred had arrested my attention and excited my imagination to the exclusion of all minor topics.

How could I plod through the dull routine of an agent's work, or interest myself in the thatch of this tenant's bothy or the sails of that one's boat, when my mind was taken up by the chain of events which I have described, and was still busy seeking an explanation for them.

Go where I would over the countryside, I could see the square, white tower shooting out from among the trees, and beneath that tower this ill-fated family were watching and waiting, waiting and watching—and for what? That was still the question which stood like an impassable barrier at the end of every train of thought.

Regarded merely as an abstract problem, this mystery of the Heatherstone family had a lurid fascination about it, but when the woman whom I loved a thousandfold better than I did myself proved to be so deeply interested in the solution, I felt that it was impossible to turn my thoughts to anything else until it had been finally cleared up.

My good father had received a letter from the laird, dated from Naples, which told us that he had derived much benefit from the change, and that he had no intention of returning to Scotland for some time. This was satisfactory to all of us, for my father had found Branksome such an excellent place for study that it would have been a sore trial to him to return to the noise and tumult of a city. As to my dear sister and myself, there were, as I have shown, stronger reasons still to make us love the Wigtownshire moors.

In spite of my interview with the general—or perhaps I might say on account of it—I took occasion at least twice a day to walk towards Cloomber and satisfy myself that all was well there. He had begun by resenting my intrusion, but he had ended by taking me into a sort of half-confidence, and even by asking my assistance, so I felt that I stood upon a different footing with him than I had done formerly, and that he was less likely to be annoyed by my presence. Indeed, I met him pacing round the inclosure a few days afterwards, and his manner towards me was civil, though he made no allusion to our former conversation.

He appeared to be still in an extreme state of nervousness, starting from time to time, and gazing furtively about him, with little frightened, darting glances to the right and the left. I hoped that his daughter was right in naming the fifth of October as the turning point of his complaint, for it was evident to me as I looked at his gleaming eyes and quivering hands, that a man could not live long in such a state of nervous tension.

I found on examination that he had had the loose rails securely fastened so as to block up our former trysting-place, and though I prowled round the whole long line of fencing, I was unable to find any other place where an entrance could be effected.

Here and there between the few chinks left in the barrier I could catch glimpses of the Hall, and once I saw a rough-looking, middle-aged man standing at a window on the lower floor, whom I supposed to be Israel Stakes, the coachman. There was no sign, however, of Gabriel or of Mordaunt, and their absence alarmed me. I was convinced that, unless they were under some restraint, they would have managed to communicate with my sister or myself. My fears became more and more acute as day followed day without our seeing or hearing anything of them.

One morning—it was the second day of October—I was walking towards the Hall, hoping that I might be fortunate enough to learn some news of my darling, when I observed a man perched upon a stone at the side of the road.

As I came nearer to him I could see that he was a stranger, and from his dusty clothes and dilapidated appearance he seemed to have come from a distance. He had a great hunch of bread on his knee and a clasp-knife in his hand, but he had apparently just finished his breakfast, for he brushed the crumbs off his lap and rose to his feet when he perceived me.

Noticing the great height of the fellow and that he still held his weapon, I kept well to the other side of the road, for I knew that destitution makes men desperate and that the chain that glittered on my waistcoat might be too great a temptation to him upon this lonely highway. I was confirmed in my fears when I saw him step out into the centre of the road and bar my progress.

"Well, my lad," I said, affecting an ease which I by no means felt, "what can I do for you this morning?"

The fellow's face was the colour of mahogany with exposure to the weather, and he had a deep scar from the corner of his mouth to his ear, which by no means improved his appearance. His hair was grizzled, but his figure was stalwart, and his fur cap was cocked on one side so as to give him a rakish, semi-military appearance. Altogether he gave me the impression of being one of the most dangerous types of tramp that I had ever fallen in with.

Instead of replying to my question, he eyed me for some time in silence with sullen, yellow-shot eyes, and then closed his knife with a loud snick.

"You're not a beak," he said, "too young for that, I guess. They had me in chokey at Paisley and they had me in chokey at Wigtown, but by the living thunder if another of them lays a hand on me I'll make him remember Corporal

Rufus Smith! It's a darned fine country this, where they won't give a man work, and then lay him by the heels for having no visible means of subsistence."

"I am sorry to see an old soldier so reduced," said I. "What corps did you serve in?"

"H Battery, Royal Horse Artillery. Bad cess to the Service and every one in it! Here I am nigh sixty years of age, with a beggarly pension of thirty-eight pound ten—not enough to keep me in beer and baccy."

"I should have thought thirty-eight pound ten a year would have been a nice help to you in your old age," I remarked.

"Would you, though?" he answered with a sneer, pushing his weather-beaten face forward until it was within a foot of my own.

"How much d'ye think that slash with a tulwar is worth? And my foot with all the bones rattling about like a bagful of dice where the trail of the gun went across it. What's that worth, eh? And a liver like a sponge, and ague whenever the wind comes round to the east—what's the market value of that? Would you take the lot for a dirty forty pound a year—would you now?"

"We are poor folk in this part of the country," I answered. "You would pass for a rich man down here."

"They are fool folk and they have fool tastes," said he, drawing a black pipe from his pocket and stuffing it with tobacco. "I know what good living is, and, by cripes! While I have a shilling in my pocket I like to spend it as a shilling should be spent. I've fought for my country and my country has done darned little for me. I'll go to the Rooshians, so help me! I could show them how to cross the Himalayas so that it would puzzle either Afghans or British to stop 'em. What's that secret worth in St. Petersburg, eh, mister?"

"I am ashamed to hear an old soldier speak so, even in jest," said I sternly.

"Jest, indeed!" he cried, with a great, roaring oath. "I'd have done it years ago if the Rooshians had been game to take it up. Skobeloff was the best of the bunch, but he's been snuffed out. However, that's neither here nor there. What I want to ask you is whether you've ever heard anything in this quarter of a man called Heatherstone, the same who used to be colonel of the 41st Bengalis? They told me at Wigtown that he lived somewhere down this way."

"He lives in that large house over yonder," said I, pointing to Cloomber Tower. "You'll find the avenue gate a little way down the road, but the general isn't over fond of visitors."

The last part of my speech was lost upon Corporal Rufus Smith; for the instant that I pointed out the gate he set off hopping down the road.

His mode of progression was the most singular I have ever seen, for he would only put his right foot to the ground once in every half-dozen strides, while he worked so hard and attained such a momentum with the other limb that he got over the ground at an astonishing speed.

I was so surprised that I stood in the roadway gazing after this hulking figure until the thought suddenly struck me that some serious result might come from a meeting between a man of such blunt speech and the choleric, hot-headed general. I therefore followed him as he hopped along like some great, clumsy bird, and overtook him at the avenue gate, where he stood grasping the ironwork and peering through at the dark carriage-drive beyond.

"He's a sly old jackal," he said, looking round at me and nodding his head in the direction of the Hall. "He's a deep old dog. And that's his bungalow, is it, among the trees?"

"That is his house," I answered; "but I should advise you to keep a more civil tongue in your head if you intend to speak with the general. He is not a man to stand any nonsense."

"Right you are. He was always a hard nut to crack. But isn't this him coming down the avenue?"

I looked through the gate and saw that it was indeed the general, who, having either seen us or been attracted by our voices, was hurrying down towards us. As he advanced he would stop from time to time and peer at us through the dark shadow thrown by the trees, as if he were irresolute whether to come on or no.

"He's reconnoitering!" whispered my companion with a hoarse chuckle. "He's afraid—and I know what he's afraid of. He won't be caught in a trap if he can help it, the old 'un. He's about as fly as they make 'em, you bet!"

Then suddenly standing on his tip-toes and waving his hand through the bars of the gate, he shouted at the top of his voice:

"Come on, my gallant commandant! Come on! The coast's clear, and no enemy in sight."

This familiar address had the effect of reassuring the general, for he came right for us, though I could tell by his heightened colour that his temper was at boiling point.

"What, you here, Mr. West?" he said, as his eye fell upon me. "What is it you want, and why have you brought this fellow with you?"

"I have not brought him with me, sir," I answered, feeling rather disgusted at being made responsible for the presence of the disreputable-looking vagabond beside me. "I found him on the road here, and he desired to be directed to you, so I showed him the way. I know nothing of him myself."

"What do you want with me, then?" the general asked sternly, turning to my companion.

"If you please, sir," said the ex-corporal, speaking in a whining voice, and touching his moleskin cap with a humility which contrasted strangely with the previous rough independence of his bearing, "I'm an old gunner in the Queen's service, sir, and knowing your name by hearing it in India I thought that maybe you would take me as your groom or gardener, or give me any other place as happened to be vacant."

"I am sorry that I cannot do anything for you, my man," the old soldier answered impressively.

"Then you'll give me a little just to help me on my way, sir," said the cringing mendicant. "You won't see an old comrade go to the bad for the sake of a few rupees? I was with Sale's brigade in the Passes, sir, and I was at the second taking of Cabul."

General Heatherstone looked keenly at the supplicant, but was silent to his appeal.

"I was in Ghuznee with you when the walls were all shook down by an earthquake, and when we found forty thousand Afghans within gunshot of us. You ask me about it, and you'll see whether I'm lying or not. We went through all this when we were young, and now that we are old you are to live in a fine bungalow, and I am to starve by the roadside. It don't seem to me to be fair."

"You are an impertinent scoundrel," said the general. "If you had been a good soldier you would never need to ask for help. I shall not give you a farthing."

"One word more, sir," cried the tramp, for the other was turning away, "I've been in the Tarada Pass."

The old soldier sprang round as if the words had been a pistol-shot.

"What—what d'ye mean?" he stammered.

"I've been in the Tarada Pass, sir, and I knew a man there called Ghoolab Shah."

These last were hissed out in an undertone, and a malicious grin overspread the face of the speaker.

Their effect upon the general was extraordinary. He fairly staggered back from the gateway, and his yellow countenance blanched to a livid, mottled grey. For a moment he was too overcome to speak. At last he gasped out:

"Ghoolab Shah? Who are you who know Ghoolab Shah?"

"Take another look," said the tramp, "your sight is not as keen as it was forty years ago."

The general took a long, earnest look at the unkempt wanderer in front of him, and as he gazed I saw the light of recognition spring up in his eyes.

"God bless my soul!" he cried. "Why, it's Corporal Rufus Smith."

"You've come on it at last," said the other, chuckling to himself. "I was wondering how long it would be before you knew me. And, first of all, just unlock this gate, will you? It's hard to talk through a grating. It's too much like ten minutes with a visitor in the cells."

The general, whose face still bore evidences of his agitation, undid the bolts with nervous, trembling fingers. The recognition of Corporal Rufus Smith had, I fancied, been a relief to him, and yet he plainly showed by his manner that he regarded his presence as by no means an unmixed blessing.

"Why, Corporal," he said, as the gate swung open, "I have often wondered whether you were dead or alive, but I never expected to see you again. How have you been all these long years?"

"How have I been?" the corporal answered gruffly. "Why, I have been drunk for the most part. When I draw my money I lay it out in liquor, and as long as that lasts I get some peace in life. When I'm cleaned out I go upon tramp, partly in the hope of picking up the price of a dram, and partly in order to look for you."

"You'll excuse us talking about these private matters, West," the general said, looking round at me, for I was beginning to move away. "Don't leave us. You know something of this matter already, and may find yourself entirely in the swim with us some of these days."

Corporal Rufus Smith looked round at me in blank astonishment.

"In the swim with us?" he said. "However did he get there?"

"Voluntarily, voluntarily," the general explained, hurriedly sinking his voice. "He is a neighbour of mine, and he has volunteered his help in case I should ever need it."

This explanation seemed, if anything, to increase the big stranger's surprise.

"Well, if that don't lick cock-fighting!" he exclaimed, contemplating me with admiration. "I never heard tell of such a thing."

"And now you have found me, Corporal Smith," said the tenant of Cloomber, "what is it that you want of me?"

"Why, everything. I want a roof to cover me, and clothes to wear, and food to eat, and, above all, brandy to drink."

"Well, I'll take you in and do what I can for you," said the general slowly. "But look here, Smith, we must have discipline. I'm the general and you are the corporal; I am the master and you are the man. Now, don't let me have to remind you of that again."

The tramp drew himself up to his full height and raised his right hand with the palm forward in a military salute.

"I can take you on as gardener and get rid of the fellow I have got. As to brandy, you shall have an allowance and no more. We are not deep drinkers at the Hall."

"Don't you take opium, or brandy, or nothing yourself, sir?" asked Corporal Rufus Smith.

"Nothing," the general said firmly.

"Well, all I can say is, that you've got more nerve and pluck than I shall ever have. I don't wonder now at your winning that Cross in the Mutiny. If I was to go on listening night after night to them things without ever taking a drop of something to cheer my heart—why, it would drive me silly."

General Heatherstone put his hand up, as though afraid that his companion might say too much.

"I must thank you, Mr. West," he said, "for having shown this man my door. I would not willingly allow an old comrade, however humble, to go to the bad, and if I did not acknowledge his claim more readily it was simply because I had my doubts as to whether he was really what he represented himself to be. Just walk up to the Hall, Corporal, and I shall follow you in a minute."

"Poor fellow!" he continued, as he watched the newcomer hobbling up the avenue in the ungainly manner which I have described. "He got a gun over his foot, and it crushed the bones, but the obstinate fool would not let the doctors take it off. I remember him now as a smart young soldier in Afghanistan. He and I were associated in some queer adventures, which I may tell you of someday, and I naturally feel sympathy towards him, and would befriend him. Did he tell you anything about me before I came?"

"Not a word," I replied.

"Oh," said the general carelessly, but with an evident expression of relief, "I thought perhaps he might have said something of old times. Well, I must go and look after him, or the servants will be frightened, for he isn't a beauty to look at. Good-bye!"

With a wave of the hand the old man turned away from me and hurried up the drive after this unexpected addition to his household, while I strolled on round the high, black paling, peering through every chink between the planks, but without seeing a trace either of Mordaunt or of his sister.

I have now brought this statement down to the coming of Corporal Rufus Smith, which will prove to be the beginning of the end.

I have set down soberly and in order the events which brought us to Wigtownshire, the arrival of the Heatherstones at Cloomber, the many strange incidents which excited first our curiosity and finally our intense interest in that family, and I have briefly touched upon the circumstances which brought my sister and myself into a closer and more personal relationship with them. I think that there cannot be a better moment than this to hand the narrative over to those who had means of knowing something of what was going on inside Cloomber during the months that I was observing it from without.

Israel Stakes, the coachman, proved to be unable to read or write, but Mr. Mathew Clark, the Presbyterian Minister of Stoneykirk, has copied down his deposition, duly attested by the cross set opposite to his name. The good clergyman has, I fancy, put some slight polish upon the narrator's story, which I rather regret, as it might have been more interesting, if less intelligible, when reported verbatim. It still preserves, however, considerable traces of Israel's individuality, and may be regarded as an exact record of what he saw and did while in General Heatherstone's service.

CHAPTER 8 - *STATEMENT OF ISRAEL STAKES*

(Copied and authenticated by the Reverend Mathew Clark, Presbyterian Minister of Stoneykirk, in Wigtownshire)

Maister Fothergill West and the meenister say that I maun tell all I can aboot General Heatherstone and his hoose, but that I maunna say muckle aboot mysel' because the readers wouldna care to hear aboot me or my affairs. I am na sae sure o' that, for the Stakes is a family weel kenned and respecked on baith sides o' the Border, and there's mony in Nithsdale and Annandale as would be gey pleased to hear news o' the son o' Archie Stakes, o' Ecclefechan.

I maun e'en do as I'm tauld, however, for Mr. West's sake, hoping he'll no forget me when I chance to hae a favour tae ask.(1) I'm no able tae write mysel' because my feyther sent me oot to scare craws instead o' sendin' me tae school, but on the ither hond he brought me up in the preenciples and practice o' the real kirk o' the Covenant, for which may the Lord be praised!

It way last May twel'month that the factor body, Maister McNeil, cam ower tae me in the street and speered whether I was in want o' a place as a coachman and gairdner. As it fell oot I chanced tae be on the look oot for something o' the sort mysel' at the time, but I wasna ower quick to let him see that I wanted it.

"Ye can tak it or leave it," says he sharp like. "It's a guid place, and there's mony would be glad o't. If ye want it ye can come up tae my office at twa the morn and put your ain questions tae the gentleman."

That was a' I could get frae him, for he's a close man and a hard one at a bargain—which shall profit him leetle in the next life, though he lay by a store o' siller in this. When the day comes there'll be a hantle o' factors on the left hand o' the throne, and I shouldna be surprised if Maister McNeil found himsel' amang them.

Weel, on the morn I gaed up to the office and there I foond the factor and a lang, thin, dour man wi' grey hair and a face as brown and crinkled as a walnut. He looked hard at me wi' a pair o' een that glowed like twa spunks, and then he says, says he:

"You've been born in these pairts, I understan'?"

"Aye," says I, "and never left them neither."

"Never been oot o' Scotland?" he speers.

"Twice to Carlisle fair," says I, for I am a man wha loves the truth; and besides I kenned that the factor would mind my gaeing there, for I bargained fur twa steers and a stirk that he wanted for the stockin' o' the Drumleugh Fairm.

"I learn frae Maister McNeil," says General Heatherstone—for him it was and nane ither—"that ye canna write."

"Na," says I.

"Nor read?"

"Na," says I.

"It seems tae me," says he, turnin' tae the factor, "that this is the vera man I want. Servants is spoilt noo-a-days," says he, "by ower muckle eddication. I hae nae doobt, Stakes, that ye will suit me well enough. Ye'll hae three pund a month and a' foond, but I shall resairve the right o' givin' ye twenty-four hoors' notice at any time. How will that suit ye?"

"It's vera different frae my last place," says I, discontented-like.

And the words were true enough, for auld Fairmer Scott only gave me a pund a month and parritch twice a day.

"Weel, weel," says he, "maybe we'll gie ye a rise if ye suit. Meanwhile here's the han'sel shillin' that Maister McNeil tells me it's the custom tae give, and I shall expec' tae see ye at Cloomber on Monday."

When the Monday cam roond I walked oot tae Cloomber, and a great muckle hoose it is, wi' a hunderd windows or mair, and space enough tae hide awa' half the parish.

As tae gairdening, there was no gairden for me tae work at, and the horse was never taken oot o' the stables frae week's end tae week's end. I was busy enough for a' that, for there was a deal o' fencing tae be put up, and one thing or anither, forbye cleanin' the knives and brushin' the boots and such-like jobs as is mair fit for an auld wife than for a grown man.

There was twa besides mysel' in the kitchen, the cook Eliza, and Mary the hoosemaid, puir, benighted beings baith o' them, wha had wasted a' their lives in London, and kenned leetle aboot the warld or the ways o' the flesh.

I hadna muckle tae say to them, for they were simple folk who could scarce understand English, and had hardly mair regard for their ain souls than the tods on the moor. When the cook said she didna think muckle o' John Knox, and the ither that she wouldna give saxpence tae hear the discourse o' Maister Donald McSnaw o' the true kirk, I kenned it was time for me tae leave them tae a higher Judge.

There was four in family, the general, my leddy, Maister Mordaunt, and Miss Gabriel, and it wasna long before I found that a' wasna just exactly as it should be. My leddy was as thin and as white as a ghaist, and many's the time as I've come on her and found her yammerin' and greetin' all by hersel'. I've watched her walkin' up and doon in the wood where she thought nane could see her and wringin' her honds like one demented.

There was the young gentleman, tae, and his sister— they baith seemed to hae some trouble on their minds, and the general maist of a', for the ithers were up ane day and down anither; but he was aye the same, wi' a face as dour and sad as a felon when he feels the tow roond his neck.

I speered o' the hussies in the kitchen whether they kenned what was amiss wi' the family, but the cook she answered me back that it wasna for her tae inquire into the affairs o' her superiors, and that it was naething to her as long as she did her work and had her wages. They were puir, feckless bodies, the twa o' them, and would scarce gie an answer tae a ceevil question, though they could clack lood eneugh when they had a mind.

Weel, weeks passed into months and a' things grew waur instead o' better in the Hall. The general he got mair nairvous, and his leddy mair melancholy every day, and yet there wasna any quarrel or bickering between them, for when they've been togither in the breakfast room I used often tae gang round and prune the rose-tree alongside o' the window, so that I couldna help hearin' a great pairt o' their conversation, though sair against the grain.

When the young folk were wi' them they would speak little, but when they had gone they would aye talk as if some waefu' trial ere aboot to fa' upon them, though I could never gather from their words what it was that they were afeared o'.

I've heard the general say mair than ance that he wasna frighted o' death, or any danger that he could face and have done wi', but that it was the lang, weary waitin' and the uncertainty that had taken a' the strength and the mettle oot o' him. Then my leddy would console him and tell him that maybe it wasna as bad as he thocht, and that a' would come richt in the end—but a' her cheery words were clean throwed away upon him.

As tae the young folks, I kenned weel that they didna bide in the groonds, and that they were awa' whenever they got a chance wi' Maister Fothergill West tae Branksome, but the general was too fu' o' his ain troubles tae ken aboot it, and it didna seem tae me that it was pairt o' my duties either as coachman or as gairdner tae mind the bairns. He should have lairnt that if ye forbid a lassie and a laddie to dae anything it's just the surest way o' bringin' it aboot. The Lord foond that oot in the gairden o' Paradise, and there's no muckle change between the folk in Eden and the folk in Wigtown.

There's ane thing that I havena spoke aboot yet, but that should be set doon.

The general didna share his room wi' his wife, but slept a' alane in a chamber at the far end o' the hoose, as distant as possible frae everyone else. This room was aye lockit when he wasna in it, and naebody was ever allowed tae gang into it. He would mak' his ain bed, and red it up and dust it a' by himsel', but he wouldna so much as allow one o' us to set fut on the passage that led tae it.

At nicht he would walk a' ower the hoose, and he had lamps hung in every room and corner, so that no pairt should be dark.

Many's the time frae my room in the garret I've heard his futsteps comin' and gangin', comin' and gangin' doon one passage and up anither frae midnight till cockcraw. It was weary wark to lie listenin' tae his clatter and wonderin' whether he was clean daft, or whether maybe he'd lairnt pagan and idolatrous tricks oot in India, and that his conscience noo was like the worm which gnaweth and dieth not. I'd ha' speered frae him whether it wouldna ease him to speak wi' the holy Donald McSnaw, but it might ha' been a mistake, and the general wasna a man that you'd care tae mak' a mistake wi'.

Ane day I was workin' at the grass border when he comes up and he says, says he:

"Did ye ever have occasion tae fire a pistol, Israel?"

"Godsakes!" says I, "I never had siccan a thing in my honds in my life."

"Then you'd best not begin noo," says he. "Every man tae his ain weepon," he says. "Now I warrant ye could do something wi' a guid crab-tree cudgel!"

"Aye, could I," I answered blithely, "as well as ony lad on the Border."

"This is a lonely hoose," says he, "and we might be molested by some rascals. It's weel tae be ready for whatever may come. Me and you and my son Mordaunt and Mr. Fothergill West of Branksome, who would come if he was required, ought tae be able tae show a bauld face—what think ye?"

"'Deed, sir," I says, "feastin' is aye better than fechtin'—but if ye'll raise me a pund a month, I'll no' shirk my share o' either."

"We won't quarrel ower that," says he, and agreed tae the extra twal' pund a year as easy as though it were as many bawbees. Far be it frae me tae think evil, but I couldna help surmisin' at the time that money that was so lightly pairted wi' was maybe no' so very honestly cam by.

I'm no' a curious or a pryin' mun by nature, but I was sair puzzled in my ain mind tae tell why it was that the general walked aboot at nicht and what kept him frae his sleep.

Weel, ane day I was cleanin' doon the passages when my e'e fell on a great muckle heap o' curtains and auld cairpets and sic' like things that were piled away in a corner, no vera far frae the door o' the general's room. A' o' a sudden a thocht came intae my heid and I says tae mysel':

"Israel, laddie," says I, "what's tae stop ye frae hidin' behind that this vera nicht and seein' the auld mun when he doesna ken human e'e is on him?"

The mair I thocht o't the mair seemple it appeared, and I made up my mind tae put the idea intae instant execution.

When the nicht cam roond I tauld the women-folk that I was bad wi' the jawache, and would gang airly tae my room. I kenned fine when ance I got there that there was na chance o' ony ane disturbin' me, so I waited a wee while, and then when a' was quiet, I slippit aff my boots and ran doon the ither stair until I cam tae the heap o' auld clothes, and there I lay doon wi' ane e'e peepin' through a kink and a' the rest covered up wi' a great, ragged cairpet.

There I bided as quiet as a mouse until the general passed me on his road tae bed, and a' was still in the hoose.

My certie! I wouldna gang through wi' it again for a' the siller at the Union Bank of Dumfries, I canna think o't noo withoot feelin' cauld a' the way doon my back.

It was just awfu' lyin' there in the deid silence, waitin' and waitin' wi' never a soond tae break the monotony, except the heavy tickin' o' an auld clock somewhere doon the passage.

First I would look doon the corridor in the one way, and syne I'd look doon in t'ither, but it aye seemed to me as though there was something coming up frae the side that I wasna lookin' at. I had a cauld sweat on my broo, and my hairt was beatin' twice tae ilka tick o' the clock, and what feared me most of a' was that the dust frae the curtains and things was aye gettin' doon intae my lungs, and it was a' I could dae tae keep mysel' frae coughin'.

Godsakes! I wonder my hair wasna grey wi' a' that I went through. I wouldna dae it again to be made Lord Provost o' Glasgie.

Weel, it may have been twa o'clock in the mornin' or maybe a little mair, and I was just thinkin' that I wasna tae see onything after a'—and I wasna very sorry neither—when all o' a sudden a soond cam tae my ears clear and distinct through the stillness o' the nicht.

I've been asked afore noo tae describe that soond, but I've aye foond that it's no' vera easy tae gie a clear idea o't, though it was unlike any other soond that ever I hearkened tae. It was a shairp, ringin' clang, like what could be caused by flippin' the rim o' a wineglass, but it was far higher and thinner than that, and had in it, tae, a kind o' splash, like the tinkle o' a rain-drop intae a water-butt.

In my fear I sat up amang my cairpets, like a puddock among gowan-leaves, and I listened wi' a' my ears. A' was still again noo, except for the dull tickin' o' the distant clock.

Suddenly the soond cam again, as clear, as shrill, as shairp as ever, and this time the general heard it, for I heard him gie a kind o' groan, as a tired man might wha has been roosed oot o' his sleep.

He got up frae his bed, and I could make oot a rustling noise, as though he were dressin' himsel', and presently his footfa' as he began tae walk up and doon in his room.

Mysakes! it didna tak lang for me tae drap doon amang the cairpets again and cover mysel' ower. There I lay tremblin' in every limb, and sayin' as mony prayers as I could mind, wi' my e'e still peepin' through the keek-hole, and fixed upon the door o' the general's room.

I heard the rattle o' the handle presently, and the door swung slowly open. There was a licht burnin' in the room beyond, an' I could just catch a glimpse o' what seemed tae me like a row o' swords stuck alang the side o' the wa', when the general stepped oot and shut the door behind him. He was dressed in a dressin' goon, wi' a red smokin'-cap on his heid, and a pair o' slippers wi' the heels cut off and the taes turned up.

For a moment it cam into my held that maybe he was walkin' in his sleep, but as he cam towards me I could see the glint o' the licht in his e'en, and his face was a' twistin', like a man that's in sair distress o' mind. On my conscience, it gies me the shakes noo when I think o' his tall figure and his yelley face comin' sae solemn and silent doon the lang, lone passage.

I haud my breath and lay close watchin' him, but just as he cam tae where I was my vera hairt stood still in my breast, for "ting!"—loud and clear, within a yaird o' me cam the ringin', clangin' soond that I had a'ready hairkened tae.

Where it cam frae is mair than I can tell or what was the cause o't. It might ha' been that the general made it, but I was sair puzzled tae tell hoo, for his honds were baith doon by his side as he passed me. It cam frae his direction, certainly, but it appeared tae me tae come frae ower his heid, but it was siccan a thin, eerie, high-pitched, uncanny kind o' soond that it wasna easy tae say just exactly where it did come frae.

The general tuk nae heed o't, but walked on and was soon oot o' sicht, and I didna lose a minute in creepin' oot frae my hidin' place and scamperin' awa' back tae my room, and if a' the bogies in the Red Sea were trapesin' up and doon the hale nicht through, I wud never put my heid oot again tae hae a glimpse o' them.

I didna say a word tae anybody aboot what I'd seen, but I made up my mind that I wudna stay muckle langer at Cloomber Ha'. Four pund a month is a good wage, but it isna enough tae pay a man for the loss o' his peace o' mind, and maybe the loss o' his soul as weel, for when the deil is aboot ye canna tell what sort o' a trap he may lay for ye, and though they say that Providence is stronger than him, it's maybe as weel no' to risk it.

It was clear tae me that the general and his hoose were baith under some curse, and it was fit that that curse should fa' on them that had earned it, and no' on a righteous Presbyterian, wha had ever trod the narrow path.

My hairt was sair for young Miss Gabriel—for she was a bonnie and winsome lassie—but for a' that, I felt that my duty was tae mysel' and that I should gang forth, even as Lot ganged oot o' the wicked cities o' the plain.

That awfu' cling-clang was aye dingin' in my lugs, and I couldna bear to be alane in the passages for fear o' hearin' it ance again. I only wanted a chance or an excuse tae gie the general notice, and tae gang back to some place where I could see Christian folk, and have the kirk within a stone-cast tae fa' back upon.

But it proved tae be ordained that, instead o' my saying the word, it should come frae the general himsel'.

It was ane day aboot the beginning of October, I was comin' oot o' the stable, after giein' its oats tae the horse, when I seed a great muckle loon come hoppin' on ane leg up the drive, mair like a big, ill-faured craw than a man.

When I clapped my een on him I thocht that maybe this was ane of the rascals that the maister had been speakin' aboot, so withoot mair ado I fetched oot my bit stick with the intention o' tryin' it upon the limmer's heid. He seed me comin' towards him, and readin' my intention frae my look maybe, or frae the stick in my hand, he pu'ed oot a lang knife frae his pocket and swore wi' the most awfu' oaths that if I didna stan' back he'd be the death o' me.

Ma conscience! The words the chiel used was eneugh tae mak' the hair stand straight on your heid. I wonder he wasna struck deid where he stood.

We were still standin' opposite each ither—he wi' his knife and me wi' the stick—when the general he cam up the drive and foond us. Tae my surprise he began tae talk tae the stranger as if he'd kenned him a' his days.

"Put your knife in your pocket, Corporal," says he. "Your fears have turned your brain."

"Blood an' wounds!" says the other. "He'd ha' turned my brain tae some purpose wi' that muckle stick o' his if I hadna drawn my snickersnee. You shouldna keep siccan an auld savage on your premises."

The maister he frooned and looked black at him, as though he didna relish advice comin' frae such a source. Then turnin' tae me—"You won't be wanted after to-day, Israel," he says; "you have been a guid servant, and I ha' naething tae complain of wi' ye, but circumstances have arisen which will cause me tae change my arrangements."

"Vera guid, sir," says I.

"You can go this evening," says he, "and you shall have an extra month's pay tae mak up t'ye for this short notice."

Wi' that he went intae the hoose, followed by the man that he ca'ed the corporal, and frae that day tae this I have never clapped een either on the ane or the ither. My money was sent oot tae me in an envelope, and havin' said a few pairtin' words tae the cook and the wench wi' reference tae the wrath tae come and the treasure that is richer than rubies, I shook the dust o' Cloomber frae my feet for ever.

Maister Fothergill West says I maunna express an opeenion as tae what cam aboot afterwards, but maun confine mysel' tae what I saw mysel'. Nae doubt he has his reasons for this—and far be it frae me tae hint that they are no' guid anes—but I maun say this, that what happened didna surprise me. It was just as I expeckit, and so I said tae Maister Donald McSnaw.

I've tauld ye a' aboot it noo, and I havena a word tae add or tae withdraw. I'm muckle obleeged tae Maister Mathew Clairk for puttin' it a' doon in writin' for me, and if there's ony would wish tae speer onything mair o' me I'm well kenned and respeckit in Ecclefechan, and Maister McNeil, the factor o' Wigtown, can aye tell where I am tae be foond.

(1) The old rascal was well paid for his trouble, so he need not have made such a favour of it.—J.F.W.

CHAPTER 9 - *NARRATIVE OF JOHN EASTERLING, F.R.C.P.EDIN.*

Having given the statement of Israel Stakes *in extenso*, I shall append a short memorandum from Dr. Easterling, now practising at Stranraer. It is true that the doctor was only once within the walls of Cloomber during its tenancy by General Heatherstone, but there were some circumstances connected with this visit which made it valuable, especially when considered as a supplement to the experiences which I have just submitted to the reader.

The doctor has found time amid the calls of a busy country practice to jot down his recollections, and I feel that I cannot do better than subjoin them exactly as they stand.

I have very much pleasure in furnishing Mr. Fothergill West with an account of my solitary visit to Cloomber Hall, not only on account of the esteem which I have formed for that gentleman ever since his residence at Branksome, but also because it is my conviction that the facts in the case of General Heatherstone are of such a singular nature that it is of the highest importance that they should be placed before the public in a trustworthy manner.

It was about the beginning of September of last year that I received a note from Mrs. Heatherstone, of Cloomber Hall, desiring me to make a professional call upon her husband, whose health, she said, had been for some time in a very unsatisfactory state.

I had heard something of the Heatherstones and of the strange seclusion in which they lived, so that I was very much pleased at this opportunity of making their closer acquaintance, and lost no time in complying with her request.

I had known the Hall in the old days of Mr. McVittie, the original proprietor, and I was astonished on arriving at the avenue gate to observe the changes which had taken place.

The gate itself, which used to yawn so hospitably upon the road, was now barred and locked, and a high wooden fence, with nails upon the top, encircled the whole grounds. The drive itself was leaf-strewn and uncared-for, and the whole place had a depressing air of neglect and decay.

I had to knock twice before a servant-maid opened the door and showed me through a dingy hall into a small room, where sat an elderly, careworn lady, who introduced herself as Mrs. Heatherstone. With her pale face, her grey hair, her sad, colourless eyes, and her faded silk dress, she was in perfect keeping with her melancholy surroundings.

"You find us in much trouble, doctor," she said, in a quiet, refined voice. "My poor husband has had a great deal to worry him, and his nervous system for a long time has been in a very weak state. We came to this part of the country in the hope that the bracing air and the quiet would have a good effect upon him. Instead of improving, however, he has seemed to grow weaker, and this morning he is in a high fever and a little inclined to be delirious. The children and I were so frightened that we sent for you at once. If you will follow me I will take you to the general's bedroom."

She led the way down a series of corridors to the chamber of the sick man, which was situated in the extreme wing of the building.

It was a carpetless, bleak-looking room, scantily furnished with a small truckle bed, a campaigning chair, and a plain deal table, on which were scattered numerous papers and books. In the centre of this table there stood a large object of irregular outline, which was covered over with a sheet of linen.

All round the walls and in the corners were arranged a very choice and varied collection of arms, principally swords, some of which were of the straight pattern in common use in the British Army, while among the others were scimitars, tulwars, cuchurries, and a score of other specimens of Oriental workmanship. Many of these were richly mounted, with inlaid sheaths and hilts sparkling with precious stones, so that there was a piquant contrast between the simplicity of the apartment and the wealth which glittered on the walls.

I had little time, however, to observe the general's collection, since the general himself lay upon the couch and was evidently in sore need of my services.

He was lying with his head turned half away from us. Breathing heavily, and apparently unconscious of our presence. His bright, staring eyes and the deep, hectic flush upon his cheek showed that his fever was at its height.

I advanced to the bedside, and, stooping over him, I placed my fingers upon his pulse, when immediately he sprang up into the sitting position and struck at me frenziedly with his clenched hands. I have never seen such intensity of fear and horror stamped upon a human face as appeared upon that which was now glaring up at me.

"Bloodhound!" he yelled; "let me go—let me go, I say! Keep your hands off me! Is it not enough that my life has been ruined? When is it all to end? How long am I to endure it?"

"Hush, dear, hush!" said his wife in a soothing voice, passing her cool hand over his heated forehead. "This is Doctor Easterling, from Stranraer. He has not come to harm you, but to do you good."

The general dropped wearily back upon his pillow, and I could see by the changed expression of his face that his delirium had left him, and that he understood what had been said.

I slipped my clinical thermometer into his armpit and counted his pulse rate. It amounted to 120 per minute, and his temperature proved to be 104 degrees. Clearly it was a case of remittent fever, such as occurs in men who have spent a great part of their lives in the tropics.

"There is no danger," I remarked. "With a little quinine and arsenic we shall very soon overcome the attack and restore his health."

"No danger, eh?" he said. "There never is any danger for me. I am as hard to kill as the Wandering Jew. I am quite clear in the head now, Mary; so you may leave me with the doctor."

Mrs. Heatherstone left the room—rather unwillingly, as I thought—and I sat down by the bedside to listen to anything which my patient might have to communicate.

"I want you to examine my liver," he said when the door was closed. "I used to have an abscess there, and Brodie, the staff-surgeon, said that it was ten to one that it would carry me off. I have not felt much of it since I left the East. This is where it used to be, just under the angle of the ribs."

"I can find the place," said I, after making a careful examination; "but I am happy to tell you that the abscess has either been entirely absorbed, or has turned calcareous, as these solitary abscesses will. There is no fear of its doing you any harm now."

He seemed to be by no means overjoyed at the intelligence.

"Things always happen so with me," he said moodily. "Now, if another fellow was feverish and delirious he would surely be in some danger, and yet you will tell me that I am in none. Look at this, now." He bared his chest and showed me a puckered wound over the region of the heart. "That's where the jezail bullet of a Hillman went in. You would think that was in the right spot to settle a man, and yet what does it do but glance upon a rib, and go clean round and out at the back, without so much as penetrating what you medicos call the pleura. Did ever you hear of such a thing?"

"You were certainly born under a lucky star," I observed, with a smile.

"That's a matter of opinion," he answered, shaking his head. "Death has no terrors for me, if it will but come in some familiar form, but I confess that the anticipation of some strange, some preternatural form of death is very terrible and unnerving."

"You mean," said I, rather puzzled at his remark, "that you would prefer a natural death to a death by violence?"

"No, I don't mean that exactly," he answered. "I am too familiar with cold steel and lead to be afraid of either. Do you know anything about odyllic force, doctor?"

"No, I do not," I replied, glancing sharply at him to see if there were any signs of his delirium returning. His expression was intelligent, however, and the feverish flush had faded from his cheeks.

"Ah, you Western scientific men are very much behind the day in some things," he remarked. "In all that is material and conducive to the comfort of the body you are pre-eminent, but in what concerns the subtle forces of Nature and the latent powers of the human spirit your best men are centuries behind the humblest coolies of India. Countless generations of beef-eating, comfort loving ancestors have given our animal instincts the command over our spiritual ones. The body, which should have been a mere tool for the use of the soul, has now become a degrading prison in which it is confined. The Oriental soul and body are not so welded together as ours are, and there is far less wrench when they part in death."

"They do not appear to derive much benefit from this peculiarity in their organisation," I remarked incredulously.

"Merely the benefit of superior knowledge," the general answered. "If you were to go to India, probably the very first thing you would see in the way of amusement would be a native doing what is called the mango trick. Of course you have heard or read of it. The fellow plants a mango seed, and makes passes over it until it sprouts and bears leaves and fruit—all in the space of half-an-hour. It is not really a trick—it is a power. These men know more than your Tyndalls or Huxleys do about Nature's processes, and they can accelerate or retard her workings by subtle means of which we have no conception. These low-caste conjurers—as they are called—are mere vulgar dabblers, but the men who have trod the higher path are as far superior to us in knowledge as we are to the Hottentots or Patagonians."

"You speak as if you were well acquainted with them," I remarked.

"To my cost, I am," he answered. "I have been brought in contact with them in a way in which I trust no other poor chap ever will be. But, really, as regards odyllic force, you ought to know something of it, for it has a great future before it in your profession. You should read Reichenbach's 'Researches on Magnetism and Vital Force,' and Gregory's 'Letters on Animal Magnetism.' These, supplemented by the twenty-seven Aphorisms of Mesmer, and the works of Dr. Justinus Kerner, of Weinsberg, would enlarge your ideas."

I did not particularly relish having a course of reading prescribed for me on a subject connected with my own profession, so I made no comment, but rose to take my departure. Before doing so I felt his pulse once more, and found that the fever had entirely left him in the sudden, unaccountable fashion which is peculiar to these malarious types of disease.

I turned my face towards him to congratulate him upon his improvement, and stretched out my hand at the same time to pick my gloves from the table, with the result that I raised not only my own property, but also the linen cloth which was arranged over some object in the centre.

I might not have noticed what I had done had I not seen an angry look upon the invalid's face and heard him utter an impatient exclamation. I at once turned, and replaced the cloth so promptly that I should have been unable to say what was underneath it, beyond having a general impression that it looked like a bride-cake.

"All right, doctor," the general said good-humouredly, perceiving how entirely accidental the incident was. "There is no reason why you should not see it," and stretching out his hand, he pulled away the linen covering for the second time.

I then perceived that what I had taken for a bride-cake was really an admirably executed model of a lofty range of mountains, whose snow-clad peaks were not unlike the familiar sugar pinnacles and minarets.

"These are the Himalayas, or at least the Surinam branch of them," he remarked, "showing the principal passes between India and Afghanistan. It is an excellent model. This ground has a special interest for me, because it is the scene of my first campaign. There is the pass opposite Kalabagh and the Thul valley, where I was engaged during the summer of 1841 in protecting the convoys and keeping the Afridis in order. It wasn't a sinecure, I promise you."

"And this," said I, indicating a blood-red spot which had been marked on one side of the pass which he had pointed out—"this is the scene of some fight in which you were engaged."

"Yes, we had a skirmish there," he answered, leaning forward and looking at the red mark. "We were attacked by—"

At this moment he fell back upon his pillow as if he had been shot, while the same look of horror came over his face which I had observed when I first entered the room. At the same instant there came, apparently from the air immediately above his bed, a sharp, ringing, tinkling sound, which I can only compare with the noise made by a bicycle alarm, though it differed from this in having a distinctly throbbing character. I have never, before or since, heard any sound which could be confounded with it.

I stared round in astonishment, wondering where it could have come from, but without perceiving anything to which it could be ascribed.

"It's all right, doctor," the general said with a ghastly smile. "It's only my private gong. Perhaps you had better step downstairs and write my prescription in the dining-room."

He was evidently anxious to get rid of me, so I was forced to take my departure, though I would gladly have stayed a little longer, in the hope of learning something as to the origin of the mysterious sound.

I drove away from the house with the full determination of calling again upon my interesting patient, and endeavouring to elicit some further particulars as to his past life and his present circumstances. I was destined, however, to be disappointed, for I received that very evening a note from the general himself, enclosing a handsome fee for my single visit, and informing me that my treatment had done him so much good that he considered himself to be convalescent, and would not trouble me to see him again.

This was the last and only communication which I ever received from the tenant of Cloomber.

I have been asked frequently by neighbours and others who were interested in the matter whether he gave me the impression of insanity. To this I must unhesitatingly answer in the negative. On the contrary, his remarks gave me the idea of a man who had both read and thought deeply.

I observed, however, during our single interview, that his reflexes were feeble, his arcus senilis well marked, and his arteries atheromatous—all signs that his constitution was in an unsatisfactory condition, and that a sudden crisis might be apprehended.

CHAPTER 10 - *OF THE LETTER WHICH CAME FROM THE HALL*

Having thrown this side-light upon my narrative, I can now resume the statement of my own personal experiences. These I had brought down, as the reader will doubtless remember, to the date of the arrival of the savage-looking wanderer who called himself Corporal Rufus Smith. This incident occurred about the beginning of the month of October, and I find upon a comparison of dates that Dr. Easterling's visit to Cloomber preceded it by three weeks or more.

During all this time I was in sore distress of mind, for I had never seen anything either of Gabriel or of her brother since the interview in which the general had discovered the communication which was kept up between us. I had no doubt that some sort of restraint had been placed upon them; and the thought that we had brought trouble on their heads was a bitter one both to my sister and myself.

Our anxiety, however, was considerably mitigated by the receipt, a couple of days after my last talk with the general, of a note from Mordaunt Heatherstone. This was brought us by a little, ragged urchin, the son of one of the fishermen, who informed us that it had been handed to him at the avenue gate by an old woman—who, I expect, must have been the Cloomber cook.

"MY DEAREST FRIENDS," it ran, "Gabriel and I have grieved to think how concerned you must be at having neither heard from nor seen us. The fact is that we are compelled to remain in the house. And this compulsion is not physical but moral.

"Our poor father, who gets more and more nervous every day, has entreated us to promise him that we will not go out until after the fifth of October, and to allay his fears we have given him the desired pledge. On the other hand, he has promised us that after the fifth—that is, in less than a week— we shall be as free as air to come or go as we please, so we have something to look forward to.

"Gabriel says that she has explained to you that the governor is always a changed man after this particular date, on which his fears reach a crisis. He apparently has more reason than usual this year to anticipate that trouble is brewing for this unfortunate family, for I have never known him to take so many elaborate precautions or appear so thoroughly unnerved. Who would ever think, to see his bent form and his shaking hands, that he is the same man who used some few short years ago to shoot tigers on foot among the jungles of the Terai, and would laugh at the more timid sportsmen who sought the protection of their elephant's howdah?

"You know that he has the Victoria Cross, which he won in the streets of Delhi, and yet here he is shivering with terror and starting at every noise, in the most peaceful corner of the world. Oh, the pity of it. West! Remember what I have already told you—that it is no fanciful or imaginary peril, but one which we have every reason to suppose to be most real. It is, however, of such a nature that it can neither be averted nor can it profitably be expressed in words. If all goes well, you will see us at Branksome on the sixth.

"With our fondest love to both of you, I am ever, my dear friends, your attached

"MORDAUNT."

This letter was a great relief to us as letting us know that the brother and sister were under no physical restraint, but our powerlessness and inability even to comprehend what the danger was which threatened those whom we had come to love better than ourselves was little short of maddening.

Fifty times a day we asked ourselves and asked each other from what possible quarter this peril was to be expected, but the more we thought of it the more hopeless did any solution appear.

In vain we combined our experiences and pieced together every word which had fallen from the lips of any inmate of Cloomber which might be supposed to bear directly or indirectly upon the subject.

At last, weary with fruitless speculation, we were fain to try to drive the matter from our thoughts, consoling ourselves with the reflection that in a few more days all restrictions would be removed, and we should be able to learn from our friends' own lips.

Those few intervening days, however, would, we feared, be dreary, long ones. And so they would have been, had it not been for a new and most unexpected incident, which diverted our minds from our own troubles and gave them something fresh with which to occupy themselves.

CHAPTER 11 - OF THE CASTING AWAY OF THE BARQUE "BELINDA"

The third of October had broken auspiciously with a bright sun and a cloudless sky. There had in the morning been a slight breeze, and a few little white wreaths of vapour drifted here and there like the scattered feathers of some gigantic bird, but, as the day wore on, such wind as there was fell completely away, and the air became close and stagnant.

The sun blazed down with a degree of heat which was remarkable so late in the season, and a shimmering haze lay upon the upland moors and concealed the Irish mountains on the other side of the Channel.

The sea itself rose and fell in a long, heavy, oily roll, sweeping slowly landward, and breaking sullenly with a dull, monotonous booming upon the rock-girt shore. To the inexperienced all seemed calm and peaceful, but to those who are accustomed to read Nature's warnings there was a dark menace in air and sky and sea.

My sister and I walked out in the afternoon, sauntering slowly along the margin of the great, sandy spit which shoots out into the Irish Sea, flanking upon one side the magnificent Bay of Luce, and on the other the more obscure inlet of Kirkmaiden, on the shores of which the Branksome property is situated.

It was too sultry to go far, so we soon seated ourselves upon one of the sandy hillocks, overgrown with faded grass-tufts, which extend along the coast-line, and which form Nature's dykes against the encroachments of the ocean.

Our rest was soon interrupted by the scrunching of heavy boots upon the shingle, and Jamieson, the old man-o'-war's man whom I have already had occasion to mention, made his appearance, with the flat, circular net upon his back which he used for shrimp-catching. He came towards us upon seeing us, and said in his rough, kindly way that he hoped we would not take it amiss if he sent us up a dish of shrimps for our tea at Branksome.

"I aye make a good catch before a storm," he remarked.

"You think there is going to be a storm, then?" I asked.

"Why, even a marine could see that," he answered, sticking a great wedge of tobacco into his cheek. "The moors over near Cloomber are just white wi' gulls and kittiewakes. What d'ye think they come ashore for except to escape having all the feathers blown out o' them? I mind a day like this when I was wi' Charlie Napier off Cronstadt. It well-nigh blew us under the guns of the forts, for all our engines and propellers."

"Have you ever known a wreck in these parts?" I asked.

"Lord love ye, sir, it's a famous place for wrecks. Why, in that very bay down there two o' King Philip's first-rates foundered wi' all hands in the days o' the Spanish war. If that sheet o' water and the Bay o' Luce round the corner could tell their ain tale they'd have a gey lot to speak of. When the Jedgment Day comes round that water will be just bubbling wi' the number o' folks that will be coming up frae the bottom."

"I trust that there will be no wrecks while we are here," said Esther earnestly.

The old man shook his grizzled head and looked distrustfully at the hazy horizon.

"If it blows from the west," he said, "some o' these sailing ships may find it no joke to be caught without sea-room in the North Channel. There's that barque out yonder— I daresay her maister would be glad enough to find himsel' safe in the Clyde."

"She seems to be absolutely motionless," I remarked, looking at the vessel in question, whose black hull and gleaming sails rose and fell slowly with the throbbing of the giant pulse beneath her. "Perhaps, Jamieson, we are wrong, and there will be no storm after all."

The old sailor chuckled to himself with an air of superior knowledge, and shuffled away with his shrimp-net, while my sister and I walked slowly homewards through the hot and stagnant air.

I went up to my father's study to see if the old gentleman had any instructions as to the estate, for he had become engrossed in a new work upon Oriental literature, and the practical management of the property had in consequence devolved entirely upon me.

I found him seated at his square library table, which was so heaped with books and papers that nothing of him was visible from the door except a tuft of white hair.

"My dear son," he said to me as I entered, "it is a great grief to me that you are not more conversant with Sanscrit. When I was your age, I could converse not only in that noble language, but also in the Tamulic, Lohitic, Gangelic, Taic, and Malaic dialects, which are all offshoots from the Turanian branch."

"I regret extremely, sir," I answered, "that I have not inherited your wonderful talents as a polyglot."

"I have set myself a task," he explained, "which, if it could only be continued from generation to generation in our own family until it was completed, would make the name of West immortal. This is nothing less than to publish an English translation of the Buddhist Djarmas, with a preface giving an idea of the position of Brahminism before the coming of Sakyamuni. With diligence it is possible that I might be able myself to complete part of the preface before I die."

"And pray, sir," I asked, "how long would the whole work be when it was finished?"

"The abridged edition in the Imperial Library of Pekin," said my father, rubbing his hands together, "consists of 325 volumes of an average weight of five pounds. Then the preface, which must embrace some account of the Rig-veda, the Sama-veda, the Yagur-veda, and the Atharva-veda, with the Brahmanas, could hardly be completed in less than ten volumes. Now, if we apportion one volume to each year, there is every prospect of the family coming to an end of its task about the date 2250, the twelfth generation completing the work, while the thirteenth might occupy itself upon the index."

"And how are our descendants to live, sir," I asked, with a smile, "during the progress of this great undertaking:"

"That's the worst of you, Jack," my father cried petulantly. "There is nothing practical about you. Instead of confining your attention to the working out of my noble scheme, you begin raising all sorts of absurd objections. It is a mere matter of detail how our descendants live, so long as they stick to the Djarmas. Now, I want you to go up to the bothy of Fergus McDonald and see about the thatch, and Willie Fullerton has written to say that his milk-cow is bad. You might took in upon your way and ask after it."

I started off upon my errands, but before doing so I took a look at the barometer upon the wall. The mercury had sunk to the phenomenal point of twenty-eight inches. Clearly the old sailor had not been wrong in his interpretation of Nature's signs.

As I returned over the moors in the evening, the wind was blowing in short, angry puffs, and the western horizon was heaped with sombre clouds which stretched their long, ragged tentacles right up to the zenith.

Against their dark background one or two livid, sulphur-coloured splotches showed up malignant and menacing, while the surface of the sea had changed from the appearance of burnished quicksilver to that of ground glass. A low, moaning sound rose up from the ocean as if it knew that trouble was in store for it.

Far out in the Channel I saw a single panting, eager steam vessel making its way to Belfast Lough, and the large barque which I had observed in the morning still beating about in the offing, endeavouring to pass to the northward.

At nine o'clock a sharp breeze was blowing, at ten it had freshened into a gale, and before midnight the most furious storm was raging which I can remember upon that weather-beaten coast.

I sat for some time in our small, oak-panelled sitting-room listening to the screeching and howling of the blast and to the rattle of the gravel and pebbles as they pattered against the window. Nature's grim orchestra was playing its world-old piece with a compass which ranged from the deep diapason of the thundering surge to the thin shriek of the scattered shingle and the keen piping of frightened sea birds.

Once for an instant I opened the lattice window, but a gust of wind and rain came blustering through, bearing with it a great sheet of seaweed, which flapped down upon the table. It was all I could do to close it again with a thrust of my shoulder in the face of the blast.

My sister and father had retired to their rooms, but my thoughts were too active for sleep, so I continued to sit and to smoke by the smouldering fire.

What was going on in the Hall now, I wondered? What did Gabriel think of the storm, and how did it affect the old man who wandered about in the night? Did he welcome these dread forces of Nature as being of the same order of things as his own tumultuous thoughts?

It was only two days now from the date which I had been assured was to mark a crisis in his fortunes. Would he regard this sudden tempest as being in any way connected with the mysterious fate which threatened him?

Over all these things and many more I pondered as I sat by the glowing embers until they died gradually out, and the chill night air warned me that it was time to retire.

I may have slept a couple of hours when I was awakened by someone tugging furiously at my shoulder. Sitting up in bed, I saw by the dim light that my father was standing half-clad by my bedside, and that it was his grasp which I felt on my night-shirt.

"Get up, Jack, get up!" he was crying excitedly. "There's a great ship ashore in the bay, and the poor folk will all be drowned. Come down, my boy, and let us see what we can do."

The good old man seemed to be nearly beside himself with excitement and impatience. I sprang from my bed, and was huddling on a few clothes, when a dull, booming sound made itself heard above the howling of the wind and the thunder of the breakers.

"There it is again!" cried my father. "It is their signal gun, poor creatures! Jamieson and the fishermen are below. Put your oil-skin coat on and the Glengarry hat. Come, come, every second may mean a human life!"

We hurried down together and made our way to the beach, accompanied by a dozen or so of the inhabitants of Branksome.

The gale had increased rather than moderated, and the wind screamed all round us with an infernal clamour. So great was its force that we had to put our shoulders against it, and bore our way through it, while the sand and gravel tingled up against our faces.

There was just light enough to make out the scudding clouds and the white gleam of the breakers, but beyond that all was absolute darkness.

We stood ankle deep in the shingle and seaweed, shading our eyes with our hands and peering out into the inky obscurity.

It seemed to me as I listened that I could hear human voices loud in intreaty and terror, but amid the wild turmoil of Nature it was difficult to distinguish one sound from another.

Suddenly, however, a light glimmered in the heart of the tempest, and next instant the beach and sea and wide, tossing bay were brilliantly illuminated by the wild glare of a signal light.

The ship lay on her beam-ends right in the centre of the terrible Hansel reef, hurled over to such an angle that I could see all the planking of her deck. I recognised her at once as being the same three-masted barque which I had observed in the Channel in the morning, and the Union Jack which was nailed upside down to the jagged slump of her mizzen proclaimed her nationality.

Every spar and rope and writhing piece of cordage showed up hard and clear under the vivid light which spluttered and flickered from the highest portion of the forecastle. Beyond the doomed ship, out of the great darkness came the long, rolling lines of big waves, never ending, never tiring, with a petulant tuft of foam here and there upon their crests. Each as it reached the broad circle of unnatural light appeared to gather strength and volume and to hurry on more impetuously until with a roar and a jarring crash it sprang upon its victim.

Clinging to the weather shrouds we could distinctly see ten or a dozen frightened seamen who, when the light revealed our presence, turned their white faces towards us and waved their hands imploringly. The poor wretches had evidently taken fresh hope from our presence, though it was clear that their own boats had either been washed away or so damaged as to render them useless.

The sailors who clung to the rigging were not, however, the only unfortunates on board. On the breaking poop there stood three men who appeared to be both of a different race and nature from the cowering wretches who implored our assistance.

Leaning upon the shattered taff-rail they seemed to be conversing together as quietly and unconcernedly as though they were unconscious of the deadly peril which surrounded them.

As the signal light flickered over them, we could see from the shore that these immutable strangers wore red fezes, and that their faces were of a swarthy, large-featured type, which proclaimed an Eastern origin.

There was little time, however, for us to take note of such details. The ship was breaking rapidly, and some effort must be made to save the poor, sodden group of humanity who implored our assistance.

The nearest lifeboat was in the Bay of Luce, ten long miles away, but here was our own broad, roomy craft upon the shingle, and plenty of brave fisher lads to form a crew. Six of us sprang to the oars, the others pushed us off, and we fought our way through the swirling, raging waters, staggering and recoiling before the great, sweeping billows, but still steadily decreasing the distance between the barque and ourselves.

It seemed, however, that our efforts were fated to be in vain.

As we mounted upon a surge I saw a giant wave, topping all the others, and coming after them like a driver following a flock, sweep down upon the vessel, curling its great, green arch over the breaking deck.

With a rending, riving sound the ship split in two where the terrible, serrated back of the Hansel reef was sawing into her keel. The after-part, with the broken mizzen and the three Orientals, sank backwards into deep water and vanished, while the fore-half oscillated helplessly about, retaining its precarious balance upon the rocks.

A wail of fear went up from the wreck and was echoed from the beach, but by the blessing of Providence she kept afloat until we made our way under her bowsprit and rescued every man of the crew.

We had not got half-way upon our return, however, when another great wave swept the shattered forecastle off the reef, and, extinguishing the signal light, hid the wild denouement from our view.

Our friends upon the shore were loud in congratulation and praise, nor were they backward in welcoming and comforting the castaways. They were thirteen in all, as cold and cowed a set of mortals as ever slipped through Death's fingers, save, indeed, their captain, who was a hardy, robust man, and who made light of the affair.

Some were taken off to this cottage and some to that, but the greater part came back to Branksome with us, where we gave them such dry clothes as we could lay our hands on, and served them with beef and beer by the kitchen fire. The captain, whose name was Meadows, compressed his bulky form into a suit of my own, and came down to the parlour, where he mixed himself some grog and gave my father and myself an account of the disaster.

"If it hadn't been for you, sir, and your brave fellows," he said, smiling across at me, "we should be ten fathoms deep by this time. As to the *Belinda*, she was a leaky old tub and well insured, so neither the owners nor I are likely to break our hearts over her."

"I am afraid," said my father sadly, "that we shall never see your three passengers again. I have left men upon the beach in case they should be washed up, but I fear it is hopeless. I saw them go down when the vessel split, and no man could have lived for a moment among that terrible surge."

"Who were they?" I asked. "I could not have believed that it was possible for men to appear so unconcerned in the face of such imminent peril."

"As to who they are or were," the captain answered, puffing thoughtfully at his pipe, "that is by no means easy to say. Our last port was Kurrachee, in the north of India, and there we took them aboard as passengers for Glasgow. Ram Singh was the name of the younger, and it is only with him that I have come in contact, but they all appeared to be quiet, inoffensive gentlemen. I never inquired their business, but I should judge that they were Parsee merchants from Hyderabad whose trade took them to Europe. I could never see why the crew should fear them, and the mate, too, he should have had more sense."

"Fear them!" I ejaculated in surprise.

"Yes, they had some preposterous idea that they were dangerous shipmates. I have no doubt if you were to go down into the kitchen now you would find that they are all agreed that our passengers were the cause of the whole disaster."

As the captain was speaking the parlour door opened and the mate of the barque, a tall, red-bearded sailor, stepped in. He had obtained a complete rig-out from some kind-hearted fisherman, and looked in his comfortable jersey and well-greased seaboots a very favourable specimen of a shipwrecked mariner.

With a few words of grateful acknowledgment of our hospitality, he drew a chair up to the fire and warmed his great, brown hands before the blaze.

"What d'ye think now, Captain Meadows?" he asked presently, glancing up at his superior officer. "Didn't I warn you what would be the upshot of having those niggers on board the *Belinda*?"

The captain leant back in his chair and laughed heartily.

"Didn't I tell you?" he cried, appealing to us. "Didn't I tell you?"

"It might have been no laughing matter for us," the other remarked petulantly. "I have lost a good sea-kit and nearly my life into the bargain."

"Do I understand you to say," said I, "that you attribute your misfortunes to your ill-fated passengers?"

The mate opened his eyes at the adjective.

"Why ill-fated, sir?" he asked.

"Because they are most certainly drowned," I answered.

He sniffed incredulously and went on warming his hands.

"Men of that kind are never drowned," he said, after a pause. "Their father, the devil, looks after them. Did you see them standing on the poop and rolling cigarettes at the time when the mizzen was carried away and the quarter-boats stove? That was enough for me. I'm not surprised at you landsmen not being able to take it in, but the captain here, who's been sailing since he was the height of the binnacle, ought to know by this time that a cat and a priest are the worst cargo you can carry. If a Christian priest is bad, I guess an idolatrous pagan one is fifty times worse. I stand by the old religion, and be d—d to it!"

My father and I could not help laughing at the rough sailor's very unorthodox way of proclaiming his orthodoxy. The mate, however, was evidently in deadly earnest, and proceeded to state his case, marking off the different points upon the rough, red fingers of his left hand.

"It was at Kurrachee, directly after they come that I warned ye," he said reproachfully to the captain. "There was three Buddhist Lascars in my watch, and what did they do when them chaps come aboard? Why, they down on their stomachs and rubbed their noses on the deck—that's what they did. They wouldn't ha' done as much for an admiral of the R'yal Navy. They know who's who—these niggers do; and I smelt mischief the moment I saw them on their faces. I asked them afterwards in your presence, Captain, why they had done it, and they answered that the passengers were holy men. You heard 'em yourself."

"Well, there's no harm in that, Hawkins," said Captain Meadows.

"I don't know that," the mate said doubtfully. "The holiest Christian is the one that's nearest God, but the holiest nigger is, in my opinion, the one that's nearest the devil. Then you saw yourself, Captain Meadows, how they went on during the voyage, reading books that was writ on wood instead o' paper, and sitting up right through the night to jabber together on the quarter-deck. What did they want to have a chart of their own for and to mark the course of the vessel every day?"

"They didn't," said the captain.

"Indeed they did, and if I did not tell you sooner it was because you were always ready to laugh at what I said about them. They had instruments o' their own—when they used them I can't say—but every day at noon they worked out the latitude and longitude, and marked out the vessel's position on a chart that was pinned on their cabin table. I saw them at it, and so did the steward from his pantry."

"Well, I don't see what you prove from that," the captain remarked, "though I confess it is a strange thing."

"I'll tell you another strange thing," said the mate impressively. "Do you know the name of this bay in which we are cast away?"

"I have learnt from our kind friends here that we are upon the Wigtownshire coast," the captain answered, "but I have not heard the name of the bay."

The mate leant forward with a grave face.

"It is the Bay of Kirkmaiden," he said.

If he expected to astonish Captain Meadows he certainly succeeded, for that gentleman was fairly bereft of speech for a minute or more.

"This is really marvellous," he said, after a time, turning to us. "These passengers of ours cross-questioned us early in the voyage as to the existence of a bay of that name. Hawkins here and I denied all knowledge of one, for on the chart it is included in the Bay of Luce. That we should eventually be blown into it and destroyed is an extraordinary coincidence."

"Too extraordinary to be a coincidence," growled the mate. "I saw them during the calm yesterday morning, pointing to the land over our starboard quarter. They knew well enough that that was the port they were making for."

"What do you make of it all, then, Hawkins?" asked the captain, with a troubled face. "What is your own theory on the matter?"

"Why, in my opinion," the mate answered, "them three swabs have no more difficulty in raising a gale o' wind than I should have in swallowing this here grog. They had reasons o' their own for coming to this God-forsaken—saving your presence, sirs—this God-forsaken bay, and they took a short cut to it by arranging to be blown ashore there. That's my idea o' the matter, though what three Buddhist priests could find to do in the Bay of Kirkmaiden is clean past my comprehension."

My father raised his eyebrows to indicate the doubt which his hospitality forbade him from putting into words.

"I think, gentlemen," he said, "that you are both sorely in need of rest after your perilous adventures. If you will follow me I shall lead you to your rooms."

He conducted them with old-fashioned ceremony to the laird's best spare bedroom, and then, returning to me in the parlour, proposed that we should go down together to the beach and learn whether anything fresh had occurred.

The first pale light of dawn was just appearing in the east when we made our way for the second time to the scene of the shipwreck. The gale had blown itself out, but the sea was still very high, and all inside the breakers was a seething, gleaming line of foam, as though the fierce old ocean were gnashing its white fangs at the victims who had escaped from its clutches.

All along the beach fishermen and crofters were hard at work hauling up spars and barrels as fast as they were tossed ashore. None of them had seen any bodies, however, and they explained to us that only such things as could float had any chance of coming ashore, for the undercurrent was so strong that whatever was beneath the surface must infallibly be swept out to sea.

As to the possibility of the unfortunate passengers having been able to reach the shore, these practical men would not hear of it for a moment, and showed us conclusively that if they had not been drowned they must have been dashed to pieces upon the rocks.

"We did all that could be done," my father said sadly, as we returned home. "I am afraid that the poor mate has had his reason affected by the suddenness of the disaster. Did you hear what he said about Buddhist priests raising a gale?"

"Yes, I heard him," said I. "It was very painful to listen to him," said my father. "I wonder if he would object to my putting a small mustard plaster under each of his ears. It would relieve any congestion of the brain. Or perhaps it would be best to wake him up and give him two antibilious pills. What do you think, Jack?"

"I think," said I, with a yawn, "that you had best let him sleep, and go to sleep yourself. You can physic him in the morning if he needs it."

So saying I stumbled off to my bedroom, and throwing myself upon the couch was soon in a dreamless slumber.

CHAPTER 12 - *OF THE THREE FOREIGN MEN UPON THE COAST*

It must have been eleven or twelve o'clock before I awoke, and it seemed to me in the flood of golden light which streamed into my chamber that the wild, tumultuous episodes of the night before must have formed part of some fantastic dream.

It was hard to believe that the gentle breeze which whispered so softly among the ivy-leaves around my window was caused by the same element which had shaken the very house a few short hours before. It was as if Nature had repented of her momentary passion and was endeavouring to make amends to an injured world by its warmth and its sunshine. A chorus of birds in the garden below filled the whole air with their wonder and congratulations.

Down in the hall I found a number of the shipwrecked sailors, looking all the better for their night's repose, who set up a buzz of pleasure and gratitude upon seeing me.

Arrangements had been made to drive them to Wigtown, whence they were to proceed to Glasgow by the evening train, and my father had given orders that each should be served with a packet of sandwiches and hard-boiled eggs to sustain him on the way.

Captain Meadows thanked us warmly in the name of his employers for the manner in which we had treated them, and he called for three cheers from his crew, which were very heartily given. He and the mate walked down with us after we had broken our fast to have a last look at the scene of the disaster.

The great bosom of the bay was still heaving convulsively, and its waves were breaking into sobs against the rocks, but there was none of that wild turmoil which we had seen in the early morning. The long, emerald ridges, with their little, white crests of foam, rolled slowly and majestically in, to break with a regular rhythm—the panting of a tired monster.

A cable length from the shore we could see the mainmast of the barque floating upon the waves, disappearing at times in the trough of the sea, and then shooting up towards Heaven like a giant javelin, shining and dripping as the rollers tossed it about. Other smaller pieces of wreckage dotted the waters, while innumerable spars and packages were littered over the sands. These were being drawn up and collected in a place of safety by gangs of peasants. I noticed that a couple of broad-winged gulls were hovering and skimming over the scene of the shipwreck, as though many strange things were visible to them beneath the waves. At times we could hear their raucous voices as they cried to one another of what they saw.

"She was a leaky old craft," said the captain, looking sadly out to sea, "but there's always a feeling of sorrow when we see the last of a ship we have sailed in. Well, well, she would have been broken up in any case, and sold for firewood."

"It looks a peaceful scene," I remarked. "Who would imagine that three men lost their lives last night in those very waters?"

"Poor fellows," said the captain, with feeling. "Should they be cast up after our departure, I am sure, Mr. West, that you will have them decently interred."

I was about to make some reply when the mate burst into a loud guffaw, slapping his thigh and choking with merriment.

"If you want to bury them," he said, "you had best look sharp, or they may clear out of the country. You remember what I said last night? Just look at the top of that 'ere hillock, and tell me whether I was in the right or not?"

There was a high sand dune some little distance along the coast, and upon the summit of this the figure was standing which had attracted the mate's attention. The captain threw up his hands in astonishment as his eyes rested upon it.

"By the eternal," he shouted, "it's Ram Singh himself! Let us overhaul him!"

Taking to his heels in his excitement he raced along the beach, followed by the mate and myself, as well as by one or two of the fishermen who had observed the presence of the stranger.

The latter, perceiving our approach, came down from his post of observation and walked quietly in our direction, with his head sunk upon his breast, like one who is absorbed in thought.

I could not help contrasting our hurried and tumultuous advance with the gravity and dignity of this lonely Oriental, nor was the matter mended when he raised a pair of steady, thoughtful dark eyes and inclined his head in a graceful, sweeping salutation. It seemed to me that we were like a pack of schoolboys in the presence of a master.

The stranger's broad, unruffled brow, his clear, searching gaze, firm-set yet sensitive mouth, and clean-cut, resolute expression, all combined to form the most imposing and noble presence which I had ever known. I could not have imagined that such imperturbable calm and at the same time such a consciousness of latent strength could have been expressed by any human face.

He was dressed in a brown velveteen coat, loose, dark trousers, with a shirt that was cut low in the collar, so as to show the muscular, brown neck, and he still wore the red fez which I had noticed the night before.

I observed with a feeling of surprise, as we approached him, that none of these garments showed the slightest indication of the rough treatment and wetting which they must have received during their wearer's submersion and struggle to the shore.

"So you are none the worse for your ducking," he said in a pleasant, musical voice, looking from the captain to the mate. "I hope that your poor sailors have found pleasant quarters."

"We are all safe," the captain answered. "But we had given you up for lost—you and your two friends. Indeed, I was just making arrangements for your burial with Mr. West here."

The stranger looked at me and smiled.

"We won't give Mr. West that trouble for a little time yet," he remarked; "my friends and I came ashore all safe, and we have found shelter in a hut a mile or so along the coast. It is lonely down there, but we have everything which we can desire."

"We start for Glasgow this afternoon," said the captain; "I shall be very glad if you will come with us. If you have not been in England before you may find it awkward travelling alone."

"We are very much indebted to you for your thoughtfulness," Ram Singh answered; "but we will not take advantage of your kind offer. Since Nature has driven us here we intend to have a look about us before we leave."

"As you like," the captain said, shrugging his shoulders. "I don't think you are likely to find very much to interest you in this hole of a place."

"Very possibly not," Ram Singh answered with an amused smile. "You remember Milton's lines:

'The mind is its own place, and in itself

Can make a hell of Heaven, a heaven of Hell.'

I dare say we can spend a few days here comfortably enough. Indeed, I think you must be wrong in considering this to be a barbarous locality. I am much mistaken if this young gentleman's father is not Mr. James Hunter West, whose name is known and honoured by the pundits of India."

"My father is, indeed, a well-known Sanscrit scholar," I answered in astonishment.

"The presence of such a man," observed the stranger slowly, "changes a wilderness into a city. One great mind is surely a higher indication of civilisation than are incalculable leagues of bricks and mortar.

"Your father is hardly so profound as Sir William Jones, or so universal as the Baron Von Hammer-Purgstall, but he combines many of the virtues of each. You may tell him, however, from me that he is mistaken in the analogy which he has traced between the Samoyede and Tamulic word roots."

"If you have determined to honour our neighbourhood by a short stay," said I, "you will offend my father very much if you do not put up with him. He represents the laird here, and it is the laird's privilege, according to our Scottish custom, to entertain all strangers of repute who visit this parish."

My sense of hospitality prompted me to deliver this invitation, though I could feel the mate twitching at my sleeves as if to warn me that the offer was, for some reason, an objectionable one. His fears were, however, unnecessary, for the stranger signified by a shake of the head that it was impossible for him to accept it.

"My friends and I are very much obliged to you," he said, "but we have our own reasons for remaining where we are. The hut which we occupy is deserted and partly ruined, but we Easterns have trained ourselves to do without most of those things which are looked upon as necessaries in Europe, believing firmly in that wise axiom that a man is rich, not in proportion to what he has, but in proportion to what he can dispense with. A good fisherman supplies us with bread and with herbs, we have clean, dry straw for our couches; what could man wish for more?"

"But you must feel the cold at night, coming straight from the tropics," remarked the captain. "Perhaps our bodies are cold sometimes. We have not noticed it. We have all three spent many years in the Upper Himalayas on the border of the region of eternal snow, so we are not very sensitive to inconveniences of the sort."

"At least," said I, "you must allow me to send you over some fish and some meat from our larder."

"We are not Christians," he answered, "but Buddhists of the higher school. We do not recognise that man has a moral right to slay an ox or a fish for the gross use of his body. He has not put life into them, and has assuredly no mandate from the Almighty to take life from them save under most pressing need. We could not, therefore, use your gift if you were to send it."

"But, sir," I remonstrated, "if in this changeable and inhospitable climate you refuse all nourishing food your vitality will fail you—you will die."

"We shall die then," he answered, with an amused smile. "And now, Captain Meadows, I must bid you adieu, thanking you for your kindness during the voyage, and you, too, good-bye—you will command a ship of your own before the year is out. I trust, Mr. West, that I may see you again before I leave this part of the country. Farewell!"

He raised his red fez, inclined his noble head with the stately grace which characterised all his actions, and strode away in the direction from which he had come.

"Let me congratulate you, Mr. Hawkins," said the captain to the mate as we walked homewards. "You are to command your own ship within the year."

"No such luck!" the mate answered, with a pleased smile upon his mahogany face, "still, there's no saying how things may come out. What d'ye think of him, Mr. West?"

"Why," said I, "I am very much interested in him. What a magnificent head and bearing he has for a young man. I suppose he cannot be more than thirty."

"Forty," said the mate.

"Sixty, if he is a day," remarked Captain Meadows. "Why, I have heard him talk quite familiarly of the first Afghan war. He was a man then, and that is close on forty years ago."

"Wonderful!" I ejaculated. "His skin is as smooth and his eyes are as clear as mine are. He is the superior priest of the three, no doubt."

"The inferior," said the captain confidently. "That is why he does all the talking for them. Their minds are too elevated to descend to mere worldly chatter."

"They are the strangest pieces of flotsam and jetsam that were ever thrown upon this coast," I remarked. "My father will be mightily interested in them."

"Indeed, I think the less you have to do with them the better for you," said the mate. "If I do command my own ship I'll promise you that I never carry live stock of that sort on board of her. But here we are all aboard and the anchor tripped, so we must bid you good-bye."

The wagonette had just finished loading up when we arrived, and the chief places, on either side of the driver, had been reserved for my two companions, who speedily sprang into them. With a chorus of cheers the good fellows whirled away down the road, while my father, Esther, and I stood upon the lawn and waved our hands to them until they disappeared behind the Cloomber woods, *en route* for the Wigtown railway station. Barque and crew had both vanished now from our little world, the only relic of either being the heaps of *debris* upon the beach, which were to lie there until the arrival of an agent from Lloyd's.

CHAPTER 13 - *IN WHICH I SEE THAT WHICH HAS BEEN SEEN BY FEW*

At dinner that evening I mentioned to my father the episode of the three Buddhist priests, and found, as I had expected, that he was very much interested by my account of them.

When, however, he heard of the high manner in which Ram Singh had spoken of him, and the distinguished position which he had assigned him among philologists, he became so excited that it was all we could do to prevent him from setting off then and there to make his acquaintance.

Esther and I were relieved and glad when we at last succeeded in abstracting his boots and manoeuvring him to his bedroom, for the exciting events of the last twenty-four hours had been too much for his weak frame and delicate nerves.

I was sitting at the open porch in the gloaming, turning over in my mind the unexpected events which had occurred so rapidly—the gale, the wreck, the rescue, and the strange character of the castaways—when my sister came quietly over to me and put her hand in mine.

"Don't you think, Jack," she said, in her low, sweet voice, "that we are forgetting our friends over at Cloomber? Hasn't all this excitement driven their fears and their danger out of our heads?"

"Out of our heads, but never out of our hearts," said I, laughing. "However, you are right, little one, for our attention has certainly been distracted from them. I shall walk up in the morning and see if I can see anything of them. By the way, to-morrow is the fateful 5th of October—one more day, and all will be well with us."

"Or ill," said my sister gloomily.

"Why, what a little croaker you are, to be sure!" I cried. "What in the world is coming over you?"

"I feel nervous and low-spirited," she answered, drawing closer to my side and shivering. "I feel as if some great peril were hanging over the heads of those we love. Why should these strange men wish to stay upon the coast?"

"What, the Buddhists?" I said lightly. "Oh, these fellows have continual feast-days and religious rites of all sorts. They have some very good reason for staying, you may be sure."

"Don't you think," said Esther, in an awe-struck whisper, "that it is very strange that these priests should arrive here all the way from India just at the present moment? Have you not gathered from all you have heard that the general's fears are in some way connected with India and the Indians?"

The remark made me thoughtful.

"Why, now that you mention it," I answered, "I have some vague impression that the mystery is connected with some incident which occurred in that country. I am sure, however, that your fears would vanish if you saw Ram Singh. He is the very personification of wisdom and benevolence. He was shocked at the idea of our killing a sheep, or even a fish for his benefit—said he would rather die than have a hand in taking the life of an animal."

"It is very foolish of me to be so nervous," said my sister bravely. "But you must promise me one thing, Jack. You will go up to Cloomber in the morning, and if you can see any of them you must tell them of these strange neighbours of ours. They are better able to judge than we are whether their presence has any significance or not."

"All right, little one," I answered, as we went indoors. "You have been over-excited by all these wild doings, and you need a sound night's rest to compose you. I'll do what you suggest, however, and our friends shall judge for themselves whether these poor fellows should be sent about their business or not."

I made the promise to allay my sister's apprehensions, but in the bright sunlight of morning it appeared less than absurd to imagine that our poor vegetarian castaways could have any sinister intentions, or that their advent could have any effect upon the tenant of Cloomber.

I was anxious, myself, however, to see whether I could see anything of the Heatherstones, so after breakfast I walked up to the Hall. In their seclusion it was impossible for them to have learnt anything of the recent events. I felt, therefore, that even if I should meet the general he could hardly regard me as an intruder while I had so much news to communicate.

The place had the same dreary and melancholy appearance which always characterised it. Looking through between the thick iron bars of the main gateway there was nothing to be seen of any of the occupants. One of the great Scotch firs had been blown down in the gale, and its long, ruddy trunk lay right across the grass-grown avenue; but no attempt had been made to remove it.

Everything about the property had the same air of desolation and neglect, with the solitary exception of the massive and impenetrable fencing, which presented as unbroken and formidable an obstacle as ever to the would-be trespasser.

I walked round this barrier as far as our old trysting-place without finding any flaw through which I could get a glimpse of the house, for the fence had been repaired with each rail overlapping the last, so as to secure absolute privacy for those inside, and to block those peep-holes which I had formerly used.

At the old spot, however, where I had had the memorable interview with the general on the occasion when he surprised me with his daughter, I found that the two loose rails had been refixed in such a manner that there was a gap of two inches or more between them.

Through this I had a view of the house and of part of the lawn in front of it, and, though I could see no signs of life outside or at any of the windows, I settled down with the intention of sticking to my post until I had a chance of speaking to one or other of the inmates. Indeed, the cold, dead aspect of the house had struck such a chill into my heart that I determined to scale the fence at whatever risk of incurring the general's displeasure rather than return without news of the Heatherstones.

Happily there was no need of this extreme expedient, for I had not been there half-an-hour before I heard the harsh sound of an opening lock, and the general himself emerged from the main door.

To my surprise he was dressed in a military uniform, and that not the uniform in ordinary use in the British Army. The red coat was strangely cut and stained with the weather. The trousers had originally been white, but had now faded to a dirty yellow. With a red sash across his chest and a straight sword hanging from his side, he stood the living example of a bygone type—the John Company's officer of forty years ago.

He was followed by the ex-tramp, Corporal Rufus Smith, now well-clad and prosperous, who limped along beside his master, the two pacing up and down the lawn absorbed in conversation. I observed that from time to time one or other of them would pause and glance furtively all about them, as though guarding keenly against a surprise. I should have preferred communicating with the general alone, but since there was no dissociating him from his companion, I beat loudly on the fencing with my stick to attract their attention. They both faced round in a moment, and I could see from their gestures that they were disturbed and alarmed.

I then elevated my stick above the barrier to show them where the sound proceeded from. At this the general began to walk in my direction with the air of a man who is bracing himself up for an effort, but the other caught him by the wrist and endeavoured to dissuade him.

It was only when I shouted out my name and assured them that I was alone that I could prevail upon them to approach. Once assured of my identity the general ran eagerly towards me and greeted me with the utmost cordiality.

"This is truly kind of you, West," he said. "It is only at such times as these that one can judge who is a friend and who not. It would not be fair to you to ask you to come inside or to stay any time, but I am none the less very glad to see you."

"I have been anxious about you all," I said, "for it is some little time since I have seen or heard from any of you. How have you all been keeping?"

"Why, as well as could be expected. But we will be better tomorrow—we will be different men to-morrow, eh, Corporal?"

"Yes, sir," said the corporal, raising his hand to his forehead in a military salute. "We'll be right as the bank to-morrow."

"The corporal and I are a little disturbed in our minds just now," the general explained, "but I have no doubt that all will come right. After all, there is nothing higher than Providence, and we are all in His hands. And how have you been, eh?"

"We have been very busy for one thing," said I. "I suppose you have heard nothing of the great shipwreck?"

"Not a word," the general answered listlessly.

"I thought the noise of the wind would prevent you hearing the signal guns. She came ashore in the bay the night before last—a great barque from India."

"From India!" ejaculated the general.

"Yes. Her crew were saved, fortunately, and have all been sent on to Glasgow."

"All sent on!" cried the general, with a face as bloodless as a corpse.

"All except three rather strange characters who claim to be Buddhist priests. They have decided to remain for a few days upon the coast."

The words were hardly out of my mouth when the general dropped upon his knees with his long, thin arms extended to Heaven.

"Thy will be done!" he cried in a cracking voice. "Thy blessed will be done!"

I could see through the crack that Corporal Rufus Smith's face had turned to a sickly yellow shade, and that he was wiping the perspiration from his brow.

"It's like my luck!" he said. "After all these years, to come when I have got a snug billet."

"Never mind, my lad," the general said, rising, and squaring his shoulders like a man who braces himself up for an effort. "Be it what it may we'll face it as British soldiers should. D'ye remember at Chillianwallah, when you had to run from your guns to our square, and the Sikh horse came thundering down on our bayonets? We didn't flinch then, and we won't flinch now. It seems to me that I feel better than I have done for years. It was the uncertainty that was killing me."

"And the infernal jingle-jangle," said the corporal. "Well, we all go together—that's some consolation."

"Good-bye, West," said the general. "Be a good husband to Gabriel, and give my poor wife a home. I don't think she will trouble you long. Good-bye! God bless you!"

"Look here, General," I said, peremptorily breaking off a piece of wood to make communication more easy, "this sort of thing has been going on too long. What are these hints and allusions and innuendoes? It is time we had a little plain speaking. What is it you fear? Out with it! Are you in dread of these Hindoos? If you are, I am able, on my father's authority, to have them arrested as rogues and vagabonds."

"No, no, that would never do," he answered, shaking his head. "You will learn about the wretched business soon enough. Mordaunt knows where to lay his hand upon the papers bearing on the matter. You can consult him about it to-morrow."

"But surely," I cried, "if the peril is so imminent something may be done to avert it. If you would but tell me what you fear I should know how to act."

"My dear friend," he said, "there is nothing to be done, so calm yourself, and let things take their course. It has been folly on my part to shelter myself behind mere barriers of wood and stone. The fact is, that inaction was terrible to me, and I felt that to do anything, however futile, in the nature of a precaution, was better than passive resignation. My humble friend here and I have placed ourselves in a position in which, I trust, no poor fellow will ever find himself again. We can only recommend ourselves to the unfailing goodness of the Almighty, and trust that what we have endured in this world may lessen our atonement in the world to come. I must leave you now, for I have many papers to destroy and much to arrange. Good-bye!"

He pushed his hand through the hole which I had made, and grasped mine in a solemn farewell, after which he walked back to the Hall with a firm and decided step, still followed by the crippled and sinister corporal.

I walked back to Branksome much disturbed by this interview, and extremely puzzled as to what course I should pursue.

It was evident now that my sister's suspicions were correct, and that there was some very intimate connection between the presence of the three Orientals and the mysterious peril which hung over the towers of Cloomber.

It was difficult for me to associate the noble-faced Ram Singh's gentle, refined manner and words of wisdom with any deed of violence, yet now that I thought of it I could see that a terrible capacity for wrath lay behind his shaggy brows and dark, piercing eyes.

I felt that of all men whom I had ever met he was the one whose displeasure I should least care to face. But how could two men so widely dissociated as the foul-mouthed old corporal of artillery and the distinguished Anglo-Indian general have each earned the ill-will of these strange castaways? And if the danger were a positive physical one, why should he not consent to my proposal to have the three men placed under custody—though I confess it would have gone much against my grain to act in so inhospitable a manner upon such vague and shadowy grounds.

These questions were absolutely unanswerable, and yet the solemn words and the terrible gravity which I had seen in the faces of both the old soldiers forbade me from thinking that their fears were entirely unfounded.

It was all a puzzle—an absolutely insoluble puzzle.

One thing at least was clear to me—and that was that in the present state of my knowledge, and after the general's distinct prohibition, it was impossible for me to interfere in any way. I could only wait and pray that, whatever the danger might be, it might pass over, or at least that my dear Gabriel and her brother might be protected against it.

I was walking down the lane lost in thought, and had got as far as the wicket gate which opens upon the Branksome lawn, when I was surprised to hear my father's voice raised in most animated and excited converse.

The old man had been of late so abstracted from the daily affairs of the world, and so absorbed in his own special studies, that it was difficult to engage his attention upon any ordinary, mundane topic. Curious to know what it was that had drawn him so far out of himself, I opened the gate softly, and walking quietly round the laurel bushes, found him sitting, to my astonishment, with none other than the very man who was occupying my thoughts, Ram Singh, the Buddhist.

The two were sitting upon a garden bench, and the Oriental appeared to be laying down some weighty proposition, checking every point upon his long, quivering, brown fingers, while my father, with his hands thrown abroad and his face awry, was loud in protestation and in argument.

So absorbed were they in their controversy, that I stood within a hand-touch of them for a minute or more before they became conscious of my presence.

On observing me the priest sprang to his feet and greeted me with the same lofty courtesy and dignified grace which had so impressed me the day before.

"I promised myself yesterday," he said, "the pleasure of calling upon your father. You see I have kept my word. I have even been daring enough to question his views upon some points in connection with the Sanscrit and Hindoo tongues, with the result that we have been arguing for an hour or more without either of us convincing the other. Without pretending to as deep a theoretical knowledge as that which has made the name of James Hunter West a household word among Oriental scholars, I happen to have given considerable attention to this one point, and indeed I am in a position to say that I know his views to be unsound. I assure you, sir, that up to the year 700, or even later, Sanscrit was the ordinary language of the great bulk of the inhabitants of India."

"And I assure you, sir," said my father warmly, "that it was dead and forgotten at that date, save by the learned, who used it as a vehicle for scientific and religious works—just as Latin was used in the Middle Ages long after it had ceased to be spoken by any European nation."

"If you consult the puranas you will find," said Ram Singh, "that this theory, though commonly received, is entirely untenable."

"And if you will consult the Ramayana, and more particularly the canonical books on Buddhist discipline," cried my father, "you will find that the theory is unassailable."

"But look at the Kullavagga," said our visitor earnestly.

"And look at King Asoka," shouted my father triumphantly. "When, in the year 300 before the Christian era—before, mind you—he ordered the laws of Buddha to be engraved upon the rocks, what language did he employ, eh? Was it Sanscrit?—no! And why was it not Sanscrit? Because the lower orders of his subjects would not have been able to understand a word of it. Ha, ha! That was the reason. How are you going to get round King Asoka's edicts, eh?"

"He carved them in the various dialects," Ram Singh answered. "But energy is too precious a thing to be wasted in mere wind in this style. The sun has passed its meridian, and I must return to my companions."

"I am sorry that you have not brought them to see us," said my father courteously. He was, I could see, uneasy lest in the eagerness of debate he had overstepped the bounds of hospitality.

"They do not mix with the world," Ram Singh answered, rising to his feet. "They are of a higher grade than I, and more sensitive to contaminating influences. They are immersed in a six months' meditation upon the mystery of the third incarnation, which has lasted with few intermissions from the time that we left the Himalayas. I shall not see you again, Mr. Hunter West, and I therefore bid you farewell. Your old age will be a happy one, as it deserves to be, and your Eastern studies will have a lasting effect upon the knowledge and literature of your own country. Farewell!"

"And am I also to see no more of you?" I asked.

"Unless you will walk with me along the sea-shore," he answered. "But you have already been out this morning, and may be tired. I ask too much of you."

"Nay, I should be delighted to come," I responded from my heart, and we set off together, accompanied for some little distance by my father, who would gladly, I could see, have reopened the Sanscrit controversy, had not his stock of breath been too limited to allow of his talking and walking at the same time.

"He is a learned man," Ram Singh remarked, after we had left him behind, "but, like many another, he is intolerant towards opinions which differ from his own. He will know better someday."

I made no answer to this observation, and we trudged along for a time in silence, keeping well down to the water's edge, where the sands afforded a good foothold.

The sand dunes which lined the coast formed a continuous ridge upon our left, cutting us off entirely from all human observation, while on the right the broad Channel stretched away with hardly a sail to break its silvery uniformity. The Buddhist priest and I were absolutely alone with Nature.

I could not help reflecting that if he were really the dangerous man that the mate affected to consider him, or that might be inferred from the words of General Heatherstone, I had placed myself completely in his power.

Yet such was the majestic benignity of the man's aspect, and the unruffled serenity of his deep, dark eyes, that I could afford in his presence to let fear and suspicion blow past me as lightly as the breeze which whistled round us. His face might be stern, and even terrible, but I felt that he could never be unjust.

As I glanced from time to time at his noble profile and the sweep of his jet-black beard, his rough-spun tweed travelling suit struck me with an almost painful sense of incongruity, and I re-clothed him in my imagination with the grand, sweeping Oriental costume which is the fitting and proper frame for such a picture—the only garb which does not detract from the dignity and grace of the wearer.

The place to which he led me was a small fisher cottage which had been deserted some years before by its tenant, but still stood gaunt and bare, with the thatch partly blown away and the windows and doors in sad disrepair. This dwelling, which the poorest Scotch beggar would have shrunk from, was the one which these singular men had preferred to the proffered hospitality of the laird's house. A small garden, now a mass of tangled brambles, stood round it, and through this my acquaintance picked his way to the ruined door. He glanced into the house and then waved his hand for me to follow him.

"You have now an opportunity," he said, in a subdued, reverential voice, "of seeing a spectacle which few Europeans have had the privilege of beholding. Inside that cottage you will find two Yogis—men who are only one remove from the highest plane of adeptship. They are both wrapped in an ecstatic trance, otherwise I should not venture to obtrude your presence upon them. Their astral bodies have departed from them, to be present at the feast of lamps in the holy Lamasery of Rudok in Tibet. Tread lightly lest by stimulating their corporeal functions you recall them before their devotions are completed."

Walking slowly and on tiptoe, I picked my way through the weed-grown garden, and peered through the open doorway.

There was no furniture in the dreary interior, nor anything to cover the uneven floor save a litter of fresh straw in a corner.

Among this straw two men were crouching, the one small and wizened, the other large-boned and gaunt, with their legs crossed in Oriental fashion and their heads sunk upon their breasts. Neither of them looked up, or took the smallest notice of our presence.

They were so still and silent that they might have been two bronze statues but for the slow and measured rhythm of their breathing. Their faces, however, had a peculiar, ashen-grey colour, very different from the healthy brown of my companion's, and I observed, on stooping my head, that only the whites of their eyes were visible, the balls being turned upwards beneath the lids.

In front of them upon a small mat lay an earthenware pitcher of water and half-a-loaf of bread, together with a sheet of paper inscribed with certain cabalistic characters. Ram Singh glanced at these, and then, motioning to me to withdraw, followed me out into the garden.

"I am not to disturb them until ten o'clock," he said. "You have now seen in operation one of the grandest results of our occult philosophy, the dissociation of spirit from body. Not only are the spirits of these holy men standing at the present moment by the banks of the Ganges, but those spirits are clothed in a material covering so identical with their real bodies that none of the faithful will ever doubt that Lal Hoomi and Mowdar Khan are actually among them. This is accomplished by our power of resolving an object into its chemical atoms, of conveying these atoms with a speed which exceeds that of lightning to any given spot, and of there re-precipitating them and compelling them to retake their original form. Of old, in the days of our ignorance, it was necessary to convey the whole body in this way, but we have since found that it was as easy and more convenient to transmit material enough merely to build up an outside shell or semblance. This we have termed the astral body."

"But if you can transmit your spirits so readily," I observed, "why should they be accompanied by anybody at all?"

"In communicating with brother initiates we are able to employ our spirits only, but when we wish to come in contact with ordinary mankind it is essential that we should appear in some form which they can see and comprehend."

"You have interested me deeply in all that you have told me," I said, grasping the hand which Ram Singh had held out to me as a sign that our interview was at an end. "I shall often think of our short acquaintance."

"You will derive much benefit from it," he said slowly, still holding my hand and looking gravely and sadly into my eyes. "You must remember that what will happen in the future is not necessarily bad because it does not fall in with your preconceived ideas of right. Be not hasty in your judgments. There are certain great rules which must be carried out, at whatever cost to individuals. Their operation may appear to you to be harsh and cruel, but that is as nothing compared with the dangerous precedent which would be established by not enforcing them. The ox and the sheep are safe from us, but the man with the blood of the highest upon his hands should not and shall not live."

He threw up his arms at the last words with a fierce, threatening gesture, and, turning away from me, strode back to the ruined hut.

I stood gazing after him until he disappeared through the doorway, and then started off for home, revolving in my mind all that I had heard, and more particularly this last outburst of the occult philosopher.

Far on the right I could see the tall, white tower of Cloomber standing out clear-cut and sharp against a dark cloud-bank which rose behind it. I thought how any traveller who chanced to pass that way would envy in his heart the tenant of that magnificent building, and how little they would guess the strange terrors, the nameless dangers, which were gathering about his head. The black cloud-wrack was but the image, I reflected, of the darker, more sombre storm which was about to burst.

"Whatever it all means, and however it happens," I ejaculated, "God grant that the innocent be not confounded with the guilty."

My father, when I reached home, was still in a ferment over his learned disputation with the stranger.

"I trust, Jack," he said, "that I did not handle him too roughly. I should remember that I am *in loco magistri*, and be less prone to argue with my guests. Yet, when he took up this most untenable position, I could not refrain from attacking him and hurling him out of it, which indeed I did, though you, who are ignorant of the niceties of the question, may have failed to perceive it. You observed, however, that my reference to King Asoka's edicts was so conclusive that he at once rose and took his leave."

"You held your own bravely," I answered, "but what is your impression of the man now that you have seen him?"

"Why," said my father, "he is one of those holy men who, under the various names of Sannasis, Yogis, Sevras, Qualanders, Hakims, and Cufis have devoted their lives to the study of the mysteries of the Buddhist faith. He is, I take it, a theosophist, or worshipper of the God of knowledge, the highest grade of which is the adept. This man and his companions have not attained this high position or they could not have crossed the sea without contamination. It is probable that they are all advanced chelas who hope in time to attain to the supreme honour of adeptship."

"But, father," interrupted my sister, "this does not explain why men of such sanctity and attainments should choose to take up their quarters on the shores of a desolate Scotch bay."

"Ah, there you get beyond me," my father answered. "I may suggest, however, that it is nobody's business but their own, so long as they keep the peace and are amenable to the law of the land."

"Have you ever heard," I asked, "that these higher priests of whom you speak have powers which are unknown to us?"

"Why, Eastern literature is full of it. The Bible is an Eastern book, and is it not full of the record of such powers from cover to cover? It is unquestionable that they have in the past known many of Nature's secrets which are lost to us. I cannot say, however, from my own knowledge that the modern theosophists really possess the powers that they claim."

"Are they a vindictive class of people?" I asked. "Is there any offence among them which can only be expiated by death?"

"Not that I know of," my father answered, raising his white eyebrows in surprise. "You appear to be in an inquisitive humour this afternoon—what is the object of all these questions? Have our Eastern neighbours aroused your curiosity or suspicion in any way?"

I parried the question as best I might, for I was unwilling to let the old man know what was in my mind. No good purpose could come from his enlightenment; his age and his health demanded rest rather than anxiety; and indeed, with the best will in the world I should have found it difficult to explain to another what was so very obscure to myself. For every reason I felt that it was best that he should be kept in the dark.

Never in all my experience had I known a day pass so slowly as did that eventful 5th of October. In every possible manner I endeavoured to while away the tedious hours, and yet it seemed as if darkness would never arrive.

I tried to read, I tried to write, I paced about the lawn, I walked to the end of the lane, I put new flies upon my fishing-hooks, I began to index my father's library—in a dozen ways I endeavoured to relieve the suspense which was becoming intolerable. My sister, I could see, was suffering from the same feverish restlessness.

Again and again our good father remonstrated with us in his mild way for our erratic behaviour and the continual interruption of his work which arose from it.

At last, however, the tea was brought, and the tea was taken, the curtains were drawn, the lamps lit, and after another interminable interval the prayers were read and the servants dismissed to their rooms. My father compounded and swallowed his nightly jorum of toddy, and then shuffled off to his room, leaving the two of us in the parlour with our nerves in a tingle and our minds full of the most vague and yet terrible apprehensions.

CHAPTER 14 - *OF THE VISITOR WHO RAN DOWN THE ROAD IN THE NIGHT-TIME*

It was a quarter past ten o'clock by the parlour timepiece when my father went off to his room, and left Esther and myself together. We heard his slow steps dying away up the creaking staircase, until the distant slamming of a door announced that he had reached his sanctum.

The simple oil lamp upon the table threw a weird, uncertain light over the old room, flickering upon the carved oak panelling, and casting strange, fantastic shadows from the high-elbowed, straight-backed furniture. My sister's white, anxious face stood out in the obscurity with a startling exactness of profile like one of Rembrandt's portraits.

We sat opposite to each other on either side of the table with no sound breaking the silence save the measured ticking of the clock and the intermittent chirping of a cricket beneath the grate.

There was something awe-inspiring in the absolute stillness. The whistling of a belated peasant upon the high road was a relief to us, and we strained our ears to catch the last of his notes as he plodded steadily homewards.

At first we had made some pretence—she of knitting and I of reading—but we soon abandoned the useless deception, and sat uneasily waiting, starting and glancing at each other with questioning eyes whenever the faggot crackled in the fire or a rat scampered behind the wainscot. There was a heavy electrical feeling in the air, which weighed us down with a foreboding of disaster.

I rose and flung the hall door open to admit the fresh breeze of the night. Ragged clouds swept across the sky, and the moon peeped out at times between their hurrying fringes, bathing the whole countryside in its cold, white radiance. From where I stood in the doorway I could see the edge of the Cloomber wood, though the house itself was only visible from the rising ground some little distance off. At my sister's suggestion we walked together, she with her shawl over her head, as far as the summit of this elevation, and looked out in the direction of the Hall.

There was no illumination of the windows tonight. From roof to basement not a light twinkled in any part of the great building. Its huge mass loomed up dark and sullen amid the trees which surrounded it, looking more like some giant sarcophagus than a human habitation.

To our overwrought nerves there was something of terror in its mere bulk and its silence. We stood for some little time peering at it through the darkness, and then we made our way back to the parlour again, where we sat waiting—waiting, we knew not for what, and yet with absolute conviction that some terrible experience was in store for us.

It was twelve o'clock or thereabout when my sister suddenly sprang to her feet and held up her fingers to bespeak attention.

"Do you hear nothing?" she asked.

I strained my ears, but without success.

"Come to the door," she cried, with a trembling voice. "Now can you hear anything?"

In the deep silence of the night I distinctly heard a dull, murmuring, clattering sound, continuous apparently, but very faint and low.

"What is it?" I asked, in a subdued voice.

"It's the sound of a man running towards us," she answered, and then, suddenly dropping the last semblance of self-command, she fell upon her knees beside the table and began praying aloud with that frenzied earnestness which intense, overpowering fear can produce, breaking off now and again into half-hysterical whimperings.

I could distinguish the sound clearly enough now to know that her quick, feminine perception had not deceived her, and that it was indeed caused by a running man.

On he came, and on down the high road, his footfalls ringing out clearer and sharper every moment. An urgent messenger he must be, for he neither paused nor slackened his pace.

The quick, crisp rattle was changed suddenly to a dull, muffled murmur. He had reached the point where sand had been recently laid down for a hundred yards or so. In a few moments, however, he was back on hard ground again and his flying feet came nearer and ever nearer.

He must, I reflected, be abreast of the head of the lane now. Would he hold on? Or would he turn down to Branksome?

The thought had hardly crossed my mind when I heard by the difference of the sound that the runner had turned the corner, and that his goal was beyond all question the laird's house.

Rushing down to the gate of the lawn, I reached it just as our visitor dashed it open and fell into my arms. I could see in the moonlight that it was none other than Mordaunt Heatherstone.

"What has happened?" I cried. "What is amiss, Mordaunt?"

"My father!" he gasped—"my father!"

His hat was gone, his eyes dilated with terror, and his face as bloodless as that of a corpse. I could feel that the hands which clasped my arms were quivering and shaking with emotion.

"You are exhausted," I said, leading him into the parlour. "Give yourself a moment's rest before you speak to us. Be calm, man, you are with your best friends."

I laid him on the old horsehair sofa, while Esther, whose fears had all flown to the winds now that something practical was to be done, dashed some brandy into a tumbler and brought it to him. The stimulant had a marvellous effect upon him, for the colour began to come back into his pale cheeks and the light of recognition in his eyes.

He sat up and took Esther's hand in both of his, like a man who is waking out of some bad dream and wishes to assure himself that he is really in safety.

"Your father?" I asked. "What of him?"

"He is gone."

"Gone!"

"Yes; he is gone; and so is Corporal Rufus Smith. We shall never set eyes upon them again."

"But where have they gone?" I cried. "This is unworthy of you, Mordaunt. What right have we to sit here, allowing our private feelings to overcome us, while there is a possibility of succouring your father? Up, man! Let us follow him. Tell me only what direction he took."

"It's no use," young Heatherstone answered, burying his face in his hands. "Don't reproach me, West, for you don't know all the circumstances. What can we do to reverse the tremendous and unknown laws which are acting against us? The blow has long been hanging over us, and now it has fallen. God help us!"

"In Heaven's name tell me what has happened?" said I excitedly. "We must not yield to despair."

"We can do nothing until daybreak," he answered. "We shall then endeavour to obtain some trace of them. It is hopeless at present."

"And how about Gabriel and Mrs. Heatherstone?" I asked. "Can we not bring them down from the Hall at once? Your poor sister must be distracted with terror."

"She knows nothing of it," Mordaunt answered. "She sleeps at the other side of the house, and has not heard or seen anything. As to my poor mother, she has expected some such event for so long a time that it has not come upon her as a surprise. She is, of course, overwhelmed with grief, but would, I think, prefer to be left to herself for the present. Her firmness and composure should be a lesson to me, but I am constitutionally excitable, and this catastrophe coming after our long period of suspense deprived me of my very reason for a time."

"If we can do nothing until the morning," I said, "you have time to tell us all that has occurred."

"I will do so," he answered, rising and holding his shaking hands to the fire. "You know already that we have had reason for some time—for many years in fact—to fear that a terrible retribution was hanging over my father's head for a certain action of his early life. In this action he was associated with the man known as Corporal Rufus Smith, so that the fact of the latter finding his way to my father was a warning to us that the time had come, and that this 5th of October—the anniversary of the misdeed—would be the day of its atonement. I told you of our fears in my letter, and, if I am not mistaken, my father also had some conversation with you, John, upon the subject. When I saw yesterday morning that he had hunted out the old uniform which he had always retained since he wore it in the Afghan war, I was sure that the end was at hand, and that our forebodings would be realised.

"He appeared to be more composed in the afternoon than I have seen him for years, and spoke freely of his life in India and of the incidents of his youth. About nine o'clock he requested us to go up to our own rooms, and locked us in there—a precaution which he frequently took when the dark fit way upon him. It was always his endeavour, poor soul, to keep us clear of the curse which had fallen upon his own unfortunate head. Before parting from us he tenderly embraced my mother and Gabriel, and he afterwards followed me to my room, where he clasped my hand affectionately and gave into my charge a small packet addressed to yourself."

"To me?" I interrupted.

"To you. I shall fulfill my commission when I have told you my story. I conjured him to allow me to sit up with him and share any danger which might arise, but he implored me with irresistible earnestness not to add to his troubles by thwarting his arrangements. Seeing that I was really distressing him by my pertinacity, I at last allowed him to close the door and to turn the key upon the outside. I shall always reproach myself for my want of firmness. But what can you do when your own father refuses your assistance or co-operation? You cannot force yourself upon him."

"I am sure that you did all you could do," my sister said.

"I meant to, dear Esther, but, God help me, it was hard to tell what was right. He left me, and I heard his footsteps die away down the long corridor. It was then about ten o'clock, or a little after. For a time I paced up and down the room, and then, carrying the lamp to the head of my bed, I lay down without undressing, reading St. Thomas a Kempis, and praying from my heart that the night might pass safely over us.

"I had at last fallen into a troubled sleep when I was suddenly aroused by a loud, sonorous sound ringing in my ears. I sat up bewildered, but all was silent again. The lamp was burning low, and my watch showed me that it was going on to midnight. I blundered to my feet, and was striking a match with the intention of lighting the candles, when the sharp, vehement cry broke out again so loud and so clear that it might have been in the very room with me. My chamber is in the front of the house, while those of my mother and sister are at the back, so that I am the only one who commands a view of the avenue.

"Rushing to the window I drew the blind aside and looked out. You know that the gravel-drive opens up so as to form a broad stretch immediately in front of the house. Just in the centre of this clear space there stood three men looking up at the house.

"The moon shone full upon them, glistening on their upturned eyeballs, and by its light I could see that they were swarthy-faced and black-haired, of a type that I was familiar with among the Sikhs and Afridis. Two of them were thin, with eager, aesthetic countenances, while the third was kinglike and majestic, with a noble figure and flowing beard."

"Ram Singh!" I ejaculated.

"What, you know of them?" exclaimed Mordaunt in great surprise. "You have met them?"

"I know of them. They are Buddhist priests," I answered, "but go on."

"They stood in a line," he continued, "sweeping their arms upwards and downwards, while their lips moved as if repeating some prayer or incantation. Suddenly they ceased to gesticulate, and broke out for the third time into the wild, weird, piercing cry which had roused me from my slumber. Never shall I forget that shrill, dreadful summons swelling and reverberating through the silent night with an intensity of sound which is still ringing in my ears.

"As it died slowly away, there was a rasping and creaking as of keys and bolts, followed by the clang of an opening door and the clatter of hurrying feet. From my window I saw my father and Corporal Rufus Smith rush frantically out of the house hatless and unkempt, like men who are obeying a sudden and overpowering impulse. The three strangers laid no hands on them, but all five swept swiftly away down the avenue and vanished among the trees. I am positive that no force was used, or constraint of any visible kind, and yet I am as sure that my poor father and his companion were helpless prisoners as it I had seen them dragged away in manacles.

"All this took little time in the acting. From the first summons which disturbed my sleep to the last shadowy glimpse which I had of them between the tree trunks could hardly have occupied more than five minutes of actual time. So sudden was it, and so strange, that when the drama was over and they were gone I could have believed that it was all some terrible nightmare, some delusion, had I not felt that the impression was too real, too vivid, to be imputed to fancy.

"I threw my whole weight against my bedroom door in the hope of forcing the lock. It stood firm for a while, but I flung myself upon it again and again, until something snapped and I found myself in the passage.

"My first thought was for my mother. I rushed to her room and turned the key in her door. The moment that I did so she stepped out into the corridor in her dressing-gown, and held up a warning finger.

"'No noise,' she said, Gabriel is asleep. They have been called away?'

"'They have,' I answered.

"'God's will be done!' she cried. 'Your poor father will be happier in the next world than he has ever been in this. Thank Heaven that Gabriel is asleep. I gave her chloral in her cocoa.'

"'What am I to do?' I said distractedly.

"'Where have they gone? How can I help him? We cannot let him go from us like this, or leave these men to do what they will with him. Shall I ride into Wigtown and arouse the police?'

"'Anything rather than that,' my mother said earnestly. 'He has begged me again and again to avoid it. My son, we shall never set eyes upon your father again. You may marvel at my dry eyes, but if you knew as I know the peace which death would bring him, you could not find it in your heart to mourn for him. All pursuit is, I feel, vain, and yet some pursuit there must be. Let it be as private as possible. We cannot serve him better than by consulting his wishes.'

"'But every minute is precious,' I cried. 'Even now he may be calling upon us to rescue him from the clutches of those dark-skinned fiends.'

"The thought so maddened me that I rushed out of the house and down to the high road, but once there I had no indication in which direction to turn. The whole wide moor lay before me, without a sign of movement upon its broad expanse. I listened, but not a sound broke the perfect stillness of the night.

"It was then, my dear friends, as I stood, not knowing in which direction to turn, that the horror and responsibility broke full upon me. I felt that I was combating against forces of which I knew nothing. All was strange and dark and terrible.

"The thought of you, and of the help which I might look for from your advice and assistance, was a beacon of hope to me. At Branksome, at least, I should receive sympathy, and, above all, directions as to what I should do, for my mind is in such a whirl that I cannot trust my own judgment. My mother was content to be alone, my sister asleep, and no prospect of being able to do anything until daybreak. Under those circumstances what more natural than that I should fly to you as fast as my feet would carry me? You have a clear head, Jack; speak out, man, and tell me what I should do. Esther, what should I do?"

He turned from one to the other of us with outstretched hands and eager, questioning eyes.

"You can do nothing while the darkness lasts," I answered. "We must report the matter to the Wigtown police, but we need not send our message to them until we are actually starting upon the search, so as to comply with the law and yet have a private investigation, as your mother wishes. John Fullarton, over the hill, has a lurcher dog which is as good as a bloodhound. If we set him on the general's trail he will run him down if he had to follow him to John o' Groat's."

"It is terrible to wait calmly here while he may need our assistance."

"I fear our assistance could under any circumstances do him little good. There are forces at work here which are beyond human intervention. Besides, there is no alternative.

We have, apparently, no possible clue as to the direction which they have taken, and for us to wander aimlessly over the moor in the darkness would be to waste the strength which may be more profitably used in the morning. It will be daylight by five o'clock. In an hour or so we can walk over the hill together and get Fullarton's dog."

"Another hour!" Mordaunt groaned, "every minute seems an age."

"Lie down on the sofa and rest yourself," said I. "You cannot serve your father better than by laying up all the strength you can, for we may have a weary trudge before us. But you mentioned a packet which the general had intended for me."

"It is here," he answered, drawing a small, flat parcel from his pocket and handing it over to me, "you will find, no doubt, that it will explain all which has been so mysterious."

The packet was sealed at each end with black wax, bearing the impress of the flying griffin, which I knew to be the general's crest. It was further secured by a band of broad tape, which I cut with my pocket-knife. Across the outside was written in bold handwriting: "J. Fothergill West, Esq.," and underneath: "To be handed to that gentleman in the event of the disappearance or decease of Major-General J. B. Heatherstone, V.C., C.B., late of the Indian Army."

So at last I was to know the dark secret which had cast a shadow over our lives. Here in my hands I held the solution of it.

With eager fingers I broke the seals and undid the wrapper. A note and a small bundle of discoloured paper lay within. I drew the lamp over to me and opened the former. It was dated the preceding afternoon, and ran in this way:

MY DEAR WEST,—

I should have satisfied your very natural curiosity on the subject which we have had occasion to talk of more than once, but I refrained for your own sake. I knew by sad experience how unsettling and unnerving it is to be forever waiting for a catastrophe which you are convinced must befall, and which you can neither avert nor accelerate.

Though it affects me specially, as being the person most concerned, I am still conscious that the natural sympathy which I have observed in you, and your regard for Gabriel's father, would both combine to render you unhappy if you knew the hopelessness and yet the vagueness of the fate which threatens me. I feared to disturb your mind, and I was therefore silent, though at some cost to myself, for my isolation has not been the least of the troubles which have weighed me down.

Many signs, however, and chief among them the presence of the Buddhists upon the coast as described by you this morning, have convinced me that the weary waiting is at last over and that the hour of retribution is at hand. Why I should have been allowed to live nearly forty years after my offence is more than I can understand, but it is possible that those who had command over my fate know that such a life is the greatest of all penalties to me.

Never for an hour, night or day, have they suffered me to forget that they have marked me down as their victim. Their accursed astral bell has been ringing my knell for two-score years, reminding me ever that there is no spot upon earth where I can hope to be in safety. Oh, the peace, the blessed peace of dissolution! Come what may on the other side of the tomb, I shall at least be quit of that thrice terrible sound.

There is no need for me to enter into the wretched business again, or to detail at any length the events of October 5th, 1841, and the various circumstances which led up to the death of Ghoolab Shah, the arch adept.

I have torn a sheaf of leaves from my old journal, in which you will find a bald account of the matter, and an independent narrative was furnished by Sir Edward Elliott, of the Artillery, to the Star of India some years ago—in which, however, the names were suppressed.

I have reason to believe that many people, even among those who knew India well, thought that Sir Edward was romancing, and that he had evolved his incidents from his imagination. The few faded sheets which I send you will show you that this is not the case, and that our men of science must recognise powers and laws which can and have been used by man, but which are unknown to European civilisation.

I do not wish to whine or to whimper, but I cannot help feeling that I have had hard measure dealt me in this world. I would not, God knows, take the life of any man, far less an aged one, in cold blood. My temper and nature, however, were always fiery and headstrong, and in action when my blood is up, I have no knowledge of what I am about. Neither the corporal nor I would have laid a finger upon Ghoolab Shah had we not seen that the tribesmen were rallying behind him. Well, well, it is an old story now, and there is no profit in discussing it. May no other poor fellow ever have the same evil fortune!

I have written a short supplement to the statements contained in my journal for your information and that of any one else who may chance to be interested in the matter.

And now, adieu! Be a good husband to Gabriel, and, if your sister be brave enough to marry into such a devil-ridden family as ours, by all means let her do so. I have left enough to keep my poor wife in comfort.

When she rejoins me I should wish it to be equally divided between the children. If you hear that I am gone, do not pity, but congratulate

Your unfortunate friend,

JOHN BERTHIER HEATHERSTONE.

I threw aside the letter and picked up the roll of blue foolscap which contained the solution of the mystery. It was all ragged and frayed at the inner edge, with traces of gum and thread still adhering to it, to show that it had been torn out of a strongly bound volume. The ink with which it had been written was faded somewhat, but across the head of the first page was inscribed in bold, clear characters, evidently of later date than the rest: "Journal of Lieutenant J. B. Heatherstone in the Thull Valley during the autumn of 1841," and then underneath:

This extract contains some account of the events of the first week of October of that year, including the skirmish of the Terada ravine and the death of the man Ghoolab Shah.

I have the narrative lying before me now, and I copy it verbatim. If it contains some matter which has no direct bearing upon the question at issue, I can only say that I thought it better to publish what is irrelevant than by cutting and clipping to lay the whole statement open to the charge of having been tampered with.

CHAPTER 15 - *THE DAY-BOOK OF JOHN BERTHIER HEATHERSTONE*

Thull Valley, Oct. 1, 1841.—The Fifth Bengal and Thirty-third Queen's passed through this morning on their way to the Front. Had tiffin with the Bengalese. Latest news from home that two attempts had been made on the Queen's life by semi-maniacs named Francis and Bean.

It promises to be a hard winter. The snow-line has descended a thousand feet upon the peaks, but the passes will be open for weeks to come, and, even if they were blocked, we have established so many depots in the country that Pollock and Nott will have no difficulty in holding their own. They shall not meet with the fate of Elphinstone's army. One such tragedy is enough for a century.

Elliott of the Artillery, and I, are answerable for the safety of the communications for a distance of twenty miles or more, from the mouth of the valley to this side of the wooden bridge over the Lotar. Goodenough, of the Rifles, is responsible on the other side, and Lieutenant-Colonel Sidney Herbert of the Engineers, has a general supervision over both sections.

Our force is not strong enough for the work which has to be done. I have a company and a half of our own regiment, and a squadron of Sowars, who are of no use at all among the rocks. Elliott has three guns, but several of his men are down with cholera, and I doubt if he has enough to serve more than two.

(Note: capsicum for cholera—tried it)

On the other hand, each convoy is usually provided with some guard of its own, though it is often absurdly inefficient. These valleys and ravines which branch out of the main pass are alive with Afridis and Pathans, who are keen robbers as well as religious fanatics. I wonder they don't swoop down on some of our caravans. They could plunder them and get back to their mountain fastnesses before we could interfere or overtake them. Nothing but fear will restrain them.

If I had my way I would hang one at the mouth of every ravine as a warning to the gang. They are personifications of the devil to look at, hawk-nosed, full-lipped, with a mane of tangled hair, and most Satanic sneer. No news today from the Front.

October 2.—I must really ask Herbert for another company at the very least. I am convinced that the communications would be cut off if any serious attack were made upon us.

Now, this morning two urgent messages were sent me from two different points more than sixteen miles apart, to say that there were signs of a descent of the tribes.

Elliott, with one gun and the Sowars, went to the farther ravine, while I, with the infantry, hurried to the other, but we found it was a false alarm. I saw no signs of the Hillmen, and though we were greeted by a splutter of jezail bullets we were unable to capture any of the rascals.

Woe betide them if they fall into my hands. I would give them as short a shrift as ever a Highland cateran got from a Glasgow judge. These continued alarms may mean nothing or they may be an indication that the Hillmen are assembling and have some plan in view.

We have had no news from the Front for some time, but to-day a convoy of wounded came through with the intelligence that Nott had taken Ghuznee. I hope he warmed up any of the black rascals that fell into his hands.

No word of Pollock.

An elephant battery came up from the Punjab, looking in very good condition. There were several convalescents with it going up to rejoin their regiments. Knew none of them except Mostyn of the Hussars and young Blakesley, who was my fag at Charterhouse, and whom I have never seen since.

Punch and cigars *al fresco* up to eleven o'clock.

Letters to-day from Wills & Co. about their little bill forwarded on from Delhi. Thought a campaign freed a man from these annoyances. Wills says in his note that, since his written applications have been in vain, he must call upon me in person. If he calls upon me now he will assuredly be the boldest and most persevering of tailors.

A line from Calcutta Daisy and another from Hobhouse to say that Matilda comes in for all the money under the will. I am glad of it.

October 3.—Glorious news from the Front today. Barclay, of the Madras Cavalry, galloped through with dispatches. Pollock entered Cabul triumphantly on the 16th of last month, and, better still, Lady Sale has been rescued by

Shakespear, and brought safe into the British camp, together with the other hostages. *Te Deum laudamus!*

This should end the whole wretched business—this and the sack of the city. I hope Pollock won't be squeamish, or truckle to the hysterical party at home. The towns should be laid in ashes and the fields sown with salt. Above all, the Residency and the Palace must come down. So shall Burnes, McNaghten, and many another gallant fellow know that his countrymen could avenge if they could not save him!

It is hard when others are gaining glory and experience to be stuck in this miserable valley. I have been out of it completely, bar a few petty skirmishes. However, we may see some service yet.

A jemidar of ours brought in a Hillman today, who says that the tribes are massing in the Terada ravine, ten miles to the north of us, and intend attacking the next convoy. We can't rely on information of this sort, but there may prove to be some truth in it. Proposed to shoot our informant, so as to prevent his playing the double traitor and reporting our proceedings. Elliott demurred.

If you are making war you should throw no chance away. I hate half-and-half measures. The Children of Israel seem to have been the only people who ever carried war to its logical conclusion—except Cromwell in Ireland. Made a compromise at last by which the man is to be detained as a prisoner and executed if his information prove to be false. I only hope we get a fair chance of showing what we can do.

No doubt these fellows at the Front will have C.B.'s and knighthoods showering upon them thick and fast, while we poor devils, who have had most of the responsibility and anxiety, will be passed over completely. Elliott has a whitlow.

The last convoy left us a large packet of sauces, but as they forgot to leave anything to eat with them, we have handed them over to the Sowars, who drink them out of their pannikins as if they were liqueurs. We hear that another large convoy may be expected from the plains in the course of a day or two. Took nine to four on Cleopatra for the Calcutta Cup.

October 4.—The Hillmen really mean business this time, I think. We have had two of our spies come in this morning with the same account about the gathering in the Terada quarter. That old rascal Zemaun is at the head of it, and I had recommended the Government to present him with a telescope in return for his neutrality! There will be no Zemaun to present it to if I can but lay hands upon him.

We expect the convoy tomorrow morning, and need anticipate no attack until it comes up, for these fellows fight for plunder, not for glory, though, to do them justice, they have plenty of pluck when they get started. I have devised an excellent plan, and it has Elliott's hearty support. By Jove! if we can only manage it, it will be as pretty a ruse as ever I heard of.

Our intention is to give out that we are going down the valley to meet the convoy and to block the mouth of a pass from which we profess to expect an attack. Very good. We shall make a night-march to-night and reach their camp. Once there I shall conceal my two hundred men in the waggons and travel up with the convoy again.

Our friends the enemy, having heard that we intended to go south, and seeing the caravan going north without us, will naturally swoop down upon it under the impression that we are twenty miles away. We shall teach them such a lesson that they would as soon think of stopping a thunderbolt as of interfering again with one of Her Britannic Majesty's provision trains. I am all on thorns to be off.

Elliott has rigged up two of his guns so ingeniously that they look more like costermongers' barrows than anything else. To see artillery ready for action in the convoy might arouse suspicion. The artillerymen will be in the waggons next the guns, all ready to unlimber and open fire. Infantry in front and rear. Have told our confidential and discreet Sepoy servants the plan which we do not intend to adopt. N.B.—If you wish a thing to be noised over a whole province always whisper it under a vow of secrecy to your confidential native servant.

8.45 P.M.—Just starting for the convoy. May luck go with us!

October 5.—Seven o'clock in the evening. *Io triumphe!* Crown us with laurel—Elliott and myself! Who can compare with us as vermin killers?

I have only just got back, tired and weary, stained with blood and dust, but I have sat down before either washing or changing to have the satisfaction of seeing our deeds set forth in black and white—if only in my private log for no eye but my own. I shall describe it all fully as a preparation for an official account, which must be drawn up when Elliott gets back. Billy Dawson used to say that there were three degrees of comparison—a prevarication, a lie, and an official account. We at least cannot exaggerate our success, for it would be impossible to add anything to it.

We set out, then, as per programme, and came upon the camp near the head of the valley. They had two weak companies of the 54th with them who might no doubt have held their own with warning, but an unexpected rush of wild

Hillmen is a very difficult thing to stand against. With our reinforcements, however, and on our guard, we might defy the rascals.

Chamberlain was in command—a fine young fellow. We soon made him understand the situation, and were all ready for a start by daybreak though his waggons were so full that we were compelled to leave several tons of fodder behind in order to make room for my Sepoys and for the artillery.

About five o'clock we inspanned, to use an Africanism, and by six we were well on our way, with our escort as straggling and unconcerned as possible—as helpless-looking a caravan as ever invited attack.

I could soon see that it was to be no false alarm this time, and that the tribes really meant business.

From my post of observation, under the canvas screens of one of the waggons, I could make out turbaned heads popping up to have a look at us from among the rocks, and an occasional scout hurrying northward with the news of our approach.

It was not, however, until we came abreast of the Terada Pass, a gloomy defile bounded by gigantic cliffs, that the Afridis began to show in force, though they had ambushed themselves so cleverly that, had we not been keenly on the look-out for them, we might have walked right into the trap. As it was, the convoy halted, upon which the Hillmen, seeing that they were observed, opened a heavy but ill-directed fire upon us.

I had asked Chamberlain to throw out his men in skirmishing order, and to give them directions to retreat slowly upon the waggons so as to draw the Afridis on. The ruse succeeded to perfection.

As the redcoats steadily retired, keeping behind cover as much as possible, the enemy followed them up with yells of exultation, springing from rock to rock, waving their jezails in the air, and howling like a pack of demons.

With their black, contorted, mocking faces, their fierce gestures, and their fluttering garments, they would have made a study for any painter who wished to portray Milton's conception of the army of the damned.

From every side they pressed in until, seeing, as they thought, nothing between them and victory, they left the shelter of the rocks and came rushing down, a furious, howling throng, with the green banner of the Prophet in their van.

Now was our chance, and gloriously we utilised it.

From every cranny and slit of the waggons came a blaze of fire, every shot of which told among the close-packed mob. Two or three score rolled over like rabbits and the rest reeled for a moment, and then, with their chiefs at their head, came on again in a magnificent rush.

It was useless, however, for undisciplined men to attempt to face such a well-directed fire. The leaders were bowled over, and the others, after hesitating for a few moments, turned and made for the rocks.

It was our turn now to assume the offensive. The guns were unlimbered and grape poured into them, while our little infantry force advanced at the double, shooting and stabbing all whom they overtook.

Never had I known the tide of battle turn so rapidly and so decisively. The sullen retreat became a flight, and the flight a panic-stricken rout, until there was nothing left of the tribesmen except a scattered, demoralised rabble flying wildly to their native fastnesses for shelter and protection.

I was by no means inclined to let them off cheaply now that I had them in my power. On the contrary, I determined to teach them such a lesson that the sight of a single scarlet uniform would in future be a passport in itself.

We followed hard upon the track of the fugitives and entered the Terada defile at their very heels. Having detached Chamberlain and Elliott with a company on either side to protect my wings, I pushed on with my Sepoys and a handful of artillerymen, giving the enemy no time to rally or to recover themselves. We were so handicapped, however, by our stiff European uniforms and by our want of practice in climbing, that we should have been unable to overtake any of the mountaineers had it not been for a fortunate accident.

There is a smaller ravine which opens into the main pass, and in their hurry and confusion some of the fugitives rushed down this. I saw sixty or seventy of them turn down, but I should have passed them by and continued in pursuit of the main body had not one of my scouts come rustling up to inform me that the smaller ravine was a *cul-de-sac*, and that the Afridis who had gone up it had no possible means of getting out again except by cutting their way through our ranks.

Here was an opportunity of striking terror into the tribes. Leaving Chamberlain and Elliott to continue the pursuit of the main body, I wheeled my Sepoys into the narrow path and proceeded slowly down it in extended order, covering the whole ground from cliff to cliff. Not a jackal could have passed us unseen. The rebels were caught like rats in a trap.

The defile in which we found ourselves was the most gloomy and majestic that I have ever seen. On either side naked precipices rose sheer up for a thousand feet or more, converging upon each other so as to leave a very narrow slit of daylight above us, which was further reduced by the feathery fringe of palm trees and aloes which hung over each lip of the chasm.

The cliffs were not more than a couple of hundred yards apart at the entrance, but as we advanced they grew nearer and nearer, until a half company in close order could hardly march abreast.

A sort of twilight reigned in this strange valley, and the dim, uncertain light made the great, basalt rocks loom up vague and fantastic. There was no path, and the ground was most uneven, but I pushed on briskly, cautioning my fellows to have their fingers on their triggers, for I could see that we were nearing the point where the two cliffs would form an acute angle with each other.

At last we came in sight of the place. A great pile of boulders was heaped up at the very end of the pass, and among these our fugitives were skulking, entirely demoralised apparently, and incapable of resistance. They were useless as prisoners, and it was out of the question to let them go, so there was no choice but to polish them off.

Waving my sword, I was leading my men on, when we had a most dramatic interruption of a sort which I have seen once or twice on the boards of Drury Lane, but never in real life.

In the side of the cliff, close to the pile of stones where the Hillmen were making their last stand, there was a cave which looked more like the lair of some wild beast than a human habitation.

Out of this dark archway there suddenly emerged an old man—such a very, very old man that all the other veterans whom I have seen were as chickens compared with him. His hair and beard were both as white as snow, and each reached more than half-way to his waist. His face was wrinkled and brown and ebony, a cross between a monkey and a mummy, and so thin and emaciated were his shrivelled limbs that you would hardly have given him credit for having any vitality left, were it not for his eyes, which glittered and sparkled with excitement, like two diamonds in a setting of mahogany.

This apparition came rushing out of the cave, and, throwing himself between the fugitives and our fellows, motioned us back with as imperious a sweep of the hand as ever an emperor used to his slaves.

"Men of blood," he cried, in a voice of thunder, speaking excellent English, too—"this is a place for prayer and meditation, not for murder. Desist, lest the wrath of the gods fall upon you."

"Stand aside, old man," I shouted. "You will meet with a hurt if you don't get out of the way."

I could see that the Hillmen were taking heart, and that some of my Sepoys were flinching, as if they did not relish this new enemy. Clearly, I must act promptly if I wished to complete our success.

I dashed forward at the head of the white artillerymen who had stuck to me. The old fellow rushed at us with his arms out as if to stop us, but it was not time to stick at trifles, so I passed my sword through his body at the same moment that one of the gunners brought his carbine down upon his head. He dropped instantly, and the Hillmen, at the sight of his fall, set up the most unearthly howl of horror and consternation.

The Sepoys, who had been inclined to hang back, came on again the moment he was disposed of, and it did not take us long to consummate our victory. Hardly a man of the enemy got out of the defile alive.

What could Hannibal or Caesar have done more? Our own loss in the whole affair has been insignificant—three killed and about fifteen wounded. Got their banner, a green wisp of a thing with a sentence of the Koran engraved upon it.

I looked, after the action, for the old chap, but his body had disappeared, though how or whither I have no conception. His blood be upon his own head! He would be alive now if he had not interfered, as the constables say at home, "with an officer in the execution of his duty."

The scouts tell me that his name was Ghoolab Shah, and that he was one of the highest and holiest of the Buddhists. He had great fame in the district as a prophet and worker of miracles—hence the hubbub when he was cut down. They tell me that he was living in this very cave when Tamerlane passed this way in 1399, with a lot more bosh of that sort.

I went into the cave, and how any man could live in it a week is a mystery to me, for it was little more than four feet high, and as damp and dismal a grotto as ever was seen. A wooden settle and a rough table were the sole furniture, with a lot of parchment scrolls with hieroglyphics.

Well, he has gone where he will learn that the gospel of peace and good will is superior to all his Pagan lore. Peace go with him.

Elliott and Chamberlain never caught the main body—I knew they wouldn't—so the honours of the day rest with me. I ought to get a step for it, anyhow, and perhaps, who knows? some mention in the *Gazette*. What a lucky chance! I think Zemaun deserves his telescope after all for giving it to me. Shall have something to eat now, for I am half starved. Glory is an excellent thing, but you cannot live upon it.

October 6, 11 A.M.—Let me try to set down as calmly and as accurately as I can all that occurred last night. I have never been a dreamer or a visionary, so I can rely upon my own senses, though I am bound to say that if any other fellow had told me the same thing I should have doubted him. I might even have suspected that I was deceived at the time had I not heard the bell since. However, I must narrate what happened.

Elliott was in my tent with me having a quiet cheroot until about ten o'clock. I then walked the rounds with my jemidar, and having seen that all was right I turned in a little before eleven.

I was just dropping off to sleep, for I was dog-tired after the day's work, when I was aroused by some slight noise, and, looking round, I saw a man dressed in Asiatic costume standing at the entrance of my tent. He was motionless when I saw him, and he had his eyes fixed upon me with a solemn and stern expression.

My first thought was that the fellow was some Ghazi or Afghan fanatic who had stolen in with the intention of stabbing me, and with this idea in my mind I had all the will to spring from my couch and defend myself, but the power was unaccountably lacking.

An overpowering languor and want of energy possessed me. Had I seen the dagger descending upon my breast I could not have made an effort to avert it. I suppose a bird when it is under the influence of a snake feels very much as I did in the presence of this gloomy-faced stranger. My mind was clear enough, but my body was as torpid as though I were still asleep.

I shut my eyes once or twice and tried to persuade myself that the whole thing was a delusion, but every time that I opened them there was the man still regarding me with the same stony, menacing stare.

The silence became unendurable. I felt that I must overcome my languor so far as to address him. I am not a nervous man, and I never knew before what Virgil meant when he wrote "adhoesit faucibus ora." At last I managed to stammer out a few words, asking the intruder who he was and what he wanted.

"Lieutenant Heatherstone," he answered, speaking slowly and gravely, "you have committed this day the foulest sacrilege and the greatest crime which it is possible for man to do. You have slain one of the thrice blessed and reverend ones, an arch adept of the first degree, an elder brother who has trod the higher path for more years than you have numbered months. You have cut him off at a time when his labours promised to reach a climax and when he was about to attain a height of occult knowledge which would have brought man one step nearer to his Creator. All this you have done without excuse, without provocation, at a time when he was pleading the cause of the helpless and distressed. Listen now to me, John Heatherstone.

"When first the occult sciences were pursued many thousands of years ago, it was found by the learned that the short tenure of human existence was too limited to allow a man to attain the loftiest heights of inner life. The inquirers of those days directed their energies in the first place, therefore, to the lengthening of their own days in order that they might have more scope for improvement.

"By their knowledge of the secret laws of Nature they were enabled to fortify their bodies against disease and old age. It only remained to protect themselves against the assaults of wicked and violent men who are ever ready to destroy what is wiser and nobler than themselves. There was no direct means by which this protection could be effected, but it was in some measure attained by arranging the occult forces in such a way that a terrible and unavoidable retribution should await the offender.

"It was irrevocably ordained by laws which cannot be reversed that anyone who should shed the blood of a brother who had attained a certain degree of sanctity should be a doomed man. Those laws are extant to this day, John Heatherstone, and you have placed yourself in their power. King or emperor would be helpless before the forces which you have called into play. What hope, then, is there for you?

"In former days these laws acted so instantaneously that the slayer perished with his victim. It was judged afterwards that this prompt retribution prevented the offender from having time to realise the enormity of his offence.

"It was therefore ordained that in all such cases the retribution should be left in the hands of the *chelas*, or immediate disciples of the holy man, with power to extend or shorten it at their will, exacting it either at the time or at any future anniversary of the day when the crime was committed.

"Why punishment should come on those days only it does not concern you to know. Suffice it that you are the murderer of Ghoolab Shah, the thrice blessed, and that I am the senior of his three *chelas* commissioned to avenge his death.

"It is no personal matter between us. Amid our studies we have no leisure or inclination for personal matters. It is an immutable law, and it is as impossible for us to relax it as it is for you to escape from it. Sooner or later we shall come to you and claim your life in atonement for the one which you have taken.

"The same fate shall be meted out to the wretched soldier, Smith, who, though less guilty than yourself, has incurred the same penalty by raising his sacrilegious hand against the chosen of Buddha. If your life is prolonged, it is merely that you may have time to repent of your misdeed and to feel the full force of your punishment.

"And lest you should be tempted to cast it out of your mind and to forget it, our bell—our astral bell, the use of which is one of our occult secrets—shall ever remind you of what have been and what is to be. You shall hear it by day and you shall hear it by night, and it will be a sign to you that do what you may and go where you will, you can never shake yourself clear of the *chelas* of Ghoolab Shah.

"You will never see me more, accursed one, until the day when we come for you. Live in fear, and in that anticipation which is worse than death."

With a menacing wave of the hand the figure turned and swept out of my tent into the darkness. The instant that the fellow disappeared from my sight I recovered from my lethargy which had fallen upon me. Springing to my feet, I rushed to the opening and looked out. A Sepoy sentry was standing leaning upon his musket, a few paces off.

"You dog," I said in Hindustani. "What do you mean by letting people disturb me in this way?"

The man stared at me in amazement. "Has any one disturbed the sahib?" he asked.

"This instant—this moment. You must have seen him pass out of my tent."

"Surely the Burra Sahib is mistaken," the man answered, respectfully but firmly. "I have been here for an hour, and no one has passed from the tent."

Puzzled and disconcerted, I was sitting by the side of my couch wondering whether the whole thing were a delusion, brought on by the nervous excitement of our skirmish, when a new marvel overtook me. From over my head there suddenly sounded a sharp, tinkling sound, like that produced by an empty glass when flipped by the nail, only louder and more intense.

I looked up, but nothing was to be seen. I examined the whole interior of the tent carefully, but without discovering any cause for the strange sound. At last, worn out with fatigue, I gave the mystery up, and throwing myself on the couch was soon fast asleep.

When I awoke this morning I was inclined to put the whole of my yesternight's experiences down to imagination, but I was soon disabused of the idea, for I had hardly risen before the same strange sound was repeated in my very ear as loudly, and to all appearance as causelesly, as before. What it is or where it comes from I cannot conceive. I have not heard it since.

Can the fellow's threats have something in them and this be the warning bell of which he spoke? Surely it is impossible. Yet his manner was indescribably impressive.

I have tried to set down what he said as accurately as I can, but I fear I have omitted a good deal. What is to be the end of this strange affair? I must go in for a course of religion and holy water. Not a word to Chamberlain or Elliott. They tell me I am looking like a ghost this morning.

Evening.—Have managed to compare notes with Gunner Rufus Smith of the Artillery, who knocked the old fellow over with the butt of his gun. His experience has been the same as mine. He has heard the sound, too. What is the meaning of it all? My brain is in a whirl.

Oct. 10 (four days later).—God help us!

This last laconic entry terminated the journal. It seemed to me that, coming as it did after four days' complete silence, it told a clearer tale of shaken nerve and a broken spirit than could any more elaborate narrative. Pinned on to the journal was a supplementary statement which had evidently been recently added by the general.

"From that day to this," it said, "I have had no night or day free from the intrusion of that dreadful sound with its accompanying train of thought. Time and custom have brought me no relief, but on the contrary, as the years pass over my head my physical strength decreases and my nerves become less able to bear up against the continual strain.

"I am a broken man in mind and body. I live in a state of tension, always straining my ears for the hated sound, afraid to converse with my fellows for fear of exposing my dreadful condition to them, with no comfort or hope of comfort on this side of the grave. I should be willing, Heaven knows, to die, and yet as each 5th of October comes round, I am prostrated with fear because I do not know what strange and terrible experience may be in store for me.

"Forty years have passed since I slew Ghoolab Shah, and forty times I have gone through all the horrors of death, without attaining the blessed peace which lies beyond.

"I have no means of knowing in what shape my fate will come upon me. I have immured myself in this lonely country, and surrounded myself with barriers, because in my weaker moments my instincts urge me to take some steps for self-protection, but I know well in my heart how futile it all is. They must come quickly now, for I grow old, and Nature will forestall them unless they make haste.

"I take credit to myself that I have kept my hands off the prussic-acid or opium bottle. It has always been in my power to checkmate my occult persecutors in that way, but I have ever held that a man in this world cannot desert his post until he has been relieved in due course by the authorities. I have had no scruples, however, about exposing myself to danger, and, during the Sikh and Sepoy wars, I did all that a man could do to court Death. He passed me by, however, and picked out many a young fellow to whom life was only opening and who had everything to live for, while I survived to win crosses and honours which had lost all relish for me.

"Well, well, these things cannot depend upon chance, and there is no doubt some deep reason for it all.

"One compensation Providence has made me in the shape of a true and faithful wife, to whom I told my dreadful secret before the wedding, and who nobly consented to share my lot. She has lifted half the burden from my shoulders, but with the effect, poor soul, of crushing her own life beneath its weight!

"My children, too, have been a comfort to me. Mordaunt knows all, or nearly all. Gabriel we have endeavoured to keep in the dark, though we cannot prevent her from knowing that there is something amiss.

"I should like this statement to be shown to Dr. John Easterling of Stranraer. He heard on one occasion this haunting sound. My sad experience may show him that I spoke truth when I said that there was much knowledge in the world which has never found its way to England.

- "J. B. HEATHERSTONE."

It was going on for dawn by the time that I had finished this extraordinary narrative, to which my sister and Mordaunt Heatherstone listened with the most absorbed attention. Already we could see through the window that the stars had begun to fade and a grey light to appear in the east. The crofter who owned the lurcher dog lived a couple of miles off, so it was time for us to be on foot. Leaving Esther to tell my father the story in such fashion as she might, we thrust some food in our pockets and set off upon our solemn and eventful errand.

CHAPTER 16 - *AT THE HOLE OF CREE*

It was dark enough when we started to make it no easy matter to find our way across the moors, but as we advanced it grew lighter and lighter, until by the time we reached Fullarton's cabin it was broad daylight.

Early as it was, he was up and about, for the Wigtown peasants are an early rising race. We explained our mission to him in as few words as possible, and having made his bargain—what Scot ever neglected that preliminary?—he agreed not only to let us have the use of his dog but to come with us himself.

Mordaunt, in his desire for privacy, would have demurred at this arrangement, but I pointed out to him that we had no idea what was in store for us, and the addition of a strong, able-bodied man to our party might prove to be of the utmost consequence.

Again, the dog was less likely to give us trouble if we had its master to control it. My arguments carried the day, and the biped accompanied us as well as his four-footed companion.

There was some little similarity between the two, for the man was a towsy-headed fellow with a great mop of yellow hair and a straggling beard, while the dog was of the long-haired, unkempt breed looking like an animated bundle of oakum.

All our way to the Hall its owner kept retailing instances of the creature's sagacity and powers of scent, which, according to his account, were little less than miraculous. His anecdotes had a poor audience, I fear, for my mind was filled with the strange story which I had been reading, while Mordaunt strode on with wild eyes and feverish cheeks, without a thought for anything but the problem which we had to solve.

Again and again as we topped an eminence I saw him look eagerly round him in the faint hope of seeing some trace of the absentee, but over the whole expanse of moorland there was no sign of movement or of life. All was dead and silent and deserted.

Our visit to the Hall was a very brief one, for every minute now was of importance. Mordaunt rushed in and emerged with an old coat of his father's, which he handed to Fullarton, who held it out to the dog.

The intelligent brute sniffed at it all over, then ran whining a little way down the avenue, came back to sniff the coat again, and finally elevating its stump of a tail in triumph, uttered a succession of sharp yelps to show that it was satisfied that it had struck the trail. Its owner tied a long cord to its collar to prevent it from going too fast for us, and we all set off upon our search, the dog tugging and straining at its leash in its excitement as it followed in the general's footsteps.

Our way lay for a couple of hundred yards along the high road, and then passed through a gap in the hedge and on to the moor, across which we were led in a bee-line to the northward.

The sun had by this time risen above the horizon, and the whole countryside looked so fresh and sweet, from the blue, sparkling sea to the purple mountains, that it was difficult to realise how weird and uncanny was the enterprise upon which we were engaged.

The scent must have lain strongly upon the ground, for the dog never hesitated nor stopped, dragging its master along at a pace which rendered conversation impossible.

At one place, in crossing a small stream, we seemed to get off the trail for a few minutes, but our keen-nosed ally soon picked it up on the other side and followed it over the trackless moor, whining and yelping all the time in its eagerness. Had we not all three been fleet of foot and long of wind, we could not have persisted in the continuous, rapid journey over the roughest of ground, with the heather often well-nigh up to our waists.

For my own part, I have no idea now, looking back, what goal it was which I expected to reach at the end of our pursuit. I can remember that my mind was full of the vaguest and most varying speculations.

Could it be that the three Buddhists had had a craft in readiness off the coast, and had embarked with their prisoners for the East? The direction of their track seemed at first to favour this supposition, for it lay in the line of the upper end of the bay, but it ended by branching off and striking directly inland. Clearly the ocean was not to be our terminus.

By ten o'clock we had walked close upon twelve miles, and were compelled to call a halt for a few minutes to recover our breath, for the last mile or two we had been breasting the long, wearying slope of the Wigtown hills.

From the summit of this range, which is nowhere more than a thousand feet in height, we could see, looking northward, such a scene of bleakness and desolation as can hardly be matched in any country.

Right away to the horizon stretched the broad expanse of mud and of water, mingled and mixed together in the wildest chaos, like a portion of some world in the process of formation. Here and there on the dun-coloured surface of this great marsh there had burst out patches of sickly yellow reeds and of livid, greenish scum, which only served to heighten and intensify the gloomy effect of the dull, melancholy expanse.

On the side nearest to us some abandoned peat-cuttings showed that ubiquitous man had been at work there, but beyond these few petty scars there was no sign anywhere of human life. Not even a crow nor a seagull flapped its way over that hideous desert.

This is the great Bog of Cree. It is a salt-water marsh formed by an inroad of the sea, and so intersected is it with dangerous swamps and treacherous pitfalls of liquid mud, that no man would venture through it unless he had the guidance of one of the few peasants who retain the secret of its paths.

As we approached the fringe of rushes which marked its border, a foul, dank smell rose up from the stagnant wilderness, as from impure water and decaying vegetation—an earthy, noisome smell which poisoned the fresh upland air.

So forbidding and gloomy was the aspect of the place that our stout crofter hesitated, and it was all that we could do to persuade him to proceed. Our lurcher, however, not being subject to the delicate impressions of our higher organisation, still ran yelping along with its nose on the ground and every fibre of its body quivering with excitement and eagerness.

There was no difficulty about picking our way through the morass, for wherever the five could go we three could follow.

If we could have had any doubts as to our dog's guidance they would all have been removed now, for in the soft, black, oozing soil we could distinctly trace the tracks of the whole party. From these we could see that they had walked abreast, and, furthermore, that each was about equidistant from the other. Clearly, then, no physical force had been used in taking the general and his companion along. The compulsion had been psychical and not material.

Once within the swamp, we had to be careful not to deviate from the narrow track, which offered a firm foothold.

On each side lay shallow sheets of stagnant water overlying a treacherous bottom of semi-fluid mud, which rose above the surface here and there in moist, sweltering banks, mottled over with occasional patches of unhealthy vegetation. Great purple and yellow fungi had broken out in a dense eruption, as though Nature were afflicted with a foul disease, which manifested itself by this crop of plague spots.

Here and there dark, crab-like creatures scuttled across our path, and hideous, flesh-coloured worms wriggled and writhed amid the sickly reeds. Swarms of buzzing, piping insects rose up at every step and formed a dense cloud around our heads, settling on our hands and faces and inoculating us with their filthy venom. Never had I ventured into so pestilent and forbidding a place.

Mordaunt Heatherstone strode on, however, with a set purpose upon his swarthy brow, and we could but follow him, determined to stand by him to the end of the adventure. As we advanced, the path grew narrower and narrower until, as we saw by the tracks, our predecessors had been compelled to walk in single file. Fullarton was leading us with the dog, Mordaunt behind him, while I brought up the rear. The peasant had been sulky and surly for a little time back, hardly answering when spoken to, but he now stopped short and positively refused to go a step farther.

"It's no' canny," he said, "besides I ken where it will lead us tae."

"Where, then?" I asked.

"Tae the Hole o' Cree," he answered. "It's no far frae here, I'm thinking."

"The Hole of Cree! What is that, then?"

"It's a great, muckle hole in the ground that gangs awa' doon so deep that naebody could ever reach the bottom. Indeed there are folk wha says that it's just a door leadin' intae the bottomless pit itsel'."

"You have been there, then?" I asked.

"Been there!" he cried. "What would I be doin' at the Hole o' Cree? No, I've never been there, nor any other man in his senses."

"How do you know about it, then?"

"My great-grandfeyther had been there, and that's how I ken," Fullarton answered. "He was fou' one Saturday nicht and he went for a bet. He didna like tae talk aboot it afterwards, and he wouldna tell a' what befell him, but he was aye feared o' the very name. He's the first Fullarton that's been at the Hole o' Cree, and he'll be the last for me. If ye'll tak' my advice ye'll just gie the matter up and gang hame again, for there's na guid tae be got oot o' this place."

"We shall go on with you or without you," Mordaunt answered. "Let us have your dog and we can pick you up on our way back."

"Na, na," he cried, "I'll no' hae my dog scaret wi' bogles, and running down Auld Nick as if he were a hare. The dog shall bide wi' me."

"The dog shall go with us," said my companion, with his eyes blazing. "We have no time to argue with you. Here's a five-pound note. Let us have the dog, or, by Heaven, I shall take it by force and throw you in the bog if you hinder us."

I could realise the Heatherstone of forty years ago when I saw the fierce and sudden wrath which lit up the features of his son.

Either the bribe or the threat had the desired effect, for the fellow grabbed at the money with one hand while with the other he surrendered the leash which held the lurcher. Leaving him to retrace his steps, we continued to make our way into the utmost recesses of the great swamp.

The tortuous path grew less and less defined as we proceeded, and was even covered in places with water, but the increasing excitement of the hound and the sight of the deep footmarks in the mud stimulated us to push on. At last, after struggling through a grove of high bulrushes, we came on a spot the gloomy horror of which might have furnished Dante with a fresh terror for his "Inferno."

The whole bog in this part appeared to have sunk in, forming a great, funnel-shaped depression, which terminated in the centre in a circular rift or opening about forty feet in diameter. It was a whirlpool—a perfect maelstrom of mud, sloping down on every side to this silent and awful chasm.

Clearly this was the spot which, under the name of the Hole of Cree, bore such a sinister reputation among the rustics. I could not wonder at its impressing their imagination, for a more weird or gloomy scene, or one more worthy of the avenue which led to it, could not be conceived.

The steps passed down the declivity which surrounded the abyss, and we followed them with a sinking feeling in our hearts, as we realised that this was the end of our search.

A little way from the downward path was the return trail made by the feet of those who had come back from the chasm's edge. Our eyes fell upon these tracks at the same moment, and we each gave a cry of horror, and stood gazing speechlessly at them. For there, in those blurred footmarks, the whole drama was revealed.

Five had gone down, but only three had returned.

None shall ever know the details of that strange tragedy. There was no mark of struggle nor sign of attempt at escape. We knelt at the edge of the Hole and endeavoured to pierce the unfathomable gloom which shrouded it. A faint, sickly exhalation seemed to rise from its depths, and there was a distant hurrying, clattering sound as of waters in the bowels of the earth.

A great stone lay embedded in the mud, and this I hurled over, but we never heard thud or splash to show that it had reached the bottom.

As we hung over the noisome chasm a sound did at last rise to our ears out of its murky depths. High, clear, and throbbing, it tinkled for an instant out of the abyss, to be succeeded by the same deadly stillness which had preceded it.

I did not wish to appear superstitious, or to put down to extraordinary causes that which may have a natural explanation. That one keen note may have been some strange water sound produced far down in the bowels of the earth. It may have been that or it may have been that sinister bell of which I had heard so much. Be this as it may, it was the only sign that rose to us from the last terrible resting-place of the two who had paid the debt which had so long been owing.

We joined our voices in a call with the unreasoning obstinacy with which men will cling to hope, but no answer came back to us save a hollow moaning from the depths beneath. Footsore and heart-sick, we retraced our steps and climbed the slimy slope once more.

"What shall we do, Mordaunt?" I asked, in a subdued voice. "We can but pray that their souls may rest in peace."

Young Heatherstone looked at me with flashing eyes.

"This may be all according to occult laws," he cried, "but we shall see what the laws of England have to say upon it. I suppose a *chela* may be hanged as well as any other man. It may not be too late yet to run them down. Here, good dog, good dog--here!"

He pulled the hound over and set it on the track of the three men. The creature sniffed at it once or twice, and then, falling upon its stomach, with bristling hair and protruding tongue, it lay shivering and trembling, a very embodiment of canine terror.

"You see," I said, "it is no use contending against those who have powers at their command to which we cannot even give a name. There is nothing for it but to accept the inevitable, and to hope that these poor men may meet with some compensation in another world for all that they have suffered in this."

"And be free from all devilish religions and their murderous worshippers!" Mordaunt cried furiously.

Justice compelled me to acknowledge in my own heart that the murderous spirit had been set on foot by the Christian before it was taken up by the Buddhists, but I forbore to remark upon it, for fear of irritating my companion.

For a long time I could not draw him away from the scene of his father's death, but at last, by repeated arguments and reasonings, I succeeded in making him realise how useless and unprofitable any further efforts on our part must necessarily prove, and in inducing him to return with me to Cloomber.

Oh, the wearisome, tedious journey! It had seemed long enough when we had some slight flicker of hope, or at least of expectation, before us, but now that our worst fears were fulfilled it appeared interminable.

We picked up our peasant guide at the outskirts of the marsh, and having restored his dog we let him find his own way home, without telling him anything of the results of our expedition. We ourselves plodded all day over the moors with heavy feet and heavier hearts until we saw the ill-omened tower of Cloomber, and at last, as the sun was setting, found ourselves once more beneath its roof.

There is no need for me to enter into further details, nor to describe the grief which our tidings conveyed to mother and to daughter. Their long expectation of some calamity was not sufficient to prepare them for the terrible reality.

For weeks my poor Gabriel hovered between life and death, and though she came round at last, thanks to the nursing of my sister and the professional skill of Dr. John Easterling, she has never to this day entirely recovered her former vigour. Mordaunt, too, suffered much for some time, and it was only after our removal to Edinburgh that he rallied from the shock which he had undergone.

As to poor Mrs. Heatherstone, neither medical attention nor change of air can ever have a permanent effect upon her. Slowly and surely, but very placidly, she has declined in health and strength, until it is evident that in a very few weeks at the most she will have rejoined her husband and restored to him the one thing which he must have grudged to leave behind.

The Laird of Branksome came home from Italy restored in health, with the result that we were compelled to return once more to Edinburgh.

The change was agreeable to us, for recent events had cast a cloud over our country life and had surrounded us with unpleasant associations. Besides, a highly honourable and remunerative appointment in connection with the University library had become vacant, and had, through the kindness of the late Sir Alexander Grant, been offered to my father, who, as may be imagined, lost no time in accepting so congenial a post.

In this way we came back to Edinburgh very much more important people than we left it, and with no further reason to be uneasy about the details of housekeeping. But, in truth, the whole household has been dissolved, for I have been married for some months to my dear Gabriel, and Esther is to become Mrs. Heatherstone upon the 23rd of the month. If she makes him as good a wife as his sister has made me, we may both set ourselves down as fortunate men.

These mere domestic episodes are, as I have already explained, introduced only because I cannot avoid alluding to them.

My object in drawing up this statement and publishing the evidence which corroborates it, was certainly not to parade my private affairs before the public, but to leave on record an authentic narrative of a most remarkable series of events. This I have endeavoured to do in as methodical a manner as possible, exaggerating nothing and suppressing nothing.

The reader has now the evidence before him, and can form his own opinions unaided by me as to the causes of the disappearance and death of Rufus Smith and of John Berthier Heatherstone, V.C., C.B.

There is only one point which is still dark to me. Why the *chelas* of Ghoolab Shah should have removed their victims to the desolate Hole of Cree instead of taking their lives at Cloomber, is, I confess, a mystery to me.

In dealing with occult laws, however, we must allow for our own complete ignorance of the subject. Did we know more we might see that there was some analogy between that foul bog and the sacrilege which had been committed, and that their ritual and customs demanded that just such a death was the one appropriate to the crime.

On this point I should be sorry to be dogmatic, but at least we must allow that the Buddhist priests must have had some very good cause for the course of action which they so deliberately carried out.

Months afterwards I saw a short paragraph in the *Star of India* announcing that three eminent Buddhists—Lal Hoomi, Mowdar Khan, and Ram Singh—had just returned in the steamship *Deccan* from a short trip to Europe. The very next item was devoted to an account of the life and services of Major-General Heatherstone, "who has lately disappeared from his country house in Wigtownshire, and who, there is too much reason to fear, has been drowned."

I wonder if by chance there was any other human eye but mine which traced a connection between these paragraphs. I never showed them to my wife or to Mordaunt, and they will only know of their existence when they read these pages.

I don't know that there is any other point which needs clearing up. The intelligent reader will have already seen the reasons for the general's fear of dark faces, of wandering men (not knowing how his pursuers might come after him), and of visitors (from the same cause and because his hateful bell was liable to sound at all times).

His broken sleep led him to wander about the house at night, and the lamps which he burnt in every room were no doubt to prevent his imagination from peopling the darkness with terrors. Lastly, his elaborate precautions were, as he has himself explained, rather the result of a feverish desire to do something than in the expectation that he could really ward off his fate.

Science will tell you that there are no such powers as those claimed by the Eastern mystics. I, John Fothergill West, can confidently answer that science is wrong.

For what is science? Science is the consensus of opinion of scientific men, and history has shown that it is slow to accept a truth. Science sneered at Newton for twenty years. Science proved mathematically that an iron ship could not swim, and science declared that a steamship could not cross the Atlantic.

Like Goethe's Mephistopheles, our wise professor's forte is "stets verneinen." Thomas Didymus is, to use his own jargon, his prototype. Let him learn that if he will but cease to believe in the infallibility of his own methods, and will look to the East, from which all great movements come, he will find there a school of philosophers and of savants who, working on different lines from his own, are many thousand years ahead of him in all the essentials of knowledge.

THE END

FAMILIAR CHILLS: HORROR AND *THE MYSTERY OF CLOOMBER*

BY JOEL K. JENSEN

The popular understanding is that horror tales appeal through fright – we enjoy a good scare, and the adrenalin boost afforded by immanent peril delights us (as long as we're in fact safe). But while this is true of roller coasters, the real appeal of a horror story is altogether different. Our horrors undergird our moralities, and our horror stories are morality tales. They tell us how to live.

Take the case of Arthur Conan Doyle's "forgotten" novella, *The Mystery of Cloomber.* Doyle published this tale of terror in 1889, one of his earlier efforts.[1] The book was not commercially successful. Though it received mention in the usual places, few readers in 1889 seem to have discovered the book – Doyle was not yet the household name he would become, and *Cloomber* flew under the radar. He wasn't helped by tepid reviews. One noted that at least Doyle had the decency to avoid writing in an accent. This is back-handed praise at best, but it also turns out to have been untrue – *Cloomber* includes an entire chapter written in an approximation of the Scottish brogue (this makes for some real hilarity - try orating this chapter aloud to your children, as I do – they'll be fascinated and confounded).

---

[1] It has been suggested that Doyle actually wrote this story several years earlier. This may be at least partially true – the 1889 publication may have borrowed from materials begun at an earlier time. See Owen Dudley Edwards, "The Mystery of the Mystery of Cloomber," *Journal of the Arthur Conan Doyle Society* 2, no.2 (Autumn 1991).

Doyle himself later regarded the story as a literary mistake. It is no longer clear if he was just disappointed in the nonexistent sales, or if his misgivings were of a more literary nature. As concerns the latter, the juxtaposition of themes is ambitious – eerie Scottish moors visited by mysterious Buddhist magicians (indeed!)– and readers may take it as incongruous. Nevertheless, *The Mystery of Cloomber* has remained almost continuously in print for 125 years, and its fan base has continued to grow.[2] The reasons for its growing popularity are complex: beyond the novelty of dipping a toe into the non-Sherlock Doyle, readers will discover that Doyle knows how to reliably set a suspenseful scene – even, as we'll see, when we know full well how the drama will unfold.

Whatever its reception (or lack thereof) at the time, re-reading the story now, a century and a quarter after it rolled off the press, we're unlikely to be frightened – the peril, suspenseful as it may be, is no longer convincingly perilous. But having given that caveat, note that *Cloomber's* lack of real terror is no reason for dismissal. Quite the opposite – we ought to realize by now that bigger frights don't necessarily make better horror stories, and may in fact distract us from their real importance.[3]

Horror story villains *shouldn't* scare us. Lovecraft and King, and any number of others, are legitimately creepy. But with many supposed tales of terror, the real *raison d'etre*

---

[2] *The Mystery of Cloomber* did have at least one vocal defender in 1889 – Doyle's father, Charles Altamont Doyle, who read in while interred at the Montrose Royal Lunatic Asylum, where he painted pictures of fairies.
[3] I'm classifying *The Mystery of Cloomber* as a horror story. I'll concede that this is potentially contentious – is it a mystery, or simply a tale of suspense? Sure, it is those things, but for reasons that I hope will become clear, it's a horror story too. Don't worry about mutual exclusivity.

is not to terrify per se, but rather to legitimize our collective moral sentiments. This ultimately requires rebuilding our comforts by tale's end, even while a story arc of monsters and villains seems to knock them down. My comments won't capture all horror stories cleanly, so as a broad generalization, let's distinguish two species - those tales that reaffirm the social order, and those that unsettle it.[4] We can point to innumerable examples of either – the truly terrifying fairy tale *Hansel and Gretel* is exemplary of the latter while Doyle's *Mystery of Cloomber* fits squarely into the former designation. For simplicity's sake, let's designate the first genera H_1 and the latter H_2.

H_1 are marked by predictability and fidelity to formula (though with attendant variations). H_1 stories often feature monstrous villains, or at least some immanent evil threat. Does such a threat frighten us? Certainly, but only *temporarily*. When we're frightened by such tales, we're really frightening ourselves – we're playing along with a game whose rules we've agreed to. Invariably, the threatening evil is defeated by story's end. In this way, the virtuous and laudable protagonists arrive back where they began, but with the moral order of the universe confirmed anew. The fright of an H_1 shouldn't be carried with us. It's a fear we leave behind once the cover closes, or once we leave the theatre.

H_2 stories, on the other hand, aim to unsettle. Note the shattering moral logic of *Hansel and Gretel*. The children win in the end, but the moral landscape has been altered irrevocably: we put the book down knowing that sometimes mothers will try to kill their children, and that to get by in this

---

[4] We could easily divide the genre into further species, sub-classifications, etc, but I'll leave that to you. What I'm actuality interested in here are those stories that lay out the moral rules, and so I'll concern myself primarily with the H_1 genera.

world, children may have to kill old women. At tale's end we know the children cannot recapture their previous innocence – the world is brutal and to get along we may have to be brutal, too.

Take Woody Allen's *Crimes and Misdemeanors*, a reversal of Dostoevsky's *Crime and Punishment*. This is not ostensibly a horror story at all, but it is in fact seriously frightening. As in Dostoevsky's tale, the protagonist commits a grisly crime, but at the story's end he goes unpunished, and life returns to normal – "justice" simply doesn't occur. Or consider William Golding's *Lord of the Flies*. After a rollicking conflict between good and evil, the boys battling each other for control of the island, suddenly the Navy shows up and sends everyone home. The conflict is unresolved, the bad kids aren't punished, and readers are left with the knowledge that the children's brutality is only a mild reflection of the adults'.

While there are enduring H_2 stories, they can also leave audiences cold. H_1 stories, on the other hand, have more popular appeal.[5] They give audiences precisely what they want. This is true even of *The Mystery of Cloomber* – audiences may have taken a while to discover it, and it's true that some details are handled ham-fistedly, but the story does nevertheless ultimately complete an H_1 story trajectory.

I'll give you the setup of *Mystery of Cloomber*, and we'll see if you can divine the ending. Our narrator/protagonist, John Fothergill West, has newly arrived at Branksome Moor with his father and sister, to watch over the estate of his father's brother (the familial relationships get pretty complicated, but all that really matters is the arrival of a family on the moor). Doyle sets an eerie landscape: "Very bleak and lonely

---

[5] H_2 stories are more enduring, and are the ones we remember, but given the choice a lot of us would rather have an H_1.

it was upon this Wigtown coast. A man might walk many a weary mile and never see a living thing except the white, heavy-flapping kittiwakes which screamed and cried to each other with their shrill sad voices."[6]   Descriptions of the unwelcoming moors, an environment the Scotsman Doyle knew well, are one of the more successful aspects of the book, and are later wrapped into the climax of the story with a charming irony - I won't give it away entirely, but fans of Sherlock Holmes won't be disappointed.

The titular Cloomber refers to a great hall, abandoned and unoccupied above the cliffs over the Irish Sea, "like a headstone of some giant grave"[7]. The narrative precipitates as a new and mysterious tenant arrives at Cloomber in the dark of night, one Major-General J.B. Heatherstone. The General remains the story's central riddle, shunning all contact with the local villagers or our narrator, and contracting the erection of an impenetrable defensive barricade around Cloomber – but is he repelling an imminent threat, or imprisoning his family within?

Who is this mysterious Heatherstone? It is evident from his first appearance in the story that he is a man wracked by fear and that his peculiar behaviours anticipate some unnamed malevolence. Further, we know that Heatherstone's fears in some manner derive from his long ago service in the Indian Army.[8] This is Doyle's first use of a trope he would return to frequently throughout his career – a long forgotten evil from India returns to impose itself upon the naïve gentility

---

[6] Arthur Conan Doyle, *The Mystery of Cloomber* (London: Hesperus Press Limited, 2004), 6

[7] Ibid., 6.

[8] In case this isn't clear, the Indian Army refers to the British Army in India, and in case this isn't clear either, India mean Pakistan – Doyle is writing before Partition.

of English society (well Scottish society, anyway). *The Sign of the Four*, *The Mystery of the Crooked Man*, and *The Speckled Band* all repeat this motif in their own way. Why India? There are reasons for this, as I'll get to, but it is worth noting that *Cloomber*'s treatment of this theme is by far the most complete and, for our purposes, interesting.[9]

We build toward a climax with two unusual events: a terrible storm at sea, and the arrival of a barque, the *Belinda*, in the bay below the cliffs. In a dramatic episode, the *Belinda* is smashed apart, but not before the crew is saved by the daring peasants of Branksome Moor, led by our intrepid narrator. But while the crew averts tragedy, three mysterious passengers, Buddhist priests from India are apparently drowned as a massive wave smashes the vessel asunder.

But, of course, as we might expect, the three passengers mysteriously appear on the beach the next day, having somehow survived and remaining perfectly dry.[10] There is much time spent here by Doyle fawning over these mysterious luminaries from the Orient: their charm, their noble bearing, their obvious wisdom, the miraculous circumstances of their arrival, and on and on. But when Major-General Heatherstone is finally informed that three Buddhists are bivouacking upon the rocky shore, he is predictably panicked and prepares the action stations.

---

[9] The action of the story primarily concerns the mystery of Heatherstone, his bizarre comings and goings, and our narrator's flabbergasted response to this behaviour. In a recurring bit of unintentional comedy, Mr. West seems thick as a post – he doesn't piece together the connection with India until the tale's climax, despite that clues are littered everywhere. If he'd ever had read a horror story before he'd have the whole thing figured out.

[10] Actually, at this point in the plot's development, their survival is basically guaranteed. No reader will be surprised.

How do these dire tidings end? There won't be any bean spilling here (well, there probably will, I can't help myself), but, then, there isn't any need. Any reader will long before this point have the whole thing figured out. And of course, this is no failing on Doyle's part – this is an H_1 after all. A few particulars of the denouement might yet be surprising, but we know, more or less, how the tension will be resolved, and, more importantly, we know the cause (the mystery in the *Mystery*). But let's put this tale into context. Why villains from India?

In the second half of the 19th century, England "discovered" Buddhism, and India become the locus for a set of powerful associations, just right for a horror story. First, I should note that Indian and Tibetan Buddhism were at the time entirely and laughably misunderstood, even by the theosophist Doyle who was early on something of an apologist for Indian culture and religion. Thus we see throughout the story a host of totally erroneous associations: the three Buddhists wear fezzes (traditionally a Muslim garb), they have Muslim names, and they come from a Muslim, not Buddhist, region.[11] The practices the three Buddhists seem to be engaged in might be much more likely to be associated with Hindu yogic practices than Buddhist ones (though, more than that, their practices are simply fictional, and, by the way, they're pretty awesome), and finally Doyle seems all but unaware that Buddhism had long all but disappeared from India.

Our three arrivals from India are blessed with psychic abilities: foresight, astral projection, matter transmission, and some form of mind control, among other dark powers. Serious horror is associated with the "astral bell": the terrifying sound of a gong emanates at intervals above the

---

[11] The events seem to take place in the Pakistani foothills of the Himalayas.

heads of those upon whom the priests have directed their curse. A bit like a psychic digital alarm clock – yes, I know, it doesn't sound particularly threatening, but Doyle seems to have expected it to come across as shockingly dark magick[12].

The association of magic with Indian (and more particularly, Tibetan) Buddhism was not new or unique to Doyle. In the latter half of the 19th century, it was all the rage. Today it's zombies, vampires or werewolves (though vampires seem to have reached their nadir, and surely we'll be done with zombies in about two more years), but one hundred years ago we had the unfathomable Black Magick from the East. This is interesting in itself - the trending of our terrors - but is beyond my scope here. The mystification of the Buddhist East reached perhaps its greatest popularity with James Hilton's 1933 novel *Lost Horizon*, portraying an Edenic Buddhist kingdom encapsulated in time.[13] We shouldn't think here that Doyle's *Cloomber* started this literary trend – all the more so since it wasn't widely read at first – but it remains one of the most illustrative of a particular brand of confused romanticizing nonsense.[14]

None of this is to dismiss *Cloomber*. Far from it. Doyle uses the Indian bugaboo to reliably create a classically structured H_1. It's true his Buddhists are a bundle of contradictions – some of these confusions are simply errors,

---

[12] Doyle precedes Aleister Crowley, but I'm going to go ahead and claim this as magick with a "k".

[13] For such romanticizing, it's hard to top Herge's irresistible *Tintin in Tibet* from 1960, complete with levitating monks and a ferocious/cuddly yeti.

[14] In truth, the romanticization/mystification of the Buddhist East still continues. As evidence, witness *The Manhattan Projects*, a comic series by Jonathan Hickman, begun in 2012. The series received critical acclaim, but it's hard to look past the evil killer kamakazi zen samurai warrior robots.

as when the Buddhists seem to be associated with the "green banner of the Prophet"[15] - but chiefly the contradictions are not accidental, but essential to H[1] thematic structure.

Readily apparent are bizarre surface juxtapositions – in describing the natives he encountered on patrol in his Indian Army days, the ill-fated Heatherstone says, "They are personifications of the devil to look at: hawk-nosed, full-lipped, with a mane of tangled hair, and most Satanic sneer."[16] Or later: "...howling like a pack of demons. With their black, contorted, mocking faces, their fierce gestures, and their fluttering garments, they would have made a study for any painter who wished to portray Milton's army of the damned."[17] But contrast such descriptions with "...he raised a pair of steady, thoughtful dark eyes, and inclined his head in a sweeping salutation. It seemed to me that we were like a pack of schoolboys in the presence of a master."[18]

Further confounding, the incongruities of appearance magnify internal, moral contradictions. When we are first introduced to the three Buddhists, they explain their vegetarianism, claiming no moral right to take the life of an animal. But later (and this much should be obvious almost from the beginning of the book), we learn that they have made the long journey to Scotland on an errand of violent vengeance. On the one hand, they are depicted as morally sensitive, at a greater moral evolutionary stage than we beef-eaters in the West, but at the same time they are bidden to an ancient and bloody *lex talionis*, a law of retribution. How should we make sense of this seeming moral jumble sale?

---

[15] Doyle, *The Mystery of Cloomber*, 107.
[16] Ibid., 102.
[17] Ibid., 106.
[18] Ibid., 73.

Cloomber reflects first, the contradictions that shaped the conception of India in the popular imagination (Doyle's audience), and second, the contradictions that are *necessary* for a horror story to be successful. Which is to say, Doyle employs the contradictions wittingly; the story relies upon them. The romanticizing/demonizing of the Buddhist East has been described by Donald Lopez, in *Prisoners of Shangri-La* in this way, "we see here a play of opposites: the pristine and polluted, the authentic and the derivative, the holy and demonic, the good and the bad."[19] Such dualities were par for the course for depictions of India and Tibet at the time and are part and parcel of what made India newly compelling to audiences.[20] But notice that the moral reversal is required for a horror story to retain its punch. To explain what I mean, let's take a detour to the middle ages.

In the late Medieval, a common form of European entertainment was known as the Morality Play. As a generalization, morality plays depicted a protagonist who must choose between following a pious, godly life, or a life of sin. As he navigates these straits, he is met by personifications of virtues (and vices). The audience of a morality play always knew full well how the story would end - the result was never in question. For morality plays, the point was not to make an ambiguous story, in which the end was a guessing game, but precisely the opposite. As the virtues and vices battle for control of the protagonist, we, the audience, know that in the end virtue will prevail, and evil be vanquished. The plays served to reinforce the already-accepted morality of the time, not to challenge it. In *Everyman*, the most exemplary of the morality plays still extant, the protagonist Everyman ascends to heaven with Good Deeds by his side.

---

[19] Donald Lopez, *Prisoners of Shangri-La: Tibetan Buddhism and the West* (Chicago: University of Chicago Press, 1998), 4.
[20] To the extent that the India in the popular imagination was a fictional entity, it was also a fiction that the audience wanted.

These plays could be frightening – they were intended to frighten - but only temporarily. For any fiction, there is required a suspension of disbelief. Thus, when the actors strut and fret, we may convince ourselves the peril they pose is genuine. But in the end, everything, virtues and vices, are back in their places. The moral universe is restored (hence the *morality* play). To put it in Aristotle's terms, for a catharsis to be effected, the emotional turmoil enacted upon the boards must eventually be resolved.

Notice that for morality plays, as will later be true for horror stories, a central lesson is that individuals have power over their own fates. In the Middle Ages (as is often explicitly the case now for horror stories), this meant that audience members were reminded that the power to ascend to heaven or descend to hell was in their hands. One might think of this kind of story as scaring the audience straight, just as when we (at least if you're my age) were in high school and watched *Death on the Highway*, the point was to frighten us into obedience. If you don't drive carefully, this could happen to you! We can think of countless examples of the same. Notice, however, that it would be too simple to characterize such presentations as scary. In effect, they aren't really scary at all. Why not? Because they reaffirm a moral order that we already know exists. We already know that drinking and driving is unsafe – seeing a video making this explicit, the blood and guts might be shocking, but we're left with the appropriate message that we have control over our fate. If we follow the rules, no one gets hurt.

What would make *Death on the Highway* truly scary? If a driver who does in fact obey all the rules gets killed, through no fault of her own. We know, in fact, that this possibility is entirely real, and happens every day. But morality tales aren't much concerned with reality. In

Everyman, if our protagonist strove to be virtuous, successfully resisting lust and greed, only to burn in the underworld anyway, we'd have a very different kind of tale. Weird exceptions such as these (if they existed) would be H_2s. But again, readers and viewers don't usually want to be scared, not really. They want to *think* they've been scared. Between the two there is a big difference.[21]

Horror stories (H_1s anyway) are morality plays, and consequently do not really trade in fear. And like morality plays, horror stories are frequently allegorical. The characters embody vices or virtues with which the audience is already bluntly familiar. In this way, the audience of a morality play anticipates the story they are presented with. They know that the good will be rewarded, the bad will be punished - and the ambivalent may face punishment as well. If this isn't clear by now, just think of any of those formulaic teen slasher movies so popular in the 80s and 90s. We always know within the first few frames that the first to get axed will be the teenagers necking behind the barn. And why? Necking is morally loose behavior, and always gets punished (even with death!).

Thus, morality plays present a dyadic moral universe, in which only two sides really exist - morality plays aren't typically interested in mining the moral ambiguity of the in-between. There are exceptions, and these exceptions (when they are pulled off well) tend to be actually scary. H_1 stories, like morality plays, go for the quick scare, but do not attempt

---

[21] Compare the popularity of an ostensibly scary movie like *Friday the 13th*, for which there are 11 sequels and TV and comic book spinoffs to a more genuinely harrowing movie like *Schindler's List*. The latter is a "good" movie, but we really only watch out of a sense of collective guilt and responsibility, not because we're having a good time. Only one of these films is actually scaring us. And who would sit through 11 *Schindler's List* sequels?

to truly unsettle. They don't aim for the uncanny – the few that do are H₂s.

Take any monster story in which a rampaging menace stalks about killing the hapless. As we know, who gets punished? Only those who are morally bad or wicked (or perhaps those who are morally ambivalent – the "red shirts"). This is precisely why horror movies are easy fodder for drinking games and book-making. Often those horror stories which play against our expectations – by letting a morally ambiguous character survive while punishing the virtuous – leave us flat. We *want* the virtuous to survive.[22]

In *Mystery of Cloomber*, we are aware early on that Heatherstone is awaiting some unnamed evil, whose source remains opaque. (Well, it's *supposed* to be a mysterious evil, but if you can't figure it out immediately, you may be reading the wrong book). Readers of Doyle will be familiar with this trope. Take *The Adventure of the Dancing Men*, for instance, in which we await the appearance of an evil visitor. Nothing is particularly wrong with Doyle's recycling – it's good fun, and more importantly, there is nothing wrong with repeating a formula when it's done well. We might actually say here that horror stories *must* be formulaic. Why? Because they concern themselves with morality, and morality is more easily

---

[22] While horror stories ought to be predictable, detective shows on TV often fail to be predictable, when really they ought as well. One should to be able to look backward at the cast of suspects and see that the plot is really consistent, and the crime really solvable. Often though, detective shows err on the side of trying to surprise us. The result is that the character least likely to have committed the crime is the one to have done it. Thus, to predict the murderer, you just need to identify the person, in the first 5 minutes of the show, for whom the crime is totally implausible and with whose character the crime is totally inconsistent. That's your man.

understood when condensed to sets of rules. But, these rules don't apply to all situations equally. There are exceptions – or, rather, we deal with exceptions in order to make the rules clear. This is the same way we do research in clinical psychology – not by looking at the normal cases, but by examining the exceptional or aberrant. Horror stories do the same. The point, in the long run, is to reaffirm the normal circumstances: here are the accepted moral rules – if you break them, woe betide you!

The chief victim of the monster's rampage should himself (or herself) possess some character flaw which itself is responsible for awakening the horror in the first place, thus exposing the community to its hidden danger. Ultimately, this character who awakens the horror must also succumb to its wrath – as will those others in the community who are themselves guilty of moral transgressions. All of which means Heatherstone has it coming (big surprise). But for the formula to work, those who are morally virtuous must succeed in combating the evil, and returning it to its box. [23] The violence of a horror story is not meted randomly – it falls upon those who are already guilty, and most particularly, upon those who cause the horror in the first place. They are stories of comeuppance.

Almost all horror stories make use of this trope, at least: a person of high social standing and respectability (Heatherstone) is brought low by the reverberations of their own hidden moral flaws (note that it is important that the moral flaws must be hidden, and not immediately apparent – otherwise the cathartic process will remain incomplete). Notice the reversal here – the monster in the horror story is not really to blame for its actions. Rather, it follows

---

[23] Notice that Pandora's Box is an H_2 not an H_1. Hope may be left in the box at the end, but we have a clear lesson about the unresolvedness of real life.

immutable natural, or moral laws. In *Cloomber*, this is actually put quite explicitly – "Be not hasty in your judgments. There are certain great rules which must be carried out, at whatever cost to individuals. Their operation may appear to you to harsh and cruel, but that is nothing as compared with the dangerous precedent which would be established by not enforcing them."[24]

But if a horror story is really pulling its weight, then there should be a further hidden cause of the violence, a further hidden monster, only revealed at the end (even though an informed audience will already know this). This latent monster is in fact the community itself. It should be the case that some moral contradiction exists in the community itself, which is exposed by the horror. The monster is thus is a mirror image of the community, one in which the moral sense has been reversed.[25] How does this play out in *The Mystery of Cloomber*?

I said I wouldn't spoil anything, but really I already have, so why stop here? *Cloomber* is a revenge story. The explicit "monster" of the film, the magicians from India, have journeyed to the moors to right a past wrong. Without going into too many specifics, let's note that Heatherstone's own acts of evil from the past can't have been anomalous. That is to say, Heatherstone's evil can't exist in contradistinction to a morally pure society from which he comes. Rather, his behavior is a symptom. Heatherstone is in fact noble as per the rules of the game he's playing. The evil arising from India exposes the flaw in the society itself. That this comeuppance should arise from a "backward" or "barbarian" state is no accident – only the seeming opposite can expose the inherent flaw.

---

[24] Doyle, *The Mystery of Cloomber*, 88.
[25] Note that a mirror image is not a replica, it is a reversal.

An aside: we should pause here to try to digest what, for many readers, is the most hard to swallow difficulty of *Cloomber*. I've already revealed that the Buddhists, ostensibly the villains of the tale, are seeking revenge. To readers of today who are more politically correct, more aware of the diversity of cultural and religious expression (call it what you like), this seems more than just an error – it seems to contradict Buddhist ethics at its core. What reading of Buddhism advocates an eye for an eye calculus? Not all revenge stories are horror stories, but certainly a great many horror stories are revenge stories – the violation of natural laws (in this case *karma*) that must be eventually atoned for. We like revenge stories, particularly when the law must be subverted in order to balance the more primal moral scales. And certainly plenty of Buddhists might enjoy the revenge trope on offer here explicitly on its own terms. But many readers might also find the pairing philosophically incompatible, or else a real head scratcher. Put plainly, we might just find it funny. And yes, it is funny. But *The Mystery of Cloomber* has more to offer than just ironic, self-aware amusement. As a revenge story, and as a horror story, *Cloomber* offers a surprisingly progressive social critique, one interesting for its own sake (and once again, the Doyle's suspense is reliably engaging).

Note the critique undergirding Doyle's romanticizing. The civilized West is set in opposition to the sneering barbarian hordes of the Orient, but how is our civilization sustained? It is only possible with a certain amount of cruelty – our level of comfort and refinement here in the West disguises, but also depends upon, some indiscriminate blood-spilling. In *Cloomber,* this critique is never explicit, Doyle keeps it always below the surface, but nevertheless this moral reversal is crucial to the story.

Doyle lays the contradictions most bare in his descriptions of the powers of the Buddhist priests. While I have above referred to their powers as magick, Doyle in fact does the opposite – the powers displayed are described as the products of scientific advance, not spell-casting. This is put in fairly explicit terms, and gives early explication to a conundrum that would later flummox generations of fans of Sherlock Holmes. How was it the creator of the coldly rational Holmes could also believe in all that theosophist silliness – he was later in life a defender of the existence of fairies, for instance?

Doyle did not in fact separate theosophy from science. *Cloomber* at times reads as a defense of theosophy's grounding in science (in fact an early edition of the book apparently included an appendix with the comments of theosophists defending the book's scientific claims).[26] As a work of fiction, this isn't consistently successful – there are substantial passages in which the fiction/nonfiction divide seems to break down. An early instance is a speech by Heatherstone on the nature of "odylic force" – a supposed vital but invisible life energy - complete with references to contemporary scientists whose works we might want to read.[27]

---

[26] Daniel Stashower, *Teller of Tales: The Life of Arthur Conan Doyle* (New York: Holt, 1999).

[27] In a curious set of references, he refers to the work of Hans Reichenbach. This is a genuine reference, Hans Reichenbach really did do work on odylic force, but it curiously presages Reichenbach Falls, where Holmes ostensibly meets his death in *The Final Solution*. But this Reichenbach turns out to be genuine, too – it's a real place.

The Mystery of Cloomber is often remembered for the last passage,[28] in which the critique of Western science is made explicit: "For what is science? Science is the consensus of opinion of scientific men, and history has shown that it is slow to accept a truth. Science sneered at Newton for twenty years. Science proved mathematically that an iron ship could not swim, and science declared that a steamship could not cross the Atlantic."[29]

The critique of the prejudices of scientific inquiry is sometimes clumsy, though it is curiously in service to a surprisingly modern agenda. Ultimately, Doyle is urging that with our scientific advance, and its coupled moral assumptions, we may have gotten used to prejudices that in fact blind us to new possibilities. But again, notice that the critique does keep the basic moral framework in place. We are challenged as a community to avoid mental laxity, but we are not challenged to avoid two basic moral assumptions – the legitimacy of scientific inquiry itself, and the certainty that cruelty will eventually be met with justice.

It would be a rare reader indeed who, after reading *The Mystery of Cloomber*, was kept up nights worrying about astral bells or evil Buddhists on the high seas. Nor would Doyle want it that way – it would be a misunderstanding of the H_1 formula, a formula intended to be easily understood. But notice possible endings that would indeed have been scary – go ahead and imagine your own. Suppose Heatherstone's past indiscretions go entirely unpunished? Or if in a final brutal scene Heatherstone bludgeons to death the Buddhist adepts? Or with the revelation that our faith in science was somehow irredeemably in error?

---

[28] And this might indicate, unfortunately, that reviewers and biographers, or at least those who write dust jacket copy, have skipped all the content and gone straight to the end.
[29] Doyle, *The Mystery of Cloomber*, 126.

Works Cited

Anonymous. *Everyman*. Ed. A.C. Cawley. Manchester: Manchester University Press, 1961. Print.

Crimes and Misdemeanors. Dir. Woody Allen. Perf. Caroline Aaron, Alan Alda, Martin S. Bergmann, Bill Bernstein, Claire Bloom. Orion, 1989. Film.

Crowley, Alistair. *Magick in Theory and Practice*. New York: Dover, 1976.

Dostoevsky, Fyodor. *Crime and Punishment*. Trans. Richard Pevear and Larissa Volokhonsky. New York: Knopf, 1993. Print.

Doyle, Arthur Conan. *The Complete Sherlock Holmes*. Garden City, NY: Doubleday & Co., 1930. Print.

Doyle, Arthur Conan, *The Mystery of Cloomber* London: Hesperus Press Limited, 2004. Print.

Edwards, Owen Dudley. "The Mystery of the Mystery of Cloomber," *Journal of the Arthur Conan Doyle Society* 2.2 (Autumn 1991). Printed.

Friday the 13th. Dir. Sean Cunningham. Perf. Kevin Bacon, Adrienne King, Betsy Palmer. Paramount: 1980. Film.

Golding, William. *Lord of the Flies*. New York: Coward-McCann, 1962. Print.

Hergé. *The Adventures of Tintin: Tintin in Tibet*. Boston: Little, Brown and Co., 1992. Print.

Hickman, Jonathan, and Nick Pitarra. *The Manhattan Projects*. Berkeley, CA: Image Comics, 2012. Print.

Hilton, James. *Lost Horizon*. Pleasantville, NY: Reader's Digest Association, 1990. Print.

Lopez, Donald. *Prisoners of Shangri-La: Tibetan Buddhism and the West*. Chicago: University of Chicago Press, 1998. Print.

Schindler's List. Dir. Steven Spielberg. Perf. Ralph Fiennes, Ben Kingsley, Liam Neeson. Univeral. 1993. Film.

Stashower, David. *Teller of Tales: The Life of Arthur Conan Doyle*. New York: Holt, 1999. Print.

Anthology Conclusion

On July 13th, 1930, a memorial service was held for Sir Arthur Conan Doyle at the Royal Albert Hall in London. Over 8,000 people attended the service, though most did not actually come to pay their respects for the great author. Doyle's beliefs in the afterlife were well-known, and the public came to hear the deceased personally describe to them what life is like after death. Through the medium Estelle Roberts, Doyle supposedly entered the hall in spirit form and left a spoken message for his newly-widowed wife, Mary. Whether the message was for Mary Doyle, Doyle's late mother (also named Mary), or for an unknown woman by the same name, no one knows for certain. Due to noise in the hall, the only person to hear the message was Sir Arthur's wife Lady Conan Doyle, and for personal reasons, she refused to speak of it.

For the next fifty years, relatives of Sir Arthur Conan Doyle, spiritualists, and even the purchaser of Doyle's Bignell Woods property claimed to be visited by the author. While Doyle's life after his death is justly met with great skepticism, no one can deny the immortality he has reached through the publications of his written works. His character Sherlock Holmes is now one of the most well-known literary figures throughout the world. His novel *The Lost World* had a tremendous influence, inspiring countless variations from the original *King Kong* through today's *Jurassic Park* novels and films. His stories of monstrous mummies revolutionized a genre. This anthology has shown the rich variety of Doyle's writing and should be taken as an introduction to the intriguing worlds the author has created. Readers should seek out important works by the author in historical fiction, drama, nonfiction, and poetry as well as further tales in the genres included in this collection.

Sir Arthur Conan Doyle was a master of his craft; one of the finest writers in the English language. It is my hope that this anthology sparks a renaissance in Doyle's non-Sherlock Holmes tales. Please share the text with others! Let everyone enjoy the power of these forgotten tales, and perhaps one day soon Cloomber Hall will be just as well-known as 221 B Baker Street.

--Derrick Belanger

About the Authors

Sir Arthur Conan Doyle

Sir Arthur Conan Doyle is considered one of the greatest writers or the Victorian and Edwardian time periods. He is most famous for creating Sherlock Holmes, the world's greatest detective. As this anthology shows, Doyle also wrote great fiction through genres beyond mysteries such as horror, science fiction, historical fiction, nonfiction, poetry and romances. It is fair to say that the world is a better place because of his writing.

Derrick Belanger, M.A.T.

Author Derrick Belanger's publications include an eclectic mix: book reviews, articles for education journals, short stories, poems, comic books, and the graphic novel, *Twenty-Three Skidoo!* A former instructor at Washington State University, and a current middle school Language Arts teacher, Derrick lives in Broomfield, Colorado with his wife Abigail Gosselin and their two daughters, Rhea and Phoebe. Currently, Derrick is working on several Sherlockian projects: the children's book series, *The Baker Street Youth* Detectives, the Young Adult novel *Sherlock Holmes and the Transformers of Time*, the teaching guide *Sherlock Holmes for Teachers*, the pastiche novel *The Funeral of Sherlock Holmes,* and the film studies book *The Hound of the Baskervilles: From Page to Screen*. He also co-authors the web site *Mystery Aircraft.com* with author Chuck Davis.

Joel K. Jensen, Ph. D.

Joel K Jensen is the author of <u>There Exists an X, X is a Sandwich</u>, available from Sandwich Bar Press. He is interested in applying the methodologies of deductive logic to everyday life with both humor and intellectual rigor. Jensen studied philosophy and architecture at the University of Colorado, and teaches philosophy at North Hennepin Community College. He lives in Minneapolis.

Special Thanks

First, a big thank you from all of us to Steve Emecz and MX Publishing for making this two volume anthology possible and allowing us to scratch one line off of our respective bucket lists. We also thank Sir Arthur Conan Doyle for writing these brilliant stories.

Derrick Belanger would like to thank his wife Abby, daughters Rhea and Phoebe, and parents Dennis and Ellen for their love and support; Jennifer Petkus, Chris Redmond, Matthew Goodman, Tim Hillmer, Merrily Taylor, Eric Pellerin, and Steve Seitz for the positive feedback and comments; Carla Stockton and Ed Ludvigsen for planting the seed of this anthology in my brain; Dantalion for your assistance; the students and staff at Century Middle School for being awesome; Jamil Scott for your insights into Buddhism; and anyone who offered support, heard me complain, or helped me out over the past few years while I assembled this eclectic collection.

Joel Jensen would like to thank Derrick Belanger for being the brainchild of this anthology, and for his tireless efforts in bringing the project to fruition.

Also from MX Publishing

MX Publishing is the world's largest specialist Sherlock Holmes publisher, with over a hundred and fity titles and sixty authors creating the latest in Sherlock Holmes fiction and non-fiction.

The collections includes traditional short story collections and novels through to travel guides and quiz books.

Our leading biography titles include the #1 bestseller *Benedict Cumberbatch In Transition* and *The Norwood Author* which won the 2011 Howlett Award (Sherlock Holmes Book of the Year).

Join our Facebook page for the latest Sherlock Holmes book news. www.facebook.com/BooksSherlockHolmes

www.mxpublishing.co.uk (UK)
www.mxpublishing.com (USA)

Also from MX Publishing

From the editor of the Sherlock Holmes Society of London comes an award winning collection of supernatural and ghost stories......

Tales of phantoms, demons and alien gods, including all the stories from the out-of-print collection A Ghostly Crew: Tales from the Endeavour, winner of the Dracula Society's Children of the Night Award for 2001.

Also from MX Publishing

Two supernatural Sherlock Holmes novels from Tracy Revels. Shadowfall is now available in Italian and audio book.

"Tracy Revels has a clever and delicious way with words, and the world of Shadowfall is fully formed and beautifully imagined - from the dazzling and terrifying Queen Titania who steals Watson's soul, to Holmes's tiny and ethereal honeybee familiar. Revels' story is carefully and artfully constructed".

Better Holmes and Gardens